The Keys:
Voice of the Turtle

by

Karen Hulene Bartell

Sacred Emblems

The Keys:
Voice of the Turtle

Cover Art by *Kim Mendoza*

The Wild Rose Press, Inc.
PO Box 708
Adams Basin, NY 14410-0708
Visit us at www.thewildrosepress.com

Publishing History
First Mainstream Fantasy Rose Edition, 2019
Print ISBN 978-1-5092-2790-7
Digital ISBN 978-1-5092-2791-4

Sacred Emblems
Published in the United States of America

"Conveying this land to the turtles would be my way of leaving the world a better place." She turned toward Ruth. "Does that make sense?"

Ruth nodded and gazed at Keya as if for the first time. Her cousin's intentions were clear. "But legally, how can you will the property to the turtles?"

"Easy. I leave it to the Turtle Refuge." Keya laughed inwardly as they meandered along the beach. "And this is where you come in. When you're writing the brochure, add a few paragraphs about planned giving and charitable bequests…" Her words broke off as Keya stared as if in a trance.

Ruth looked at her. "What's wrong?"

Her hand shaking, Keya pointed to a shady patch of beach half hidden by sand dunes. A lifeless hand lay tangled in seaweed, its fingernails broken and bloodied.

Racing behind the sandbanks to help, Ruth skidded to a halt, her heels digging into the sand. A woman's bloated body lay staring at the sun, her eyes opaque and unseeing. "Do you recognize her?"

"No." Keya shook her head as the cat gingerly approached, sniffing and meowing. "But Earnestine said she smells familiar."

Dedication

To my husband and travel companion through life,
Peter William Bartell

Chapter 1

Miami to Key West

Brett drove past row after row of spiny lobster traps stacked like wooden pallets before arriving at the marina restaurant.

"We're here, Auggie." Ruth ended her call while she glanced in the sun visor's mirror. As she finger-combed her dark, shoulder-length hair into place, her sea-green eyes stared back, and she smiled at her reflection, eager to begin her working vacation.

Then she took in the harbor. Sailboats and fishing boats with massive marlin towers stood in sharp relief against the Florida Keys' azure sky as they lay anchored behind the brightly painted waterfront eatery.

Stepping out of the car's air-conditioning into the bright sunlight, she beamed at her dark-haired fiancé. "This really is the Sunshine State."

Brett nodded while his tawny brown eyes fixed on a place-your-face standee. "Auggie?"

With just their faces showing, a man and his dog posed behind a plywood cutout painted to look like a mermaid and a fish wearing a chef's hat. Carrying a small dog in his arms, the man stepped out from behind the stand-up painting. "Good to see you." While he shook hands with Brett, he introduced his furry companion. "This is Diesel."

"Hello, Diesel." Brett shook the dog's paw as it reached over to lick him. Then, smiling, he turned toward Ruth. "This is my fiancée, Ruth, and this is my uncle, Auggie, the one who's been giving you directions."

"So, you're the adventurous uncle I've heard so much about. It's great to put a face to a voice." Smiling, she offered her hand, but Auggie reached his arm around her to hug her. Pressed between them, Diesel licked her face while she chuckled at the dog's tickling tongue and peered at his owner.

Early forties, tanned, sun-bleached hair, wearing a devil-may-care smile, Auggie had the look of a man who had not worn a business suit in decades. His shirt collar unbuttoned, a coin hanging at his neck, he held the wiry, tricolored dog against his chest as if a part of him.

"*Uncle*." Auggie groaned as he broke away. "It sounds so *old*."

"Nonsense." Ruth smiled at her future husband. "According to Brett, you're as ageless as the sea."

"You're not calling me an old salt, *are you?*" Arching a brow, he faked a frown.

Ruth shook her head at his sense of humor. "Never."

"In that case"—he led them to a thatch-roofed bar a flight up, overlooking the Gulf—"come on upstairs to the best oyster and stone-crab bar in Marathon. Shellfish are cracked to order, and it's Happy Hour all day."

After he placed their order, he led them to a corner table in the back with a panoramic view of the Gulf. "What can I get you to drink? Beer? Wine?" He glanced at Ruth.

"A dark local beer's good," she said.

Setting his dog on the chair, Auggie turned toward his nephew. "How 'bout you?"

"Same here." As Auggie sauntered toward the bar, Brett turned toward Ruth. "He's my mother's younger brother, from the *Maehkaenah*, the Turtle Clan. Though he's closer in age to an older cousin than an uncle, he taught me everything I know about fishing and boating."

Diesel kept his eyes peeled on his person, barely acknowledging either of them until Auggie returned with the drinks. As soon as he sat, Diesel climbed on his lap.

"This dog sure does love you." Ruth reached over to pet the dog's wiry fur.

Auggie gave Diesel an affectionate hug. "He's a rat terrier mix, descended from the first refugee stowaway during the 1980 Cuban boatlift."

"That's quite a pedigree," said Ruth, tongue-in-cheek, as her phone pinged. She glanced at it. "My cousin Keya's here." She texted back.

—*We're upstairs*—

Three minutes later, a thirty-something woman appeared at the head of the stairs, wearing sunglasses, a kaftan, a wide-brimmed raffia sunhat over her blonde chignon, and a matching bag.

A striped golden cat peeked from her handbag, and its eyes grew enormous as it took in the scene.

Removing her dark glasses, the woman spotted Ruth and dashed toward her in a whirlwind of woven straw and trailing silk.

Diesel let out a warning yelp, while the cat, still

peeking from the bag, hissed back.

"Earnestine," scolded the woman. "Behave."

Auggie held Diesel closer, petting him until he calmed down.

When Ruth stood to hug her, Keya's gaze traveled to her left hand, where she inspected the diamond ring. "Lovely, but where's the wedding band?"

Ruth caught Brett's eye before answering. "We just got engaged."

Keya hugged her, then gave her another affectionate squeeze before letting go. "One ring's good, but two are better, so encore! Encore!"

"Encore..." Ruth cracked a smile. "You haven't changed a bit—still the theater major."

"*Theatre*, love." Keya affected a British pronunciation tinged with a certain melancholy. "All the world's a stage."

Ruth did a double take at her tone as she introduced the group. "This is my husband-*to-be* Brett and his uncle Auggie, and this is my *infamous* cousin Keya, who's always had a flair for the theatrical. When we were kids, we must have put on dozens of shows for our parents, improvising one-act plays whenever our families got together. After graduation, she left for the bright lights of Broadway."

"Got as far as off-Broadway, love." Keya added with an ironic smile, "Close, but not *quite* the same."

Brett stood to hug her. "I almost feel I know you. Ruth's told me so much about you."

Her violet eyes twinkling, Keya glanced at Ruth. "All good, I hope?"

"I've never heard the name *Keya* before," said Auggie. "What's it mean?"

She shared a smile with Ruth before answering. "Turtle."

"Okay, I'll take the bait." He gave her a skeptical smile. "Why did your parents name you after a turtle?"

"They were hippies living in a California commune." Keya shrugged. "When my mother dreamt of a turtle walking down a rocky path, she went to a Sioux medicine woman to interpret the dream.

"The woman reminded her that turtles carry their homes on their backs, but people don't. She said a turtle on the move meant it was looking for a place to nest, and my mother should 'make haste slowly' to find a nest of her own because she was pregnant with a daughter. Finally, she advised her to name me Keya in honor of the dream."

"The medicine woman sounds like she had a good eye for reading people." Auggie gave her a congenial smile. "Can I get you a drink?"

"Definitely!" Keya turned toward him, pausing a beat as she seemed to appraise his sun-burnished face and amber-brown eyes. "A pineapple cinnamon mojito would be lovely."

He set down his dog and pulled up a chair for Keya. "Be right back."

"Thank you." Then she lifted her index finger as if remembering something important. "Tell the bartender to be sure to muddle the pineapple with a *wooden* spoon and to add a generous dollop of whipped cream." She winked.

It was Auggie's turn to do an amused double take. "Work like a captain, play like a pirate, eh?"

Keya's eyes glinted as she nodded. "Something like that."

"So," asked Brett, "what brought you to the Florida Keys?"

Her violet-blue eyes lost their sparkle and glazed over. Her shoulders slumped, as if the wind had been knocked out of her sails, and the cat climbed on her lap, nuzzling her. "My husband," she whispered.

Responding to Brett's panicked glance for help, Ruth filled in. "Keya's husband passed away three months ago after he'd been in a coma for over a year."

"Fourteen months, to be exact," said Keya. "He had a stroke just after he inherited the house." She shook her head. "If his aunt hadn't left him that property, I believe he'd still be alive today."

"Why do you say that?" Ruth scrutinized her.

"The stress of dealing with his family's lawsuit killed him. Relatives crawled out of the woodwork for that phony inheritance claim. Every second cousin, twice removed, wanted his or her cut, and it had nothing to do with any sentiment for Aunt Libby *or* the house." Sighing in frustration, she grimaced. "They just wanted their piece of the pie."

"Why did she leave her house to Jules?" asked Ruth. "Was he her closest relative?"

"From what he told me, Jules and one other cousin were her closest kin, as well as the only ones to keep in touch with her through the years. Though she left it to them both, his cousin disclaimed it."

"*Disclaimed it*. I'm not familiar with the term." Brett squinted as he examined her. "You mean, the cousin refused it?"

Keya nodded. "After he walked away, the estate passed to Jules, who was immediately served with a lawsuit, contesting his aunt's will. Dozens of distant relatives' names appeared on it, mostly people he didn't know and hadn't met. All the aggravated stress brought on a stroke. He lingered for fourteen months in a coma. Then when he passed away, leaving his estate to me, his family filed *another* lawsuit contesting *his* will."

Brett shook his head. "Sometimes family can treat you worse than strangers."

Her mouth taut, Keya nodded.

"Here you go." Auggie placed her drink in front of her.

Keya's smile seemed forced as she looked from him to her cream-topped drink, sprinkled with cinnamon and garnished with fresh mint leaves and a cinnamon stick. "Thanks, love." She took a sip and licked her lips. "Delicious." Then, holding her drink as if in a toast, she called to the bartender. "My compliments."

The man bobbed his head in a good-natured nod.

As it sniffed the drink, the cat stood on her lap and meowed.

Keya sighed. "All right, Earnestine, one sip, but be quick. We're in public." The cat lapped at the mojito's cream while Keya explained. "Since Jules passed, she's become my drinking buddy and insists on tasting every drink."

As Brett's eyebrows rose, Ruth swallowed a smile. "Keya's always had a certain…affinity for animals, ever since we were kids."

Keya nodded. "It's true, although now more than ever. Animals never let you down. People might, but animals never do."

"Hear, hear," said Auggie, raising his beer. "I'll drink to that."

Keya lifted her glass away from the cat, who was still lapping at the cream. "Excuse me, Earnestine." Then, clinking her drink against his bottle, she sipped while she cuddled the cat.

Mewing, Earnestine curled on her lap, while Diesel appeared content on Auggie's lap. Both seemed relaxed in the group's company.

A waiter brought smoked mullet dip with a variety of crisp crackers to start. Another brought a platter of cracked stone-crab claws and peel-and-eat shrimp on a bed of crushed ice with ramekins of tangy mustard and cocktail sauce, while a third waiter brought oysters on the half shell with lemon slices and mignonette sauce, along with paper plates, plastic seafood forks, and plenty of napkins.

Ruth peeled off the shell of a cracked stone-crab claw and dipped it in the mustard sauce. As she bit into the firm, sweet meat, she groaned. "Delicious. Tastes something like lobster—yet different."

They passed the platters family style, sampling the seafood finger foods as they chatted.

Auggie held the dog on his lap throughout their meal, sneaking him bits of shellfish while Keya put slivers of shrimp on a cocktail napkin for the cat.

As she shelled a shrimp, Keya asked, "Do you live in Marathon, Auggie?"

He shook his head. "Diesel and I live aboard a houseboat in Key West."

Keya's violet eyes dilated as she studied him. "So, the sea's your mistress."

Seeming to gather his thoughts, Auggie laughed self-consciously as he glanced at Diesel. "It *is* where my heart is—" he gave her an enigmatic smile "—and it's home."

"Don't you ever tire of sailing and want to settle in one place?"

"Maybe someday." He shrugged. "Just not yet."

"I understand the call of the unknown, the wanderlust." She breathed deeply as if reliving memories. "I've always spent a year or two traveling, exploring, and then a year or two regrouping at home." Keya caught Auggie's eye as she laughed. "I need both—first flitting about, seeing the world, and then relaxing in my nest—just not concurrently."

"Plot your own course, I always say." The glow in Auggie's eyes flickered. "For Diesel and me, home is where the anchor drops. We're just two seadogs happy to sail the high seas."

"Brett will be living at sea this week." Ruth turned toward Auggie. "He's going on a fishing trip with five old college friends. Let's see if he finds his sea-legs."

"You're in for a treat, Brett." Auggie's eyes lit up. "Nothing compares to a sea voyage." Then he glanced at Ruth. "What'll you be doing while he's off fishing?"

"Keya landed me a freelance writing assignment where she volunteers at the Turtle Refuge." Ruth glanced at her cousin. "She's always had a special gift, and from what I understand, she puts it to good use at the refuge."

Shrugging, Keya gave a modest laugh. "I don't do much."

"That's not what I hear." Ruth shook her head before turning to Auggie. "She communicates with animals."

"Is that so?" Auggie cocked an eyebrow.

Keya nodded. "I help the veterinarians find out

what's wrong with the turtles by talking to them."

"Talking to the vets?" Auggie's brow creased.

Keya shook her head. "Talking to the *turtles*. A turtle's heart beats only 20 times per hour, so surgery's limited to an hour, tops, leaving just minutes to explore. To save time and suffering, I ask the turtles where they hurt."

Auggie's cynical stare spoke for him.

"You don't believe me?" Shoulders straightening as she met his gaze, Keya challenged him.

"Let's just say—" He shrugged. "—I'm skeptical."

"Then allow me to demonstrate." Keya scarcely concealed a sneer as she whispered to Earnestine, "Sit on Ruth's lap while I chat with Diesel."

The cat gave a low, throaty growl but climbed off her lap onto Ruth's.

Then Keya fixed her gaze on Diesel. Making no sound, she seemed to mentally engage him as he first perked his ears and then cocked his head, studying her. After a few moments, he crossed from Auggie's lap to hers.

Then Keya petted the dog rhythmically, methodically covering his body with her hands. As she touched one point on his rear thigh, he yelped. Keya nodded and massaged the area. "He pulled a muscle yesterday."

Sitting up straight, Auggie blinked. "He was limping a little last night now that you mention it."

After a few minutes, Diesel sighed and relaxed against Keya.

"Well, I'll be." Auggie laughed. "I've never seen him take a liking to anyone so fast."

"He just needed a woman's touch." Still petting the

dog, Keya gave Auggie an impish smile. "Convinced?"

"Dogs don't lie." He shook his head. "You can't buy their affection."

"Unlike some people." Her mouth twisted in a bitter frown. "Sorry. I just thought of the Erskines' lawsuit." She took a cleansing breath and let it go.

Auggie sat up straight. "Did you just say Erskine?"

Keya nodded. "My late husband's family. Why? Do you—"

"You'd said Jules earlier…" He hit his forehead with the flat of his hand. "You weren't married to Jules Erskine by any chance, were you?"

"I was." Stiffening, Keya blinked. "Why?"

"I'm his cousin, August Erskine."

Keya's jaw dropped. "I didn't recognize the name Auggie, but I know 'August Erskine' from the paperwork." Pushing back her chair, she scowled at him. "You're part of that family's lawsuit. You and your clan killed my husband with your litigation."

"Now just a doggone minute!" Auggie reached for Diesel as Keya stood. "I had nothing to do with that lawsuit."

"No?" She stared him down. "Your name's on it!"

Auggie shook his head. "An early version of that document included my name—without my consent—but I had it removed. I want nothing to do with that lawsuit—or those shirttail relatives contesting the will." He glanced at Brett. "Your mother and I'd never heard of that side of the family. They only surfaced after a hotel chain tracked them down and contacted them—*and me*—about buying the property." He turned back to Keya. "We share the same name, but that's it. They're a distant branch of the family I'd never even met."

"Are you telling me you don't want your *fair share* of Aunt Libby's place like the others?" Her lip curling, Keya dared him to deny it.

Again, he shook his head. "Diesel and I are happy living away from all that. If I'd wanted Aunt Libby's house, I would've accepted it when she willed it to me."

Her jaw dropped. "You mean *you're* the cousin that disclaimed her house?"

"That's right."

Keya took her seat and studied him as if assessing him. "Why did you refuse the inheritance?"

"Diesel and I aren't landlubbers. We don't need any fancy beach house...although..." He drew a deep breath.

Her eyes narrowed. "Although *what?*"

"As kids, Jules and I used to spend summers there, hunt for *treasure* on our aunt's property." Seeming to look inward, his smile became wistful, nostalgic. "I did regret not seeing the place again..." Then as his smile changed into a grimace, he turned toward Keya. "After what you've just told me, I wouldn't blame you if you wanted nothing to do with me." He sighed. "But nothing ventured, nothing gained. Would you mind if I visited the beach one last time?"

Keya squinted. "Why?"

"I don't know—" Auggie shrugged. "—for old time's sake." He lifted his gaze, silently imploring.

While Keya stared, seeming to wage an internal debate, Earnestine meowed. Keya glanced at the cat, arched her eyebrow, and then turned back to Auggie with a curt nod. "All right."

His surprised laugh was a cross between a snort and a puppy's bark. "What convinced you?"

"Earnestine trusts you." She gave him a begrudging half smile. "Who am I to question her instincts?"

He stretched out his hand to the cat. "Put her there, Earnestine." As the cat touched her paw to his palm, Auggie studied it. "She has six toes."

"Of course she does. She's a descendent of the Hemingway cat."

"Hence the name Earnestine." Auggie snickered.

Nodding, Keya returned his smile.

As Auggie removed his hand, he glanced at his watch. "I hate to break up this party." He turned to Brett. "Don't you have to be in Key West before five?"

Brett checked the time and winced. "Yeah, I have to put the deposit on the boat."

"It's a good hour-and-a-half, two-hour drive," said Auggie. "Give yourself enough time."

Ruth asked, "What about your friends? Can't they—"

"Their plane doesn't arrive until later." Brett gave her a crooked smile.

If meant to be reassuring, his plan did not work—he seemed to grimace. A week would pass before she saw him again, and an ache began radiating from her chest. "I'll miss you, you know." She reached for his hand.

He gave her fingertips a gentle tug. "You, too." Then, standing, he added, "I'd better put your suitcases in Keya's car."

"Let me settle the bill," said Auggie, "and I'll help you."

Five minutes later, their group was downstairs, saying goodbye. The separation beginning, Ruth hugged Brett, reluctant to let go.

"Come by tomorrow for dinner." Keya gave Auggie directions to her house. "I make a mean conch chowder."

Another five minutes, and Ruth was speeding toward Keya's home in her cousin's fire-engine-red convertible. The cat nestled on her lap as she turned one last time to watch Brett's rental car turn south toward Key West.

"Is this your first time in the Keys?" Keya glanced at her through her oversized sunglasses.

Ruth nodded. "It's my first time in Florida. Period."

"In that case"—her eyes on the road, Keya smiled—"Earnestine and I'll have to be your tour guides."

"Sounds great." Ruth glanced from the highway's passing scenery to her cousin and smirked. "Just leave me enough time to write the brochure for the Turtle Refuge."

"You'll have plenty of time." Keya reached over to rub the cat's ears. "Won't she, Earnestine?" At the cat's meow, Keya said, "First on the agenda, a tour of the house." With that, she turned onto a private road, waited for the electric gate to open, and drove through a palm-tree-lined lane toward a contemporary beach house, all angles and glass.

After Keya parked, Earnestine jumped out and led the way along the manicured path.

"The landscaping's beautiful." Ruth admired the shiny foliage and fragrant flowers as they strolled toward the house. "Do you take care of this yourself?"

"Oh, heaven's no," said Keya, unlocking the door.

"I wouldn't know where to begin. A gardener comes once a week."

Inside the house, everything was white—white-painted walls, white-tiled floors, and an ash-white stone fireplace. The plush, overstuffed sofas and chairs were such a subtle tint of pale blue, they seemed off-white. Glass, stone, and chrome elements infused the rooms.

Then the two window walls came into view. Perpendicular glass walls let the outside in. The beach view filled the house, letting in the warmth the furnishings lacked. A monochrome palette inside, the imposing seashore and sky lent the rooms panache with a vivid turquoise seascape.

It took Ruth a moment to adjust to the stark furnishings, but then she smiled. "I get it."

Tilting her head, Keya regarded her through one eye. "Get what?"

"Your style." Ruth nodded as she peered at the beach through the glass walls. "You haven't decorated as much as you've let nature do the honors. You're letting the landscape shine through."

A slow smile lit up Keya's face. "Flamboyance has its place, but not in competition with nature." She slid open a glass door. "Now let me show you the real beauty of this place."

They followed a cement path through white sand to a hot-tub and kidney-shaped pool. From there, they walked to the sandy beach, following its contours over a narrow isthmus that led to a bridge, which opened onto a secluded island.

"This." Keya's violet eyes glowed as she spread her arms to encompass the beach. "This is the real beauty of the place. My own little key."

Staring out at the sea, glancing from the palm-fringed beach to the sailboats in the distance, Ruth nodded. "I can see why you say that. It's beautiful, truly a jewel."

Keya's smile became mischievous as she shook her head. "You haven't seen the best part." With that, she pointed out the footprints in the sand. "Know what these are?"

Ruth shrugged. "Some kind of animal tracks?"

"Sea turtles!" Keya's eyes crinkled into a smile. "Because they're not disturbed, the endangered loggerheads nest here. *I love it!*"

After glimpsing the inner workings of her cousin's mind, Ruth glanced at the cordoned-off area. "Is that a turtle nest?"

"Yes. I marked the spot the day I noticed it—May first. Since leatherback turtle eggs take seventy to eighty days to hatch"—she shot Ruth a gleeful smile— "they may hatch while you're here."

"Wouldn't that be something!" Ruth grinned in wonder as she took in the protected beach. "So, this is the real reason you live here?"

"Partly." Keya frowned as if struggling to put her thoughts into words. "These nesting grounds are the reason I've fought to keep this property intact. The Erskines are only contesting the will so they can flip the land." She grimaced. "If this beach is developed, the impact will destroy it. I can't let that happen. I *won't* let that happen, but fighting the lawsuit is expensive. I'd hate to have to sell this place to pay court costs."

Ruth gave her a sympathetic smile. "But you said keeping the nesting grounds intact is only part of the reason you stay." Ruth gazed at her. "What's the rest of it?"

"Call it my *legacy*." Keya stood up straight. "When I'm gone, I'd like this beach to remain as nature intended it…for the turtles. Since I've never had children—"

Earnestine meowed.

Keya gave a dry laugh. "That is, except for my furry, four-legged kids, I've never had children. I have no one to leave the property to—other than who or *what* will make the best use of it. Conveying this land to the turtles would be my way of leaving the world a better place." She turned toward Ruth. "Does that make sense?"

Ruth nodded and gazed at Keya as if for the first time. Her cousin's intentions were clear. "But legally, how can you will the property to the turtles?"

"Easy. I leave it to the Turtle Refuge." Keya laughed inwardly as they meandered along the beach. "And this is where you come in. When you're writing the brochure, add a few paragraphs about planned giving and charitable bequests…" Her words broke off as Keya stared as if in a trance.

Ruth looked at her. "What's wrong?"

Her hand shaking, Keya pointed to a shady patch of beach half hidden by sand dunes. A lifeless hand lay tangled in seaweed, its fingernails broken and bloodied.

Racing behind the sandbanks to help, Ruth skidded to a halt, her heels digging into the sand. A woman's bloated body lay staring at the sun, her eyes opaque and unseeing. "Do you recognize her?"

"No." Keya shook her head as the cat gingerly approached, sniffing and meowing. "But Earnestine said she smells familiar."

Chapter 2

Body of Water

Two squad cars and an ambulance pulled in the drive, sirens blaring, disrupting the seaside serenity. As police officers retrieved the body and canvassed the shore for clues, a detective questioned Keya and Ruth inside the house.

"We just arrived here minutes before we found the body," said Ruth.

"Where were you before then?"

"At the Fisheries having lunch."

"Can anyone corroborate your story?" asked the officer.

Ruth nodded, giving them Brett's and Auggie's cell phone numbers. Then, smiling, she recalled her cousin's signature drink. "If you question the bartender at the seafood bar upstairs, I'm sure he'll remember my cousin's Pineapple Cinnamon Mojito."

The officer nodded. "Where were you before that?"

"Driving down US Highway 1 from the Miami airport." She got out her flight pass. "My fiancé and I arrived in Florida just a few hours ago."

"Yet in that brief time, you managed to discover a dead body."

Ruth blinked. *How do I respond?*

He turned his attention to Keya. "How long have

you lived at this residence?"

"Less than two years." She held Earnestine against her chest, as if drawing comfort.

"Do you know the deceased?"

Keya shook her head. "I don't recognize her, although Earnestine thinks she smells familiar."

"Earnestine?" The officer raised his head questioningly. "Who's Earnestine?"

Keya held out the cat toward him. "This is Miss Earnestine Hemingway, descended from—"

"I see…" The officer scratched his chin and started again. "So, the deceased seems familiar to you?"

"Not to me," said Keya. "I don't believe I've ever met the young woman, but Earnestine has a sophisticated sense of smell. If she—"

The officer's smile verged on a sneer. As if humoring her, he asked, "How does your cat know the deceased?"

Keya turned Earnestine toward her and gazed into her eyes. After a moment, the cat meowed. "The woman spent time next door." Keya pointed.

He all but rolled his eyes. "She frequented the house next door, but you don't recognize her…have I got that right?"

Keya nodded.

"Has anyone been reported missing?" asked Ruth.

The detective shot her a sharp look. "Why do you ask?"

Ruth shrugged. "Wouldn't it make sense to associate a body with a missing person's report?"

He scratched his ear. "A capsized sailboat was found beached this morning with no one aboard. We traced the sloop to a rental agency, where a woman answering the deceased's description had leased it."

"Do you think that's the same person?"

"It's premature to venture a guess, but…" He grimaced.

"It makes sense." Ruth finished his sentence. "Yet no missing person's report was filed for her?"

The detective shook his head. "Not yet."

"The boat rental agency must have her identification on record." Ruth studied him.

He checked his notes. "A Miss Rogers listed her place of employment as…" Then looking from his notes, he turned toward Keya. "The house number here is 57550, right?"

She nodded.

"Miss Rogers listed her place of employment as 57546." With an ironic laugh, he glanced at Earnestine. "It seems your cat's right. She worked next door."

Keya frowned. "I thought the place was vacant."

****

Two hours later, the police left, and Keya turned to Ruth. "How about a mojito?"

Carrying their drinks outside, they reclined on chaise lounges, watching the sun melt through the sky until it sizzled into the sea and turned the waves into molten gold.

Ruth scanned the horizon from the sandy beach with its palm trees silhouetted against the ruddy sky to the heavens morphing from aquamarine to a fiery opal, and she began to relax after the interrogation. "What an idyllic location. It's so different from the beaches at home along Lake Michigan." She sipped her mojito. "Living here must be like staying at a resort every day, only better. It's private—just you, Earnestine, and the turtles."

Keya drew in a sharp breath. "Those first few months were paradise when Jules was here, but after the lawsuits, Jules's stroke, coma, and passing..." She grimaced. "And now a body washed onshore..." She shook her head. "It's Paradise Lost."

Earnestine cocked her head and stiffened as she growled in her throat.

"Knock, knock," called a man's voice.

Ruth flinched at the sound.

"Who's there?" called Keya, her tone curt.

A tall, thin man wearing khakis and a nautical polo shirt waved from the property line next door. Then he stepped over the low row of pilings and picked his way through the thorny pyracantha bushes that served as a boundary between the properties. After pointing to the house behind him, he brushed his salt-and-pepper hair from his eyes. "I'm your next-door neighbor, Gerald Granger, but call me Gerry. Hope this isn't an inopportune time to introduce myself."

"I didn't realize anyone lived there." Her smile stiff, Keya stood, seeming to gather her shaken nerves about her like a flowing kaftan. "We made a fresh pitcher of mojitos. Would you care for a drink?"

"I would, at that."

"I'm Keya Erskine, and this is my cousin Ruth Bernard." Her back toward him as she poured his drink, she added, "Join us."

His stony, calculating eyes looked Keya up and down as if appraising her. "Pleased to meet you both." He crossed toward Keya, accepted the offered glass, and as he took a sip, his eyes lit up. "What an unusual flavor. What is it?"

Keya shot Ruth a sly look. "A Pineapple Cinnamon Mojito." Then she gestured toward the patio chairs. "Have a seat."

Though the neighbor's familiarity did not seem to faze her cousin, Ruth took an instant disliking to the man. "Did I understand correctly, Gerald? Did Miss Rogers work at your house?"

"Gerry," he corrected with a smile. Then his expression drooped. "Unfortunately, Maita was my bookkeeper."

Ruth held her head back to better observe him. "Hadn't you filed a missing person's report?"

"Why? Maita was fine when she left the office yesterday…seemed in high spirits." He shrugged. "She'd mentioned something about going sailing, so I didn't expect to see her again—"

"What do you mean you 'didn't expect to see her again'?" *Why do I find him so distasteful?*

"—until Monday morning at work," he finished, his tone sharp, his stretched lips pinched at one corner, as if mildly irritated. "I was called to the morgue this afternoon to identify her body." He shook his head. "Poor girl. She didn't have any family in the Keys. I gave the police her HR information, but her nearest relative is in Saint Augustine—a cousin, I believe."

Ruth studied him. "Did she work for you long?"

The muscles around his eyes contracted. "Do you moonlight for the police, Miss Bernard, or are you always this inquisitive?"

Her cheeks warmed. "No."

"Could've fooled me." His smile was shrewd as he scrutinized her with beady eyes. "You have a knack for interrogation."

"We don't find a dead body every day." Ruth hunched her shoulders as she sipped her drink.

"Of course not, and I apologize for being brusque." Gerry grimaced. "I'm afraid poor Maita's unexpected death has put us all on edge." He set down his drink as he sighed. "This is a dreadful way to meet new neighbors. Let me make it up to you both." He looked from one woman's face to the other. "Be my guests tomorrow for lunch?"

Keya spoke for them. "Say noon?" Then like a queen rising from her throne, she stood, signaling the audience had ended.

He scrambled to his feet, a quick smile materializing at his thin lips as he held out his hand. "I look forward to it."

Keya's smile taut and regal, she folded her hands in front of her, seeming to block further interaction.

As if unsure what to do with his outstretched hand, he raised it in a mock salute. "Till tomorrow then."

Keya called after him, "Careful of the firethorn." Then she whispered to Earnestine, "What do you think?"

The cat hissed.

Keya nodded. "I thought so."

"I don't trust something about him," said Ruth. "What is it?"

Keya shook her head. "I don't know, but all three of us picked up negative vibes."

"Then why did you accept his lunch invitation?"

"Just a hunch." Keya shrugged. "Maybe we'll learn something tomorrow."

They finished their drinks while the sky morphed from periwinkle and amethyst to burgundy and plum.

Then they went inside, where Keya set the security alarm and turned on the recessed lighting. "How about a light dinner, maybe a salad?"

"Perfect. I'm still full from lunch. Can I help?"

"No, relax. I'll just be a minute."

Ruth stepped toward the window walls, watching the last glimmer of sunlight fade on the horizon, when a shadow crossed the beach. She immediately stepped back, turned out the lights, and screened herself from view as she peered out.

A moment later, Keya flipped on the dining-room light that softly filtered into the living room. "What are you doing in the dark?"

Ruth gave a nervous laugh. "I thought someone was nosing around your beach."

"A trespasser?" Keya dashed to the windows, squinting through the gloom.

The hairs rose on the back of Ruth's neck. Shuddering, she eyed the wide-open window walls. "Don't these windows have shades?"

"Nope." Keya shook her head. "They're smart windows."

Ruth tilted her head. *Did I hear wrong?* "Smart windows?"

"Yup." Keya flipped another switch, and the clear windows became opaque. She smiled. "Is that better?"

Ruth nodded as she took a deep breath. "Sitting here, I felt eyes watching me—as if the windows were for looking in, not looking out."

"I know what you mean," said Keya, "but between the smart windows and the security alarm, I feel safe here at night."

The cat meowed.

"Yes, Earnestine, you're my personal intruder alarm." Keya scratched behind her ears. "She hears and sees in the dark ten times better than I do. Nothing gets past her."

****

After a quiet dinner, Ruth hid a yawn behind her hand. "Sorry. I don't know if it's the sea air or traveling, but I feel so sleepy. Mind if I turn in early tonight?"

"Make yourself at home." Keya gave her a hug. "See you in the morning."

Before showering, Ruth called Brett to update him about the afternoon's events.

"Have to admit, I got worried when the police called, asking questions about you," he said. "I'm gone an hour, and you find a body washed up on your cousin's beach."

Ruth took a deep breath, dispelling some of the tension. "Discovering her body was unnerving, and it seemed to set the tone for the rest of the evening."

"What do you mean?"

She told him about the neighbor's visit and the shadow crossing the beach. "Both were unsettling."

"You're probably just tired, and it's affecting your perception. Try to get some sleep."

She grimaced. "These separate vacations sounded all right in theory, but I wish we weren't fifty miles apart tonight."

"You have that brochure to write." Brett's tone was patient, rational. "My buddies have been after me for years to go deep-sea-fishing with them. This seemed like the perfect solution—flying into Miami and driving through the Keys together—both on the way down and back. We're both doing what's necessary. Parallel play; we're separate but close."

"Fifty miles is anything but close." Frowning, she sighed. "And I miss you already."

"I miss you, too." The warmth came through his voice. "But next Sunday will be here before you know it."

"Not soon enough." Glancing at her phone, she got an idea. "Can we keep in touch on our cells?"

"The boat has ship-to-shore radio communication, but I'm told reception only works about fifteen nautical miles out to sea."

"How far out will you be?"

"Hard to say, but some of the reefs and uninhabited mangrove islands they want to fish are forty miles from Key West."

"Great…" Her shoulders drooped along with her spirits.

"I'll call you tomorrow before we leave and whenever we're within range," said Brett. "Don't let the distance bother you. Inches or miles apart, I love you."

She forced a smile, trying to end on a good note. "I love you, too. Talk to you tomorrow."

****

Following an al fresco breakfast of *café con leche* and Cuban toast on the patio, Keya checked the pool's temperature. "It's like bath water. Did you bring your swimsuit?"

As they splashed around the pool, Ruth's cell rang. After wiping her hands on a towel, she answered without checking Caller ID. "Brett?"

"Uh…no," said a man's voice. "It's Auggie."

"Hey, Auggie." She raised her voice for Keya's

benefit. "To what do we owe this pleasure?"

"Diesel and I caught a nice mahi-mahi this morning, and we were thinking of bringing some filets for dinner tonight. What time do you and Keya want us?"

"Good question. Keya, when would you like Auggie to come for dinner?"

"I almost forgot. I promised to make conch chowder." Staring at space, Keya thought aloud. "We can stop at the fish market on the way home from church. Tell him four o'clock."

Ruth relayed the information and glanced at the time as she hung up. "When's church?"

"Eleven," said Keya. "What time is it?"

****

As the church bells pealed and they dashed from the parking lot, Brett called. Ruth barely had time to wish him fair winds and calm seas before they hurried inside, finding seats in the back row. Then as she joined the opening hymn, she gazed at the island church's low, rounded ceiling. *It looks like an upside-down ship.*

Ruth nudged her cousin after the readings. "Maybe because Brett's going sea fishing, I have boats on my mind," she whispered, "but with its rafters, beams, and ribs, doesn't this ceiling remind you of a ship's inverted hull?"

Keya looked up, nodding as the homily began.

"If you're visiting us today, welcome aboard!" The priest smiled. "It's fitting in this seaside community that the early church architects were shipbuilders. In fact, they called the area where you're sitting *the nave* from the same root word as navy. They compared the church to a ship with a crew but no passengers. No one

27

had a free ride. Every member had a responsibility, a task."

Ruth gazed again at the ceiling. *Functional* and *symbolic.*

"If you think about it, a ship and a church share many similarities. We have a Captain of our ship, of our soul. We're all aboard a vessel, headed toward the kingdom of heaven.

"With each member contributing a different skill, we need to join forces, not rock the boat or cause division. Some members believe in discipline, wearing solemn expressions because they believe serving the Captain is serious business. They tend to congregate in the back of the boat, which happens to be called the stern." A smile lit his face.

"The prayer warriors believe in kneeling and bowing. They're found in the ship's bow." His eyes twinkled. "Another group forms the maintenance crew, often working in the galley or below deck, making sure everything in church is ship shape.

"No matter who does what, all crewmembers are essential. All hands must be *on deck*, and no one's more important to the journey than anyone else. We all need to be onboard, although sometimes we also need to rescue members who've fallen overboard and find themselves adrift.

"As with any voyage, adjustments are necessary. Courses don't sail in straight lines. Corrections are needed to reach our destination. Sometimes, we must zigzag across the sea, tacking our sailboat into the wind, and sometimes we need to trim the sails.

"Our Captain knows which corrections to make for our course. Our task as the crew is to pay close attention and listen for His instructions. Then when the sails have been set through prayer, the Holy Spirit—*the wind*—moves us along the course the Captain charted for us."

As they left, Ruth glanced at her cousin. "I like the analogy of a church and a ship."

"*Ship!*" Keya thumped her head as she started the car. "That reminds me. We have to stop at the fish market." She glanced at the clock. "Barely enough time to get to lunch next door. I don't know when I'll have time to make the chowder."

"You'll have all afternoon," said Ruth. "How long can lunch last?"

When they got home, they dropped off the fish, picked up Earnestine, and dashed next door, carefully picking their way through the thorny pyracantha.

Gerry met them beachside and led them around to the front, where a stretch limousine waited.

Unimpressed with the luxury sedan, Ruth pursed her lips. The limo's finish was polished to such a high shine, it appeared to deflect dust. "I thought we were having lunch."

"We are." He smiled as the chauffeur opened the door for them. "But the chef's a much better cook than I am."

"We weren't expecting anything fancy," said Ruth. "Aren't we grilling outside?"

He grimaced. "After Maita's untimely death, I can't relax on the beach. I prefer to eat out, anyway." He tapped the window separating the driver's seat from the back, and the car rolled forward.

When Keya caught her eye, Ruth shrugged.

"Will Earnestine be welcome?"

"Why wouldn't she?" His smile was sly. "My company owns the restaurant."

After fifteen minutes of polite chitchat, Keya asked, "Where is this place, anyway?"

"Key Largo."

"Key Largo!" Keya scowled. "That's an hour away."

He waved off her concerns with a flick of his wrist. "Just another forty-five minutes. Besides, this gives me time to get acquainted with my new neighbor."

Ruth studied him as his lips turned up in an unpleasant smile verging on a leer.

"I'm curious," he said. "Are you planning to live there year-round, or will you be visiting occasionally?"

Keya shrugged. "I haven't decided."

"Perhaps you're planning to flip the property? I know an excellent realtor, who—

"I *haven't*...decided..." Her tone sharp, Keya let her words hang while she stared him down.

Changing his tenor, he became their tour guide as he pointed out various points of interest along the highway. "This is one of our company's investments," he said, drawing their attention to an enormous construction site.

Ruth tried to read the sign, but vegetation partially hid the unfinished framework. "What are you building?"

"A hotel." He smiled through uneven, stained teeth. "Tourism statistics show the Keys attract almost three million overnight guests each year—good news for the hospitality industry."

"So, hotels are your company's business?" asked Ruth.

He nodded. "Building hotels and flipping properties."

"Is that why you bought the house next door?" Keya studied him.

"How direct." He smiled. "Is that what you think?"

"Until yesterday, I thought the property was vacant," said Keya.

"I bought this parcel for my personal use, but I rarely use it. However"—he leered at her—"now that I've met my neighbor, I'll spend as much time there as possible."

Earnestine's tail puffed up as she emitted a low growl.

"What was Maita doing on the property?" asked Ruth pointblank.

"I told you yesterday." Turning toward her, his smile stiffened. "She was my company's bookkeeper."

Ruth thrust her chin. "Do you make a habit of using your home as a place of business?"

"Maita was an exception." His acerbic smile verged on a smirk. "She was a whiz with numbers and willing to work odd hours. Whenever I traveled on business, I brought her along." He shrugged. "The arrangement was more convenient for both of us."

"Yet she's dead." Ruth distrusted his reaction.

"Yes, that was unfortunate." His expression grim, Gerry shook his head. "A double disaster."

Ruth squinted. "What do you mean?"

"This morning, auditors notified me that Maita had 'cooked the books.' "

Ruth shook her head. "I don't follow."

"She'd double-charged numerous company accounts, skimming from them, and then hiding the transactions behind imaginative bookkeeping." He grimaced. "Not that I like to talk about the dead, but she apparently wasn't the loyal accountant I'd believed. With her aptitude for figures, I guess the temptation was just too great."

****

When they reached the restaurant, Gerry gave them a tour of the facilities.

"So, this isn't *just* a restaurant, but a full-service hotel," said Keya, carrying Earnestine.

His face lit up. "The best this side of Miami."

"Let me guess," said Ruth. "Your company owns a hotel and restaurant in Miami."

"Several." He laughed quietly as he waved over the maître d'. "Raoul, seat us in the closed area, overlooking the water. My guests and I want a quiet spot to chat."

Gerry ordered Oysters Rockefeller as appetizers while they studied the oversized menus. Hot and bubbling from the oven, the oysters gave off a slightly licorice aroma from the fresh fennel and dash of anise liquor.

Then as the waiter brought Gerry's surf n' turf, the steak sizzled on the platter as steam rose from the lobster.

Ruth inhaled the rich, wood-smoked flavor of her salmon grilled on a cedar plank. Her mouth watering, she bit into the tender fish.

Keya ordered seafood enchiladas and, after breathing in the spicy scents, sneezed. "The cumin and chilies tickle my nose." She glanced at Gerry as she sneaked Earnestine a smidgen of lobster. "And thanks for accommodating my cat."

"Well-behaved pets aren't the problem at restaurants or hotels." Smiling, he shook his head. "I'm reminded of the man who called a hotel, planning a visit with his dog—'Could I keep him in my room with me?'

"The manager said, 'I've never had a dog steal towels, pillows, or silverware. I've never evicted a dog for being drunk or disorderly, and I've never had a dog run out on a hotel bill. Yes, your dog's welcome here, and if he'll vouch for you, you're welcome, too.' "

Ruth studied him. *Did I misjudge him?*

They chatted on the drive home, and when he dropped them off, Gerry's smile seemed sincere. "We'll have to do this again. It's been a pleasure, ladies. I look forward to our next visit."

As they crossed to Keya's house, Ruth looked at the time. "Three-thirty—yikes! Auggie will be here in a half hour."

"And I haven't even started dinner, not that I'm hungry." Keya groaned. "I'm still stuffed from lunch."

"Me, too."

"It'll take an hour to make the conch chowder. Maybe by then, we'll feel like eating," said Keya. "Can you and Earnestine entertain him until then?"

Chapter 3

Key West—Cayo Hueso—*Island of Bones*

When Auggie called from the main gate promptly at four, Ruth buzzed him in.

Keya refrigerated his fish filets before asking, "How would you like a beer while I finish making the chowder?"

"Thought you'd never ask."

He and Ruth brought out their drinks and a bowl of water for Diesel as they relaxed on the patio.

Gerry gave them a neighborly wave as he puttered around his backyard beach.

When Ruth waved back, Auggie recoiled. "How do you know Gerald Granger?"

"He introduced himself last night, and today we had lunch." Still unsure of Gerry's motives, Ruth struggled to sound unbiased. "He bought the property next door."

Auggie muttered under his breath.

"Sorry, what was that?"

He grimaced as he scratched his ear. "You realize he's the reason the family's challenging the will, don't you?"

"What!" Coming to attention, Ruth sat up on her chaise lounge.

"Granger's behind the lawsuit."

She squinted. "Why?"

"Because he wants the land." Auggie's sneer was contemptuous. "Did he happen to mention how he plans to combine these two properties into a beachfront hotel property?"

Dazed, Ruth stared at him. "How do you know that?"

"Don't forget, until I told him I wasn't interested, he'd included me in the legal action." Auggie took out his phone and brought up a document. "Here's an email attachment I got from his hotel chain a while back."

Ruth shook her head as she read. "This document can't be right."

"Why not?" Auggie caught her eye. "Doesn't it mesh with the story he told you?"

"Something like that."

He scoffed. "He's smooth."

"Guess I should've stayed with my first impressions." Pursing her lips, she let the lesson sink in. "Did you know the woman who drowned worked for him?"

He shook his head. "The police didn't mention it when they questioned me."

"Maita was his bookkeeper."

"Maita." Under his breath, Auggie added, "Sorrowful Lady."

"What was that?" She read his lips.

"Maita's a Cuban name meaning Sorrowful Lady."

She grimaced. "Apparently, she lived up to her name."

"Lived…?" He finished his beer and stood. "Where did you find her body?"

"On the little island. Why?"

"My metal detector is in the car. Okay if I comb the beach?" He shrugged. "Maybe it'll uncover something the police missed."

"I'm sure Keya wouldn't mind."

Ten minutes later, after walking across the isthmus and bridge as Diesel dogged their heels, Ruth pointed out the shaded stretch of beach where they had spotted the body.

"As kids, Jules and I used to hunt treasure here." Auggie scanned the area with his metal detector. Then his wistful smile faded. "That was a long time ago."

"Did you ever find anything?" Ruth glanced at him.

He shook his head. "Nothing of any value—just a few rusty nails, bottle caps, and quarters." He swallowed a smile. "'Course, those were *treasures* to us."

When his metal detector made crackling noises, he pulled out a beach scoop and bucket, shoveling through the sand and letting it sift away.

"Various metals make different sounds," he said. "Gold and silver make a high-pitched beep, while metals like iron make a dull beep."

"Sounds like a Geiger counter to me."

"Yeah, the frequencies were on the lower end of the spectrum." Auggie let the last of the sand sift away, leaving behind a broken keychain. He grunted to himself as if thinking.

"What?"

He shrugged. "Probably nothing, but you said this was where you and Keya found the body?"

Ruth nodded.

"This chain could be a clue." He lifted it with his

handkerchief. "Just in case of any fingerprints."

"Good thinking."

He moved the detector's wand over the sand in a grid pattern, systematically covering the area. After a few minutes, the locater emitted a high-pitched beep.

Ruth caught his gaze while he scooped the sand. "That sounded different."

He nodded as the sand sifted away from his bucket, leaving behind something shiny.

"An earring," she said.

He pointed to the cross on one side, and turning it over with a stick, an imprint on the other. "Could be wrong, but this looks like a *Regala* reale."

"A what?" She squinted as she listened.

"This earring looks like a Spanish coin called a *reale*. Many were found on the *Regala*, a ship that sank in 1622."

"How can you tell?"

"Anyone on the Keys can recognize Dan Miller's finds." He opened his collar to expose the coin hanging at his neck. "This is my Key West 'dog tag.' "

"Dog tag?"

"Just about everyone who knew Dan has one of these. It's a piece of eight from the *Regala*. Dan used to pay his bar tabs with these." He gave a dry laugh. "Guys are wearing coins worth thousands of dollars— and they don't have a clue. In fact, Dan wrote the authentication certificate for this one on a cocktail napkin."

"He sounds like a *'reale'* character."

Wearing a fond smile, Auggie bobbed his head. "He was."

Something glittered on the beach, catching and

reflecting the sunlight. Ruth scooped the object in a handful of sand to avoid touching it, but as she wiped away damp grains, her palm grazed it.

Instantly, two figures appeared.

Ruth froze. Hyperventilating and wobbling on her legs, she blinked, hoping to clear her vision, but there they stood. *Great. Now I'm seeing things.*

One entity resembled the bookkeeper's body but seemed oblivious of its surroundings. Fingernails broken and bloody, its hands covered its mouth, and its chest rose and fell as if sobbing or silently weeping.

The other appeared as a gray mist with the vague outline of a man's face and physique. The hairs rose on the back of Ruth's neck, and when a dark eye peered at her from the mist's sinister face, she screamed.

Diesel barked at the apparitions, and she flinched, dropping the earring.

As fast as the two figures appeared, they vanished.

What was that?

"Are you all right?" Auggie lifted the second earring, letting the sand sift through the beach scoop. Then he dumped both silver-coin earrings into his handkerchief.

"Yeah," she fibbed, taking fast, shallow breaths, as her heart raced. *I've got to think this through.* "Why?"

"You seem a bit jumpy."

"Diesel's bark startled me. That's all." She pretended to shrug off the incident, but then she winced. "If these are clues to Maita's death, shouldn't we call the police?"

"Definitely." He nodded as the dog sniffed the earrings. "Do you smell something, Diesel?"

The dog woofed, and Auggie shook his head good-naturedly as he reached down to scratch his head. "Almost makes you think animals have a sixth sense, doesn't it?"

****

A few minutes later, they joined Keya in the kitchen, showing her the keychain and jewelry.

Though Earnestine ignored the chain, her tail puffed as she sniffed the earrings, and she meowed.

Keya considered her as if dialoguing on an intuitive level. "She thinks the earrings belonged to the drowned woman."

Auggie's lips formed the unspoken question "Wha—?"

Ruth reminded him with a gentle smile. "My cousin's always had an empathy with animals."

Keya rummaged in her purse for the detective's card, then glanced at the name. "Let's give Detective Bell a quick call." She shrugged as she dialed. "He probably won't be on duty until tomorrow, but at least we'll make the attempt."

She was wrong. Less than a half hour later, he was questioning them in the kitchen.

"Has anyone touched this chain and earrings?" He held out an opened plastic baggie.

Auggie shook his head as he carefully transferred the items from his handkerchief to the bag.

"My palm brushed against one of the earrings," said Ruth, "but I don't think I left fingerprints."

"I'll have the lab dust these for prints." Detective Bell glared at her. "Anything you want to add?"

Ruth considered mentioning the two spirits. *No, he wouldn't take me seriously—or he'd take me to the nearest loony bin.* She stifled a sigh.

"I could be wrong," said Auggie, "but these earrings look like converted *Regala reales*."

Nodding, the detective made a note.

Ruth recalled the apparition's sobbing and silent crying. "Was the young woman's drowning an accident—or foul play?"

"Why do you ask?" The detective wheeled around to face her.

Ruth shuddered as a chill passed over her. "Finding a body washed ashore gives me the willies. I can't help but wonder…"

His expression hostile, the detective studied her. "As a matter of fact, this case has been reclassified from accidental drowning to suspected homicide."

"Homicide!" Ruth caught her breath. "What makes you say that?"

"I'm not at liberty to discuss the details, but we have enough circumstantial evidence to suspect this wasn't accidental."

An image of the apparition's fingernails floated through Ruth's mind. "By any chance, did the lab find signs of a struggle?"

His eyes became slits. "Why do you ask?"

"The body's fingernails were jagged and bloodied. I just wondered—"

"I'll be in touch." The detective gave a curt nod as he shut the door.

Any remnant of a party atmosphere dispelled, Keya sighed as she turned toward her guests. "Not to be disrespectful of the dead, but we can't do anything to help her tonight. Let's just try to enjoy life, okay? Auggie, can I get you another beer?"

He wore a grim shadow of his usual smile. "I could

use one."

Keya grabbed a bottle from the fridge, opened it, and handed him the beer. "Need a glass?"

The corner of his mouth lifting, he shook his head. "No thanks. I take mine straight."

"Ruth, what can I get you?"

Helping herself, Ruth said, "A beer's good. Thanks."

Keya took a deep breath. "In that case, I'm making a mojito. How 'bout we relax on the patio?"

A few minutes later, they were seated outside, subdued, trying to make sense of the recent events while the evening breeze wafted over them. Late afternoon slipped into twilight.

Diesel sat on Auggie's lap as Earnestine curled on Keya's. Though the pets eyed each other, they seemed to settle into a wary pact, tolerating each other so long as their persons were near.

Then the fading sun reflected off Auggie's coin, making the metal glow, and Keya leaned forward for a closer look. "What's that pendant you're wearing?"

"This?" Inclining toward her, he held out the coin, but the chain was too short to reach. Instead, he took off the necklace and handed it to her. "This is my Key West dog tag, one of the original pieces of eight from the *Regala*."

Keya rubbed it, fingering the imprint and ridges as much as seeing them. "Why did they call this coin a piece of eight?"

"People broke or sliced them into eight pieces to pay smaller debts. Also called a Spanish dollar, it's the model for the US dollar."

"Really?" Ruth looked at him.

He nodded. "See those pillars wrapped with banners?"

"Oh, yeah. They look like dollar signs." Keya offered Ruth the necklace. "See? Each one looks like a big S with two lines through it."

Ruth hesitated. If she touched the pendant, what might emerge? *How silly.* Scoffing at herself, she shook off her fears. Then she ran her fingers over the coin, tactilely detecting the embossed metal's rims and ridges. "How 'bout that?"

The moment she connected with the coin, the misty gray entity appeared again. As the nebulous mist gathered into a form, a man materialized with one dark eye peering at her.

Diesel barked while Earnestine hissed, and Ruth flinched, pulling back her hand.

The figure vanished the moment she lost contact with the coin, and it rolled beneath the table.

She rubbed her hand on her thigh, wanting to wipe off all traces of the brief connection. Her heart pounding, she broke out in a cold sweat, yet despite her terror, she was intrigued.

"Earnestine," asked Keya, "what was that all about?" When the cat meowed, Keya recoiled and turned to Ruth. "Did you see some sort of—" She winced. "—presence?"

Ruth took a deep breath, debating whether to share her secret and risk sounding ridiculous. "Let me put it this way. Do you believe in ghosts?"

Keya gave a disbelieving laugh, then wrinkled her forehead as she considered the question. "I don't rule them out. I've just never seen one."

"What would you say if I told you I have?" Ruth

studied her.

"Have you?"

Ruth nodded. "I think so. At least, I can't offer any other explanation for seeing these…entities."

"Have you always seen them?" Brows drawing together, Keya's face tightened.

Ruth shook her head. "This afternoon was the first time—when I accidentally touched the earring. Handling the coin just now was the second."

"Maybe you have a *gift*," said Auggie, wearing a dubious yet receptive expression.

Ruth held her head back to better view him. "What kind of gift?"

"Psychometry." Auggie shrugged. "I've heard how some people can touch an object and visualize its past. Maybe in this case, my dog tag is connected to an apparition."

"Possibly a connection between the coin and the ship?" asked Keya. "The *Regala*?"

Ruth considered the possibility. "The figure appeared just now and earlier, when my palm brushed against the earring."

"This coin's definitely part of the *Regala* treasure," said Auggie, "and I suspect the earrings are, too. That might be the link."

Keya retrieved the necklace. "Want to try again?"

Ruth took another deep breath to steady her nerves. Finally, she accepted the chain from her cousin, letting the coin rest on her palm.

Again, a figure gradually appeared, eliciting the same hissing and barking from the animals.

"Calm down." Keya petted her cat with long, reassuring strokes.

Earnestine stopped hissing but kept flicking her tail, puffed to twice its size.

"Hey!" Auggie scolded Diesel as his low growl persisted. "He never acts this way."

"I think they both see the spirit." Ruth kept her eyes focused on the dark figure as it materialized from a nebulous form into a defined man's shadow. Struggling to maintain her composure, she swallowed. "Who are you?"

Still silent, the image became sharper bit by bit until even its clothing took on more detail—a white ruffled shirt with a lace collar, blooming pantaloons over stockings, floppy turned-down boots, and a cavalier hat that shielded its face from the dim light. Its dark eye watching her, the figure seemed to adopt a seagoing swagger as it took shape.

Ruth raised her voice as she repeated, "Who are you?"

Removing its plumed, wide-brimmed hat and making a sweeping bow, the ghost's deep masculine voice said, "Bartolomé García de Castillo at your service."

Ruth blinked at his unexpected gallantry.

As he straightened his spine, he replaced his hat at a jaunty angle, revealing the patch over his right eye.

That explains the one eye. Swallowing, she found her voice. "Why are you here?"

He paused, seeming to weigh her question. "I'm not sure." With that, his form began to disperse.

"Pleased to meet you, Bartolomé García de Castillo," she said a beat too fast, intrigue overcoming her fear. *Maybe he'll stay if I keep him talking?*

Auggie sat up straight. "The *explorer* Bartolomé

García de Castillo?"

Nearly dissolved, the apparition seemed indifferent until Auggie spoke. Then his shape returned to its form. "You've heard of me?"

As Ruth translated, Auggie nodded. "Any student of naval history has read of the García de Castillo expeditions. You charted the Straits of Magellan and navigated the passage between the Atlantic and Pacific, rounding Cape Horn just south of Tierra del Fuego."

The specter seemed to stand taller at being recognized.

"What were you doing aboard the *Regala*?" asked Ruth.

Bartolomé shook his head, his hat's plume waving with each motion. "Visiting Spain one last time before making my home here." Grimacing, he ducked his head. "But that wasn't meant to be."

Earnestine meowed.

As his gaze rested on her, he reached out to pet her. "Always liked cats." He ran his wraithlike fingers over her fur as if petting her. "If we'd had a cat aboard the *Regala*, it could've predicted the weather and kept us from sailing into a hurricane."

Ruth passed on his information while the cat sniffed him. Then her tail returned to its normal size. Earnestine seemed to relax as she began grooming her six-toed paw.

Bartolomé's one eye opened wide. "A ship's cat."

"Why do you say that?" asked Ruth.

"Her extra toes give her better balance aboard ship."

"Something like having sea legs?"

At his smile and nod, Ruth shared his information.

"Knock, knock," called a man's voice.

Startled, Ruth dropped the necklace.

Bartolomé vanished like steam on a mirror.

"Hope this isn't an inopportune time to drop by. I'd forgotten to give you this information earlier." Clasping a glossy folder, Gerry introduced his companion, an athletic-looking young man. "This is Heath Hawkins, my corporation's purchasing manager. He's staying with me at the moment."

As Heath stretched out his arm to shake hands with Keya, his long-sleeved shirt rode up, exposing multiple scratches.

Seated on Keya's lap, Earnestine laid her ears flat against her head. Then yowling, she reached out and grazed Heath, adding a scratch of her own.

The purchasing manager jerked away his hand as fresh red welts and droplets of blood appeared on his wrist.

"Earnestine!" Keya scolded as the cat's snarling intensified. "What's gotten into you?"

During the ruckus, Gerry approached Auggie. "I'm Gerald Granger." Extending his hand, he nodded to the house behind him. "I live next door."

"We've met," said Auggie, not moving.

"We have?" Gerry lowered his hand. "Who are you?"

"August"—he hissed, emphasizing the second syllable—"Erskine."

Gerry's ears perked at the name. Then he squinted, as if trying to place him. After a moment, he shook his head. "You have the advantage."

"You sent me the propaganda…"

Gerry shrugged, apparently not understanding.

His eyes bunching, Auggie scowled at him. "The paperwork for the lawsuit—"

"Lawsuit?" Stiffening, Gerry gave an uneasy smile. "I don't follow."

Auggie crossed his arms. "You mean your office didn't send my relatives or me any paperwork, offering to purchase this property for a proposed hotel?"

Shaking his head, Gerry took a step back. "Not that I'm aware of every move my office makes, but I assure you, Mr. Erskine, I know nothing about any lawsuit involving you."

"No? Then what's that promo packet in your hand?" Auggie stared him down. "It looks like the sales promotion your company sent me."

Gerry discreetly slipped the folder behind his back.

"You brought this for me?" Wearing a saccharine smile, Keya snatched the packet from his hand. "Let me have a look-see."

As she opened its contents, Auggie said, "Inside, you'll find four eight-by-ten glossy photos, architectural drafts, a brochure, and a promotional DVD." He smiled at Gerry. "Isn't that right?"

One by one, Keya took out the photos, drafts, and slick brochure. Then she held up the DVD. "All here as you described it, Auggie."

He scowled at Gerry and Heath. "People are like fish. They both get into trouble when they open their mouths."

Keya studied her neighbor. "Would you care to explain?"

Gerry addressed her, ignoring Auggie. "As I mentioned, Heath and I brought over the information I'd forgotten to give you earlier. Now that you have it"—his smile was fixed—"we'll be on our way." He started back to his property, calling over his shoulder, "Enjoy your evening."

Sighing through her nostrils, Keya pressed her lips together. "That was enlightening." She turned to Auggie. "This is what he'd sent you and the other branch of the family?"

He nodded. "This and an offer to purchase this land."

"Purchase this land!" Keya blinked. "What do you mean?"

"His attorney assured the Erskine family that they, *not you*"—Auggie grimaced—"are the rightful heirs and owners of this property."

"What!" Keya shook her head. "That's preposterous."

"If wishes were fishes, they'd have a fish fry." Auggie jerked his chin at the house next door. "It's nothing but legal mumbo-jumbo for a hostile buyout, but the Erskine family took the bait—hook, line, and sinker." He grimaced. "Most of them, anyway."

Keya sat back on the lawn chair. "He seems to want this property, one way or another." She frowned. "But that doesn't mean he'll get it."

Auggie considered her. "What do you intend to do with it? Live here?"

Her eyes crinkling in a wry smile, Keya glanced at Ruth before turning toward him. "For now, but when I pass, I want this beachfront property to be a turtle sanctuary, which is why I'm leaving it to the Turtle Refuge."

He gestured toward the island. "For the nesting beaches?" At her nod, he added, "So that's the reason you're in this legal battle."

"The problem is, the legal fees have drained my savings." Keya sighed. "Thank God the court date's next week. If the battle went on much longer, I'd have to sell the property just to pay court costs. Then nobody would win."

Auggie grimaced. "What a mess your neighbor has made of things."

"And why did he bring over his purchasing manager?" asked Ruth.

"Good question. Earnestine sure took a disliking to him." Keya lifted the cat to look at her. "Why did you scratch him?" As the cat meowed, Keya flinched. "Are you sure?"

Again, the cat meowed.

"What's wrong?" asked Ruth.

"Earnestine recognized Maita's scent on him."

"Really?" Ruth recalled Maita's bloody fingernails. "He did have scratch marks on his arms." She glanced at the cat. "Earnestine only added to the collection. Think there's any connection?"

"Let's not jump to any hasty conclusions." Auggie gave a nervous laugh. "A dozen things could have scratched his arms for a dozen reasons."

"But he was wearing long sleeves in July." Palms up, Ruth leaned forward to make her point. "I think he was hiding something…"

"Earnestine said he smelled of Maita," added Keya. "Do you think we should call Detective Bell?"

Auggie shook his head. "Granger introduced Heath as the corporation's purchasing manager. They both work together—scratch that, *worked* together. To presume Heath had anything to do with Maita's drowning is pure conjecture."

"At best, circumstantial evidence." Ruth shot them a wry smile. "Besides, Detective Bell might not appreciate Earnestine's sleuthing skills."

Conversation ceased as each seemed to weigh the facts against speculation.

After a moment's silence, Keya said, "Again, no disrespect to the dead, but let's not dwell on the negative. It's too gorgeous a night." Her smile stilted, she turned to Ruth. "What happened to your charming ghost?"

Ruth chuckled at her cousin's characterization. "I've never heard anyone call a ghost 'charming' before." She picked up Auggie's pendant resting in her lap. "Let's see if Bartolomé reappears." Despite rubbing the coin between her fingers, nothing materialized. "Besides charming, our ghost seems reluctant." She handed Auggie the chain and pendant.

As he slipped it over his head, he said, "This isn't the first time a ghost's been attributed to the *Regala*."

"Really?" Her tone persuasive, Keya coaxed him with a winning smile. "Do tell."

His sniff passed for a chuckle. "My father worked with Dan Miller's team. As a child, I heard firsthand about the treasure and its mystique." His eyes focusing on the past, his smile became wistful. "The *Regala* is legendary."

"I'd never heard of it," said Ruth. "What happened to it?"

"Departing from Havana in 1622, the ship had just begun the annual sail back to Spain when it was caught in a hurricane. Only five of the 265 aboard survived to tell of its sunken treasure, but after four centuries of salvagers searching for the *Regala*—and finding no trace—it became known as a ghost galleon. People thought the legend a mariner's tale.

"Only Dan Miller believed the stories. For years, his team researched the ship, and finally, they uncovered clues in the archives of Seville, Spain, which led them to search in a different area of the Keys. Even then, all they located were tantalizing bits of the wreckage—not the payload."

Auggie's eyes took on a distant expression. "My father had a theory when he worked with Dan in the eighties. Calling his idea the 'ghost-array' theory, he believed a second hurricane had separated the top deck from the ship's hull and sent it skimming over the surface, scattering its treasure to the east. During one sweep, Dan's team ran a mag survey to—"

"A mag?" Tilting her head at a quizzical angle, Ruth studied him.

"Magnetometer," he explained. "A sensor used to locate metal objects under water. The sea was so rough that day, a diver had to ride the instrument to control its depth. After a few passes, he surfaced because he'd heard strange voices discussing ship names and latitude and longitude coordinates. He asked the crew if they'd been in radio contact with anyone." Auggie's voice became husky. "But they'd had radio silence all day."

"Whose voices did he hear?" Keya's gaze fixed on him as she sipped her mojito.

"My father dismissed the diver's story as a mild case of narcosis." Shrugging, he shook his head. "He had no other *logical* explanation."

"Why do you emphasize 'logical'?" Keya wore a leery smile.

"That story haunted my father. Years later, as more events unfolded, he looked back on that incident as pivotal."

Keya frowned. "What do you mean?"

"Dan's son Kirk tested my father's ghost-array theory, searching an area farther east than anyone had ever looked, and he discovered a hoard of gold doubloons." Auggie shifted the dog in his arms. "That find clinched my father's theory. The ship had landed in fifty-four feet of water, laying undiscovered for over three hundred fifty years.

"Returning to Key West that night, Kirk told my dad, 'Someone will pay for this.' My father thought he meant the salvage crew would get a bonus, and he didn't think twice about the conversation until several days later."

"Why?" Ruth searched his eyes. "What happened?"

"Just before sunrise, a voice woke a crewmember who'd been dozing in the ship's wheelhouse. 'Hey, keep a sharp eye!' The man stepped out on deck, and in that shadowy gloom between moonlight and morning light, a misty gray figure emerged."

As Ruth caught Auggie's gaze, he nodded.

"The crewman couldn't believe his eyes, so he went back for his glasses. The voice called a second time. 'Keep a sharp eye!' When the figure vanished into thin air, the crewman realized the boat was listing. *Badly*.

"Long story short, the pump had malfunctioned, causing the boat to first list and then capsize. He hammered on everyone's door, trying to wake them and get them to safety, but Kirk and his wife were trapped below deck."

"What happened to them?" Ruth searched his face for a smile or the hint of a positive outcome.

He shook his head. "They didn't make it."

"Who was the gray figure?"

"That's the question we've all asked ourselves." Auggie shrugged. "The odd thing is, ten years *to the day* after Kirk's death, Dan's other son, John, found the payload. On the one hand, finding the *Regala* was a reward for Dan's determination. On the other, that quest was the cause of his misery."

Ruth studied him. "Aside from losing his son and daughter-in-law, why do you say that?"

"While the *Regala* had claimed 260 lives when it sank, the ship spared five. Including the two you mentioned, five people died during the ship's search and recovery—almost as if those five lives were traded for the original five survivors."

"So, they were the ones to 'pay' for it." Ruth slumped as she groaned. "Heartbreaking."

"Tragic though it was, finding the *Regala* had an upside. In addition to the ship being worth a king's ransom, it was a time capsule, an archaeological treasure trove."

Exhaling, Ruth sat back in her chair. "Do you mean to say that misty gray figure aboard the ship was Bartolomé?"

Auggie shrugged. "I'm just saying this isn't the first time I've heard of a ghost attached to the *Regala*."

"All this talk of death and ghosts has given me an appetite for life—and dinner." Wearing a skeptical smile, Keya stood. "Do you want to grill the mahi-mahi out here while I get the chowder?"

Auggie blinked. After a slight pause, he spoke in a shaky voice. "Okay." Then he cleared his throat as he put Diesel on the ground with unsteady hands. "Mind if I grab another beer while I grill the filets?"

****

An hour later, they were seated around the patio table, finishing dinner as the stars glimmered in the twilight. Keya turned on the string lights overhead, lending a festive mood to their conversation.

"What are you ladies doing tomorrow?"

"First thing on the agenda is a tour of the Turtle Refuge," said Keya.

"Research for the brochure I'm writing," Ruth added.

"We're scheduled for a nine o'clock educational program." Keya peered at him. "Why?"

Auggie wore an enigmatic smile. "Afterward, why don't you join me in Key West? Let me show you around town—Dan Miller's Museum, the Aquarium, and the Wreckage Museum?"

"Sounds great." Ruth glanced at her cousin. "What do you think?"

Keya nodded. "Let's plan on meeting in the afternoon. I'd like to show Ruth the Bahia Honda Park on the way down."

"Perfect," he said. "Give me a call when you leave the park, and we can decide where to meet."

"Okay." Keya nodded before turning toward Ruth. "And you've got to see Hemingway's house."

"Don't forget Duval Street, the seaport, and Mallory Square," added Auggie.

Ruth swallowed a smile. "I've never been to Key West, but the schedule already sounds like we've planned way too much for an afternoon. What do you say to staying the night and finishing our island tour the next day?"

"Great idea." Keya nodded. "I know just the place—my favorite turtle hotel."

"Turtle hotel?" Ruth squinted.

"You'll see. It's the—"

Yowling at the top of her lungs, Earnestine arched her back.

Crash! A clanging, metallic clattering competed with her caterwauling.

"Who's there?" shouted Keya.

"It's coming from the side of the house," called Auggie, running toward the commotion. Diesel followed, barking at his heels.

Keya turned on the perimeter lights, illuminating the front and back yards, as well as the driveway alongside the house. By the time she and Ruth reached Auggie, he was guarding a gray-haired man huddled on the ground, holding his leg and wincing in pain. Diesel growled at the man as Auggie spoke into his cell phone.

"We have the intruder in custody." He covered the speaker with his hand, whispering to Keya, "What's the address?" He repeated her words into the phone. "Thanks. We'll be outside, waiting for you."

As the man raised his eyes, Keya gasped. "That's the gardener."

"The gardener?" Auggie scowled at him. "What were you doing prowling around at this hour?"

The man mumbled something.

"Speak up!"

"I was watering the *Stachytarpheta jamaicensis*."

"The *what?*" Keya glared.

"The blue porterweed." Muttering, the man looked away.

"In the dark." Keya checked her watch. "At nine o'clock at night?"

"I thought the plants needed watering." Shifty-eyed, he never met their gaze.

Her mouth taut and turned down at the corners, Keya said, "You're fired, effective immediately. Don't even *think* about a reference."

Keya and Ruth righted the overturned garbage cans and gathered the scattered debris while Auggie guarded the prowler.

Diesel growled at the man's every move.

Within minutes, the flashing lights from the squad car lit up the gate.

As Keya led the police to the scene, they asked, "Do you recognize the intruder?"

She nodded. "He *was* my gardener, past tense." Watching the man, she added, "He's no longer in my employ."

"A fine howdy-do," he mumbled. "Working overtime—"

"You mean trespassing," said Keya. "Your scheduled hours *had been* Thursday mornings."

"What were you doing here?" asked the officer.

"Watering the *Stachytarpheta jamaicensis*."

The officer's eyes glittered as he swallowed a smile. "At nine o'clock at night?"

The man's face darkened. "I was working overtime."

"You mean, spying on us." Auggie pointed to the garbage cans' dented covers caked with sticky, red mud. "See the red clay?" He then pointed to the gardener's shoes, covered with the same telltale sludge. "He stood on top of these garbage cans, peering at us over the bushes—like this." Demonstrating, Auggie climbed on the cans. "Then he apparently stumbled and fell. The racket's what alerted us."

The man's face turned an angry, dark crimson. "I was watering the flowers."

"I wonder if it was his shadow on the beach last night." Ruth told the police what she had seen.

After noting her story, the officers called in the man's contact information. "We verified he works for several property owners in this community," said an officer several minutes later, "but he doesn't have any priors."

"He was trespassing—*spying*—on us," said Keya.

"Have you checked the house?" asked another of the officers. "Is anything missing?"

"Just our privacy." Keya grimaced.

Charging the man with a second-degree misdemeanor, the officers escorted him off the premises.

As they left, Auggie turned to Keya and Ruth. "Will you two be all right here tonight?"

"We'll be fine." Keya shrugged. "After you leave, I'll switch on the security system." Then she chewed her lip. "But why would he spy on us?"

"The police said he works for others in this area." Auggie lowered his brow. "I wonder if one of them is your next-door neighbor, Gerald."

Her nod was distracted. "That prospect would explain a few things."

"Want Diesel and me to scout around the property?"

"Thanks, we'll be fine." Keya shook her head.

"It wouldn't hurt to double-check the doors." Breathing rapidly, almost panting, he took out a handkerchief to mop his face and neck.

A concerned V between her eyes, Keya turned her attention to Auggie. "Are *you* all right?"

"Yeah, sure," he said a beat too fast, followed by a gruff, "Why?"

"You just seem"—she shrugged—"unnerved." She studied him. "Even in this low light, I see the tendons standing out on your neck. I can *watch* your pulse."

His chin dipping, he glanced down as if looking inward. When he looked up, his eyes were haunted. "Loud sounds sometimes trigger memories…" He moistened his lips.

Keya glanced at Ruth before asking, "What kind of memories?"

The muscles around his eyes bunching, he gave her a pained expression. "I was aboard the *USS Cole* in Yemen when terrorists bombed it in 2000." He glanced at the trash cans. "That crash tonight reminded me of the explosion."

"Post-traumatic stress disorder?"

His nod grim, he paused as if debating whether to say anything. "Earlier, when you'd asked me to grill the fish"—he grimaced—"I hesitated because even barbecue smoke reminds me of the ship's fire after the blast."

"I remember the headlines following the attack." Keya bit her lip. "It happened less than a year before the World Trade Center disaster."

"Most Americans didn't realize Al-Qaeda was responsible for bombing the *USS Cole*, at least not until

9/11, but to those of us aboard the ship, the war started October 12, 2000." He swallowed. "Seventeen of our crew died that day. Thirty-nine more sustained injuries, and for the rest of us"—he took a deep breath—"the healing continues."

She gave him an apologetic smile. "I'm sorry about all the disturbance tonight."

The glint returning to his eyes, he held her gaze a beat too long. Then he squeezed her hand. "Never let it be said your dinner parties are dull. Except when treasure diving, I haven't had such an adrenaline rush in years." He gave her a wry chuckle. "What do you have in store for tomorrow?"

Chapter 4

Trop Rock—Music in a Tropical "Key"

"Leatherbacks are the largest turtles, growing as big as subcompact cars," said the Turtle Refuge guide, pointing to the next tank. "But Kemps Ridley turtles are the most endangered of all the sea turtles. As you can see"—she gestured toward one swimming awkwardly—"Harvey's lost a flipper from a boat strike. The trauma forced the air from his lungs into his body, causing an air bubble. Since he can't dive for food, we've attached weights to his scutes to counteract the buoyancy."

"Can you release him?" asked a tourist.

"Unfortunately, turtles shed their scutes—the bony plates on their shells—so this is just a temporary fix. Harvey's a 'lifer,' a permanent resident of the refuge because he can't survive in the wild."

"Is that why they're endangered?"

"One of the reasons," said the guide. "Entanglements in fishing debris or mistaking plastic bags for food also kill sea turtles in record numbers."

"How?" asked a tourist.

"Underwater, plastic bags look just like jellyfish. When turtles eat the undigestible plastic, it creates gas, making them buoyant. If the turtles can't dive, they can't eat, and floating on top of the water, they're easy pickings for predators and boat strikes."

One of the children raised her hand. "Do you have any baby turtles?"

"Not here," said the guide, "but baby turtles have started hatching along the beaches. In fact, nesting habitat is a specialty of one of our volunteers." She turned to Keya. "Want to field this one?"

"Absolutely." Keya smiled at the group. "Baby turtles are about the size of pepperoni slices when they hatch, but when the females return a decade later to nest, they're the size of large pizzas. Turtles have swum in our oceans for over 100 million years. They survived whatever wiped out the dinosaurs, but now their numbers are dwindling at an alarming rate."

"Why's that?" asked a man wearing a tan Palm Beach Porpoises cap, its brim shading his face.

"Besides the reasons mentioned, they're losing their nesting beaches to coastal development." Keya grimaced. "It's estimated they'll lose over forty percent to urbanization and tourism. Beachfront lights disorient them. Seawalls interfere with the hatchlings' dash from the sand to the sea—"

"Can baby turtles talk?" asked one of the youngest children.

Keya exchanged a glance with Ruth and the guide before answering. "As a matter of fact, they can. Though turtles don't have vocal cords, they make low-frequency sounds. Land-dwelling tortoises hiss; female river turtles communicate with their hatchlings; and baby sea turtles talk to each other while still inside their eggs."

"Can we hear them?" he asked.

"Some of us can." Keya winked.

"Do they ever say 'cowabunga'?"

"No." Laughing quietly, Keya shook her head. "They never say 'cowabunga.' "

"And on that note, ladies and gentlemen"—the guide gestured toward the exit—"we'll conclude our tour. I hope you've enjoyed the presentation." As the tourists left, she whispered to Keya. "Got a minute?"

"Sure. What do you need?"

"A loggerhead was brought in yesterday, entangled in fishing line, and isn't responding." Hunching her shoulders as if unsure whether to ask, the guide winced. "Can you help?"

"Of course."

The girl led them to a private tank in the back, where a large sea turtle lay motionless, floating on the surface. One of its front flippers was bloody and raw.

Keya approached the turtle at a slow pace, all the while making eye contact. She seemed to communicate with it silently, making subtle head movements.

After a few minutes, the turtle raised its head, stretching its neck toward her. After another soundless minute or two, it began to paddle toward Keya, never taking its gaze from her.

Keya whispered to the guide. "They won't have to amputate her flipper, will they?"

"No. They've given her antibiotics, removed the fish line from around her flipper, cleaned her wounds, snipped away the dead tissue, and stitched her torn flipper back together."

Nodding, Keya turned toward the turtle, staring as if in silent communication. Then she whispered to the guide. "She's afraid she'll never swim in the ocean again."

"She should be fine once she heals," said the girl. "If she'd just exercise that flipper, it'd speed up her healing *and* her release."

Keya nodded and turned back to the turtle, focusing her attention.

Seeming to mentally connect, the loggerhead never took its gaze from her. Then the turtle almost appeared to wave goodbye with its good front flipper as it paddled away.

Keya's face lit up in a smile.

As the turtle made slow laps around the tank, Ruth straightened her spine. "What did you say?"

****

A half hour later, with Earnestine perched on her shoulder, Keya led Ruth into a small café along the Overseas Highway. "I thought we'd grab a light lunch before visiting the park. This place has the best Manhattan Conch Chowder in the Keys."

"Sounds good." Recognizing his Palm Beach Porpoises cap, Ruth spotted a man slide into the next booth. *Wasn't he at the Turtle Refuge?*

The waitress came to take their order, and Ruth turned her attention to the menu.

"You didn't take notes on the tour," said Keya. "Do you have enough information for your brochure?"

Smiling, Ruth held up her phone. "I recorded the whole visit. Listening is easier than trying to read my scribbled notes or recall what was said." Then scrolling through her photos, she showed her cousin. "I also took snapshots of all the exhibits, tanks, and posters, so I think I've covered the bases."

"Let me know if you have any questions or need to go back."

"Will do." Ruth paused as she studied her. "Though, I have to confess. I've wondered about something. When did you begin *talking* to animals?"

"You know I've always had an affinity for them." Keya shrugged. "Ever since we were kids."

"True." Ruth gave her a quizzical smile. "But I don't remember your communicating with them at the level I've seen these past two days."

Her eyes wistful, she glanced at Ruth. "Maybe it's because I've never had children."

Earnestine objected with a low growl.

"Two-legged children, that is. Critters have always been my babies." As Earnestine relaxed, Keya's brow puckered. "What started as an empathy developed into a knack. Then a few years ago, I attended a workshop, where my animal communication skills really improved."

"What happened?"

"Each of us brought a picture of our pet. Then we paired off, exchanged our face-down photos, and were told to guess the animal in the picture." Keya took a deep breath. "That workshop was the real beginning. Then, I started practicing on friends' pets, but the breakthrough happened at a friend's party with a tortoise named Flash."

"Flash." Ruth swallowed a smile. "No sarcasm intended…"

Keya winked. "A group of us stood in a circle with Flash in the middle. Within moments, he began walking about. I asked him where he was going, and he said, 'To meet everyone.'

"To speed the process, I carried him around, greeting the people, one by one. When we reached a quiet woman named Ellen, he said, 'I love her. I lo-o-ove her!' I told her Flash's reaction, and though she took it in stride, several others in the group burst into giggles. After we finished our way around the circle, I set Flash on the floor, and he 'raced' back to Ellen."

"Why do I get the feeling this isn't the end of his story?" Ruth gave her cousin a fond smile.

"His owner confided he was moving across country and couldn't take Flash with him. He'd been looking for someone to adopt him but hadn't had any takers. When Ellen heard about the situation, she lifted the tortoise, looked him in the eye, and asked him to come live with her."

"That's when you realized you have a gift?"

"That's when I realized I could make a difference—and I was hooked." Keya wore a lopsided smile. "It's why I volunteer at the Turtle Refuge."

"And why you feel so strongly about leaving your property to them?"

Keya nodded. "Like I said, I want to leave it to the turtles, so they have a safe place to nest. A bequest to the Turtle Refuge would be my way of making the world a better place."

****

After lunch, they drove to Bahia Honda Park, passing a sandcastle at the entrance that resembled Sol beaming down on sea critters. They parked and walked along the rocky shore in water shoes, beachcombing for washed-up sponges and small clam shells. Then, while hiking, they discovered a historic bridge overlooking the water.

When they returned to Keya's convertible, a man in a Porpoises cap slouched down behind the wheel of the jeep parked alongside them. Ruth looked again. *Is he the same man?*

"Can you text Auggie?" asked Keya. "Let him know we're an hour away?"

"Sure." Ruth started texting as Keya backed out of the parking spot.

The man straightened his spine and peeked out from under his cap. When he caught Ruth's gaze, he quickly hunched out of sight.

Is this a coincidence?

****

While they checked into the hotel, Ruth studied the lobby's décor. *Nothing here's related to turtles, not the furnishings, not the artwork...*"Why did you call this a turtle hotel?"

Keya gave her a mysterious smile. "You'll see."

"Your room's in Building Three," said the woman at the desk. "Can I offer you a glass of champagne?"

"Thank you, love." Keya accepted the wine as Earnestine leaned forward from her shoulder, her little nose sniffing. "Behave yourself," Keya whispered.

As they walked to their room, they crossed several footbridges over manmade streams flanked on both sides by pools with white sand beaches. Dozens of turtles swam in the pristine ponds or sunbathed on sandy perches.

The terrapin mystery solved, Ruth smiled to herself. "So, *this* is why it's your favorite hotel." She surveyed the turtle colony.

Keya nodded. "Most of them are red-eared sliders, although the ones with the green stripes are peninsula cooters." She pointed to the largest one. "That's Big Mama. She's a chicken turtle."

"Never heard of that kind," said Ruth. "Why do they call it a chicken turtle?"

Keya winced. "Supposedly, its meat tastes like chicken, but she has nothing to worry about here. These critters are all protected." Hunching her shoulders, she grinned like a little girl. "I just love turtles."

Earnestine meowed.

"And cats," added Keya with a wink.

Ruth's cell buzzed with Auggie's text. "He wants us to meet him for a drink."

When she shared the bar's address, Keya said, "It's two blocks away, if that. Tell him we'll be there after we unpack, in about twenty minutes or so." She opened the floor-to-ceiling curtains, exposing a wall of windows that overlooked the Atlantic-side harbor. Then she opened the door to their private balcony. "Look at this."

Ruth followed her, drinking in the panoramic sea view, beachside marina, and palm trees as she sipped her champagne. "Sure this isn't a travel brochure?"

****

They found Auggie sitting at a patio table, nursing a beer while Diesel lapped a bowl of water. The moment he spotted them, Auggie jumped up and pulled out two chairs.

"What a pet-friendly place," Keya said, noting the half-dozen canines seated near their humans.

Her ears flat against her head and her pupils dilated, Earnestine climbed from Keya's shoulder onto her lap. She apparently did not share her person's opinion.

He nodded. "It's Diesel's and my favorite watering hole."

"What can I get you?" asked the waitress.

When they ordered drinks, Auggie added, "In to-go cups, please." He turned to them. "So we can catch the sunset from Mallory Square."

"What's the attraction there?" asked Ruth.

"It's quintessential Key West. Ever since the Sunset Celebration began in the late '60s, it's been a daily party." Auggie caught Ruth's eye. "Starting two hours before sundown, it's captured the imaginations of writers like Earnest Hemingway and Tennessee Williams, triggering some of literature's more memorable sunsets."

"Why?"

"Simple." His face lit up in a warm smile. "The carnival atmosphere heightens the experience."

Only a block's stroll from the square, they chatted and people-watched as they meandered toward the immense waterfront wharf, passing buskers, living statues, sword-swallowers, fire jugglers on unicycles, and jugglers stilt walking. Artists drew charcoal caricatures or peddled watercolor paintings and handmade jewelry. Musicians lined the wharf, entertaining the crowd with every style of island music from Jimmy Buffet's trop rock to steel drums, percussion, and vocals.

Along the wharf, resourceful entrepreneurs offered chair massages, tarot-card readings, and henna tattoos.

Then as the Gulf slowly swallowed the sun, they munched on food-cart conch fritters and Key West pink shrimp scampi.

"What's next?" asked Keya, Earnestine perched on her shoulder.

Pointing away from the waterfront, Auggie said,

"The Duval Crawl."

Ruth blinked. "The *what*?"

Auggie exchanged a smile with Keya. "It's where you stroll along Duval Street, bar-hopping with a to-go cup in hand. The first stop's Sloppy Jim's. It's iconic. You can't come to Key West without seeing it."

As they crossed to Duval Street, Ruth spotted the man in the Palm Beach Porpoises cap. She did a double take, trying to glimpse him through the shoulder-to-shoulder crowds, but she lost him.

"Looking for something?" asked Auggie, carrying Diesel close to his chest.

She grimaced. "Thought I recognized someone who's popped up everywhere we've been today."

"Is that so?" He glanced where she had been looking. "He? She?"

"He," said Ruth, "and he's wearing a tan Palm Beach Porpoises cap."

His expression no-nonsense, Auggie nodded. "I'll keep my eyes peeled."

Lucky to find seats at the packed bar, they watched the show until Ruth spotted him again. Gesturing with her hands, she suggested they leave and continue their Duval Crawl.

"Anything wrong?" shouted Keya.

"Aside from the earsplitting decibel level?" Ruth sneered. "I think we're being followed."

"What?"

"The 'hat' is following us," Ruth repeated, cupping her hands as she shouted directly into her cousin's ear. She jerked her chin toward the man in the Porpoises cap, leaning against a post, standing at an oblique angle, half facing them and half facing the stage. Though he appeared to be watching the performers, he had a clear view of them.

Nodding, Keya told Auggie, finished her drink, and stood.

Wending through the maze of standing patrons took longer than expected. When they passed the man's post on their way out, Ruth searched the crowd's faces, but he had vanished.

"Let's find a beer garden or patio—someplace we can sit outdoors," said Auggie. "It'd be easier to spot our 'shadow.' "

"And easier to hear," said Ruth, her ears still ringing from the bar. *How can the critters stand it?*

Several establishments down the street, they found an open table on a courtyard. A musician strummed a guitar while the help-staff led the customers in a line dance between the tables.

"Much better," said Ruth. "At least, we don't have to shout at each other."

They ordered appetizers and drinks as they people-watched and discussed the next day's plans.

Then just as they were about to leave, Ruth's gaze connected with their stalker's. "There he is."

Handing off Diesel, Auggie jumped to his feet and ran to the sidewalk, checking in both directions, but their shadow had merged into the throng. When he returned, he was brusque. "Who's tailing you?"

Keya gave him a blank stare as she held Earnestine closer. "Haven't a clue."

"Me, either," said Ruth, handing back Diesel. "But earlier today, I saw him at the Turtle Refuge, the café at lunch, and Bahia Honda. Then tonight, I spotted him as we left Mallory Square, inside Sloppy Jim's, and now here." Counting off the times on her fingers, she grimaced. "Six encounters can't be coincidental."

"What do you suppose he wants?" Keya looked from her to Auggie.

"I don't know," said Auggie, squinting as if thinking. "Was he wearing that cap each time?"

Ruth nodded. "Why?"

"Baseball caps can hide surveillance cameras and audio-recording equipment."

She grimaced. "He's been trailing us since this morning."

"This on top of last night's prowler." Keya scowled.

"Have to agree, it's suspicious…but…" Ruth stifled a yawn. "Sorry, guys. Despite the intrigue, I really should get back to the hotel and transcribe today's notes before I conk out."

"So early?"

"The evening's still young." Keya tugged at her arm. "It's not even ten o'clock."

Wearing a crooked smile, Ruth shook her head. "This brochure won't write itself, you know."

"Ah, well." Auggie sighed as if disappointed. "Tonight was fun while it lasted, ladies. Between peeping toms and private eyes, I haven't had a dull moment with you two. Thanks for another stimulating evening."

Her eyes sparkling, Keya gave a naughty chuckle. "Then who says it has to end?"

Auggie's gaze caught hers. "Are you up for a nightcap?"

"Absolutely!"

"How 'bout we walk Ruth back to the hotel and

then go out for a drink?"

"Perfect." Keya turned to Ruth. "Would you mind cat-sitting?"

****

A half hour later, Ruth stepped out on the hotel room's balcony, calling to Earnestine. "Want to sit outside and listen to the waves while I type these notes?"

Whether or not the cat understood, it followed her out and climbed on her lap.

With the palm fronds swooshing overhead and the balmy breezes blowing off the ocean, Ruth's thoughts turned to Brett, just a few miles away—but apparently out of radio range. She sighed, inhaling the salt air as she forced herself to concentrate. Then, playing back the recordings, she transcribed the notes on her laptop.

Earnestine's hiss alerted her, followed by the click-click-click of a camera's shutter. Startled, Ruth turned toward the sound.

Their baseball-capped stalker stood on the stairway's landing just below, but in full view of the balcony. *Click-click-click.*

"Hey!"

He stepped back into the shadows, turned, and ran, his retreating footsteps pounding on the stairs.

"So much for getting any work done." She frowned. Though the ambiance was idyllic, she was exposed and vulnerable on the balcony. "Come on, kitty. Let's bolt the doors, shut the draperies, and finish typing inside." *Or will he find a way to snoop in here, too?*

****

After they dropped off Ruth and Ernestine, Keya

turned to Auggie, her pulse racing. *This is my first date since Jules's death.* "Where to?"

"Ever been to the *real* Sloppy Jim's—the one Hemingway frequented?" He wore a mischievous smile.

"Didn't know there were two." Her imagination piqued, her curiosity overcame her misgivings, and she smiled back, ready to explore the town. "Is the place nearby?"

"Just a short stroll." As Diesel relaxed in the crook of his arm, Auggie led the way. "The bar has a checkered past, starting out in the 1850s as an icehouse—and morgue."

"Morgue!" Keya shuddered at a flashback of the washed-up corpse. "Seems like an odd combination, but I guess ice *was* the only means of preservation back then."

"The bar was also a bordello and a speakeasy in previous lives—even a burial ground." A smile played at his lips. "More than a few people swear it's haunted."

"You don't say…?" Her words tongue-in-cheek, she listened with one ear as she would to a fish tale.

"Actually, it's what *they* say." His cheek dimpled as he shot her a devil-may-care smile. "Want to hear the schoolbook history or the bar-stool version?"

She rewarded him with a laugh. "Bar-stool." Intrigued more with Auggie than the stories, she peeked through her eyelashes, studying him. *He reminds me of someone. Who?*

"A gallows tree grows right through the bar's roof. Supposedly, sixteen pirates were hanged from it—and a woman."

Assuming his numbers were exaggerated, she

snickered.

"It's true!" He confirmed it with a nod. "She's the bar's most notorious ghost, the 'Lady in Blue.' "

As they paused beneath a streetlight, she stared into Auggie's golden flecked, honey-brown eyes, noting their long, dark lashes, and she tried to place him. *Who does he look like?*

"A tombstone rests beneath the tree. According to local legend, a woman's husband didn't find out about her rendezvous there till after she died."

Rendezvous. The word caught her off guard. *Auggie's the first man I've seen alone since Jules…*

"Supposedly, he ripped her tombstone from the cemetery and dumped it in the bar, saying, 'This is where she wanted to be…' "

She glanced at Auggie in horror. Guilt gripping her, Keya's mouth went dry. *I'm cheating on Jules…*

"Some say they see her ghost."

Fingering her wedding ring as they walked along, Keya accidentally bumped his shoulder, then shrank from his touch, scurrying to the sidewalk's opposite edge. After several silent minutes, she realized she had dropped the conversational ball. "Any other ghosts?"

"When the bar was a speakeasy in the '20s, a woman caught her husband in there with a flapper."

More betrayal. Her shoulders slumped. "What did *she* do—allegedly?"

"As the story goes, she lost her mind—killed her baby and hid it in the ladies' room."

"How horrible!" A chill ran down Keya's spine. "The place certainly has plenty of material for ghosts."

"You mean ectoplasm?" He gave her a sidelong smile. "From what I hear, the ladies' room is the bar's paranormal *hot* spot, what with all its *cold* spots." The corners of his eyes crinkled at his own joke. "All its doors opening and slamming shut by themselves, locking women in the stalls…"

She did a double take. "Is any of it true?"

He fluttered his eyebrows *à la* Groucho Marks. "Let me know after you visit the ladies' room."

She chuckled more at his delivery than his words as they stopped in front of a brightly painted, canary-yellow building. "What's this bar's connection with Hemingway?"

"Aside from him drinking here?" Auggie dimpled. "Some say Hemingway financed the place, keeping the marble urinal from the old bar in his garden as collateral and using it as a water fountain for his cat."

"*Really?*" Questioning how much to believe, she tilted her head.

His grin was wicked. "Let me know tomorrow when you get back from touring Hemingway's house."

****

Too keyed up to sleep, Ruth was working past midnight when Keya tiptoed in.

"You're still awake?"

Ruth's anger resurfaced as she told Keya about the P.I. and surveillance pictures.

Keya huffed through gritted teeth. "Next time I see him, I'm going to confront him. I don't know *what* he's up to or *why* he's following us, but I'm putting a stop to it."

"I hollered at him." Ruth scowled. "But he kept running without so much as a backward glance." Then noticing the time, she swallowed a smile. "*So*…how was your evening?"

"Great!" Keya's eyes glittered as she held two souvenir cups like trophies. "We went to the *original* bar where Hemingway hung out. *And* I have a new favorite drink—Pirate Punch."

Ruth laughed. "What's in it?"

"Fruit juices, rum…and gin." Keya exhaled. "What a kick!"

"Sounds like you had fun."

"We did!" She paused. "Is Auggie anything like Brett?"

"In some ways, I guess." Ruth considered it. "Like Brett, he's polite, has a sense of humor…yet he seems levelheaded." She studied her cousin. "Why?"

"He reminds me of someone…I just can't quite put my finger on *who*." She pressed her lips together, as if searching her mind. Then her eyes sparkled with mischief. "If Brett's anything like Auggie, I can see why you're marrying him." With a wink, she closed the bathroom door, turned on the shower, and began humming.

****

The next morning, they met Auggie in front of the Nautical Museum.

Her jaw slack, Keya stared at him.

"What's wrong?" Stiffening, Auggie shifted his position.

A slow smile spread across her face. "Nothing." After sharing a girlish giggle with Ruth, Keya turned back toward him. "I just figured out who you remind me of."

"Who?"

"Jules. I couldn't place it till just now, but something about your eyes reminds me of my hus—*late* husband." Splaying her fingers, she glanced at her emerald wedding ring.

His gaze followed hers as he seemed to collect his thoughts. "That resemblance makes sense. Besides being cousins, Jules and I spent a lot of time together growing up." He shrugged. "Aunt Libby always called us two peas in a pod."

As if considering his words, Keya massaged her temple, the emerald of her wedding ring gleaming in the morning sun.

Auggie studied it. "Is that ring from the *Regala*?"

A wistful smile played at her lips. "Jules was as fascinated with the ship's romance as you. He said he wanted our marriage to be a voyage of discovery, and this ring symbolized it."

"That's sweet." Ruth smiled. "Could I see it?"

"Sure." Keya held out her hand.

As Ruth turned Keya's fingers to better see the ring, she grazed the stone.

Immediately, Bartolomé García de Castillo appeared, his cavalier hat shielding his face from view.

Before Ruth had time to react, Keya moved her hand, pointing at the doors. "Look! They're opening."

Ruth glanced back, but Bartolomé had vanished in the morning light.

The three walked inside and were ushered into a small room where they watched a video of the *Regala's* discovery.

"You're right," Ruth whispered, awed with the find's historical importance. "This *is* like viewing a time capsule."

Auggie nodded. "Countless ships have gone down in the Keys, each one a snapshot of life at the time.

From the salvaged material, we know the foods they ate and the clothes they wore. The *Regala* is an archaeological treasure trove."

"That's the second time you've called it that." Keya's smile was reflective. "You seem as caught up in its history as Jules."

He sighed. "Maybe he and I were more alike than I recall."

As they looked at the displays and read the plaques, Ruth and Keya oohed and aahed over the salvaged gold chains and gem-encrusted jewelry. Then they stopped in the gift shop.

Auggie pointed to the Spanish coins. "I'd mentioned how the Spanish dollar could be broken into eight pieces, hadn't I?"

They nodded.

"That influenced American currency. Think of our half-dollars and quarters. Not just the coins, but *coined phrases* entered our language because of it, too."

"What do you mean?" Keya squinted.

"Instead of saying reales, we said bits, so two reales became known as two bits or a—"

"Quarter," said Keya and Ruth, recognizing the idiom.

"You've heard of making money hand over fist?"

They nodded.

"That expression came from when they minted coins by hand. A man held a hammer in one hand, while he held the die in his other fist. Then as he struck each coin, he made money hand over—"

"Fist." Keya and Ruth chuckled as they chimed in simultaneously.

"It's funny how those idioms worked their way

into our speech," said Keya.

"We all know the phrases"—Ruth shrugged—"but I hadn't a clue about their origin."

They glanced from one showcase to the next as they ambled through the shop. Then one display seized their attention—a magnificent gold cross inlaid with seven matching emeralds.

"Their color's gorgeous," said Keya, studying the cross from different angles to capture the light. "The stones have such sparkle, such green fire."

"It's called Muzo green," said Auggie. "These emeralds came from Colombia's Muzo mine, and that saturated color sets the standard for all emeralds."

Ruth stared at the cross. "Makes you wonder about its owner, doesn't it? Was he or she wearing it when the *Regala* sank? Possibly holding it in prayer?"

As Auggie's face lost its animation, the light dimmed in his eyes. "The last thing the *Regala's* passengers probably did was clutch their cross or rosary while they prayed. When my father worked with Dan's team, he mentioned how awed he felt at being the first person to touch those relics after all those years…"

"You mean after their owners drowned…" Ruth shook off a chill. *What did Bartolomé cling to?* Then she noticed various silver-coin earrings hanging from displays. "Those sure look like the ones we found, Auggie."

He nodded. "Can't help but wonder if Maita's earrings were made from the same mintage."

"If Detective Bell doesn't call about the fingerprints in the next day or two," said Keya, "I'll call him about the earrings—and mention our 'shadow' in case of any connection."

As they left the gift shop, Auggie turned toward them. "What's our next stop?"

"The aquarium's just around the corner." Keya caught Ruth's gaze. "You've got to see its tropical fish, stingrays, and *turtles*." She gave a dry laugh. "Maybe it's because of my mother's dream when she was pregnant with me, or maybe it's because they're my namesake. Whatever the reason, I've always been fascinated with turtles."

Earnestine made a low growl in her throat.

"And cats," added Keya, winking at the others. "Turtles and cats."

"That explains it," said Auggie.

"Explains what?" Squinting as though puzzled, Keya stared at him.

"Your tolerating me." He deadpanned. "Turtles. I'm a member of the Turtle Clan."

Keya gave him a coy smile as they passed beneath a painted arch and entered the aquarium.

An enormous touch tank loomed before them, overshadowing the interior's long gallery and marine exhibits lining its sides.

Ruth dipped her hand into the tank's water and lightly ran her fingertips over the sea creatures' smooth shells or spiky spines, touching the various textures of the conchs, sea stars, sea urchins, sea cucumbers, giant hermit crabs, and horseshoe crabs. "I can't get over the differences of their shells."

"Like comparing corn silk to thistles, isn't it?" Keya smiled as she handed over Earnestine. Then she picked up each of the critters, giving some a loving caress, while holding others close to her face as if silently communicating. One sea cucumber in particular captured her attention. Stroking it, she seemed to listen as she tilted her head, nodded, and finally replaced it in the tank.

When they moved on to the other exhibits, Ruth handed back Earnestine, whispering, "What were you doing at the touch tank?"

"Getting up close and personal with some of the most fascinating critters in the Lower Keys." Keya winked.

"Were you communicating with them?" At her nod, Ruth asked, "How?"

"I give and get mental images from them, although occasionally, they do talk to me." Keya stared off into the distance. "No, that description's not quite right. Not 'talk,' but sometimes, it's as if I 'hear' a voice with my inner ear."

Ruth nodded. "I know someone with synesthesia, who 'hears' colors and 'sees' music. We all sense things in our own way."

"What about your gift?" Keya scrutinized her. "You see spirits."

"See…" Ruth made a face, still unsure whether this newfound ability was a blessing or a curse. "This isn't so much a vision as it is a perception. In a way, what I see is like digital music. Sound is converted into numbers, and then when played back, the numbers are decoded into soundwaves your ear hears. Only with the spirits, I 'see' their presence."

Keya nodded. "It reminds me of a TV documentary I saw, showing how they made old-fashioned phonograph records. Sound vibrations caused a special stylus to cut into a wax cylinder that, when played back, sounded like music."

Ruth blinked. "Your analogy makes me wonder if what I've seen is a spirit—or two—reenacting scenes that once occurred."

Keya shook her head. "If that were the case, the spirits would recreate the same scene over and over. Since you've spoken to Bart, and he's responded, he's not playing the role by rote."

"Then I'm not sure how to characterize it. All I know is when I touch an object connected to the *Regala*, Bart appears, and when my hand touched the earring we found, a second spirit accompanied him."

"You have a gift."

"Though it's happened a few times"—Ruth let out an uneasy sigh—"I wouldn't be so arrogant as to call it a gift."

"Sounds like one to me." Keya gave her hand a reassuring squeeze as Auggie approached them.

"According to this timetable"—he pointed to his brochure—"a stingray-feeding tour starts in five minutes. Want to join it?"

****

"Cownose rays populate the Atlantic from New England to Brazil," said the speaker as the group ringed a tank of stingrays. "They eat by slurping shellfish into their mouths and then crushing the shells between their wide dental plates.

"When they're threatened, they defend themselves with a barb found at the base of their tail, but the stingrays in this tank have all been debarbed. They're safe to touch." She looked from face to face. "Who'd like to help feed the stingrays?"

"I would." Ruth raised her hand, and the guide gave her a shrimp.

"Keep your fingers close together while you hold the shrimp upright in your fist like this," said the guide, demonstrating.

As Ruth offered the shellfish, the stingray folded its wings around her hand while it sucked the shrimp from her fist. Delighted, she laughed. "It tickles."

When the feeding ended, Keya took the tour guide aside. "The sea cucumber in the touch tank is a bit sore from the handling. Could you remove her for the day?"

The guide crooked her head as she watched Keya. "What makes you say *her*?"

Keya shrugged as she smiled. "She seemed feminine."

"Visually, males are indistinguishable from females. Their sex organs are internal." Whether the guide believed Keya or humored her, she nodded. "I'll try to have her moved to another tank."

"Thanks," said Keya. "I'd appreciate it."

As the guide left, Ruth whispered, "What was that conversation about?"

"The sea cucumber needs a break from the touch tank. She's sore."

Ruth gave her a perplexed smile. "How do you know?"

"You mean, aside from her telling me?" Keya swallowed a smile. "My fingertips detected a warm spot on her back, indicating a tender area."

Ruth looked at her cousin with newfound respect. "You really can communicate with animals, can't you?"

Keya laughed out loud. "What've I been telling you?"

Whispering as she walked by, the guide pointed toward the touch tank. "They're moving the sea cucumber into her own container."

"Thanks." Keya's face lit up in a warm smile.

"I'm starting another tour if you'd liked to join." The guide returned the smile as she called to the visitors milling about—a woman wearing glasses with thick frames, a family, and a middle-aged couple. "Welcome to the sea turtle conservation tour, folks. Florida hosts almost ninety percent of the Northwest Atlantic's loggerhead turtle nests, with the Dry Tortugas National Park being the most active turtle-nesting site in the Keys.

"The rescued turtles you see here are our goodwill ambassadors since they can't survive at sea." She pointed to the tank, singling out a three-flippered turtle. "This one made history recently as the first ever to receive a prosthetic flipper. Found tangled in fishing gear in the Gulf of Mexico, she had to have her right flipper amputated, but graduate students created the world's first turtle flipper using biomechanics." The guide smiled. "Hopefully, that design can help other turtles recover from similar injuries."

After the tour, Auggie asked, "Are you ladies ready for lunch? I know a quiet rooftop restaurant, high above the streets' hustle and bustle—but with a bird's-eye view."

As they walked from the aquarium to the eatery, the woman in glasses followed close behind. Then after they were seated, the woman chose a nearby table.

Ruth stifled a sigh. "Not to alarm you, but I think we have a new shadow."

"Where?" Auggie looked left and right.

"Behind you, two tables over."

He pretended to adjust Diesel on his lap as he stole

a peek. "Are you sure?"

"She was hovering near us at the aquarium, again on the street, and now here." Ruth shrugged. "Did we trade one tail for another?"

"Maybe," he said. "Those thick frames she's wearing could hide all sorts of video and recording equipment."

"Well, I'm putting a stop to this right now!" Handing Earnestine to Ruth, Keya leapt to her feet and buttonholed the woman, demanding in a shrill voice, "Don't I know you?"

The woman's face paled.

"Yes, I'm sure I do." Pulling out a chair, Keya invited herself to sit down. "I recognize those glasses."

"I, uh, I might look familiar," mumbled the woman, shaking her head. "I don't—"

"You were in the aquarium, behind us on the street, and now you're here." Beaming as if proud of her deduction, Keya continued talking in a penetrating voice. "You aren't following us"—she paused—"*are you...?*"

"Waiter!" The woman motioned to the server. "This person's annoying me. Please ask her to leave."

The waiter approached hesitantly, addressing Keya. "I'm sorry, ma'am, but I'll have to ask you to return to your table."

Keya's cheeks blanched before turning a bright crimson. The roles reversed, she blinked, as if processing. Then straightening her spine, Keya raised her chin and scowled at the woman. "Whether or not you admit it, you've been tailing us. Now *back off!*" Wearing a saccharine smile, she strode to their table.

Second-guessing herself, Ruth grimaced. "Hope I

didn't misread the situation and accuse an innocent person."

"It's hard to say." Auggie took a deep breath. "Those wide frames could hide recording equipment—or just hold thick lenses."

"Either way," said Keya, reclaiming Earnestine, "I've made a fool of myself, but I can't shake the feeling she's watching us, eavesdropping." She huffed as she stood. "Whether or not I've confronted a stalker, I'm uncomfortable here. Let's leave."

A few minutes later, they were seated at a different restaurant.

"Better?" asked Auggie, tongue-in-cheek, an amused glint in his eye.

"You probably think I'm unreasonable," Keya gave him a sheepish grin. "Or worse, paranoid."

"Normally, I might think you're a tad eccentric." Then as his eyes flickered and lost their glow, a sympathetic smile grew on his face. "But after what's happened the past few days, I think your reaction is rational—even admirable. Approaching that woman took courage."

"Even if she wasn't guilty?" Keya made a face.

"Who knows?" He shrugged. "You did what you had to do, and for that, I applaud you."

"Thanks." She gave him a feeble smile.

"In fact"—he pursed his lips as if to conceal a smile—"if I didn't know better, I'd say you belonged to the Turtle Clan." The smile won out.

Tilting her head, Keya squinted. "What do you mean?"

"People of the Turtle Clan tend to be daring, fearless." His smile morphed into a smirk. "If not downright stubborn."

"Thanks, *I think*." Keya's forehead puckered. "I heard stubborn. Is that what you think?"

"Hear what you want." His eyes homed in on hers. "I think you're fearless."

Keya studied his features as if trying to read him. "You'd mentioned earlier you're a member of the Turtle Clan?"

Nodding, he glanced at Ruth. "Brett's mother and I were born into it."

"I'm not sure what clan I belong to, *if any*," said Keya. "Though according to my grandmother, I'm descended from Calusa Indians."

Ruth sat up straight. "I didn't know that."

"Yup, part Indian and part castaway sailor."

"Are you aware that 3.14% of all castaways"— Auggie grinned—"are *Pi*-rates?"

Keya rolled her eyes, snickering.

Seeing her cousin in a new light, Ruth studied her cheekbones and coloring for visual clues of her heritage. "I've never heard of the Calusas. Were they native to Florida?"

Keya nodded. "From what I've read, Spanish soldiers forced them south from the mainland to Key West, their last stronghold, where many were buried along its shores. Later when Spanish settlers found bones scattered on its beaches, they named it *Cayo Hueso*—Island of Bones. Then mistaking *Hueso* for West, the English colonists called it Key West.

"Island of Bones…" A shudder skidded down Ruth's spine. "The name's so menacing compared to Key West."

His eyes glimmering, Auggie turned toward Keya.

"So, you're descended from Indians and pirate castaways?"

"Not pirates, a *sailor*"—she tossed her chin—"and my grandmother hinted at Spanish nobility in the mix."

"Noble blood." Ruth sat up in her seat. "How did that happen?"

"Supposedly, my Calusa great-great-great-great-something-grandmother married a count, but he was lost at sea." Keya gave them a wistful smile. "I still have a pair of earrings that, *according to family tradition*, he'd given her before he died, before she met my great-something-step-grandfather, the castaway who was shipwrecked near here."

"Shipwrecks were common," said Auggie. "What with the coral reefs, hurricanes, and tropical storms, these waters were dangerous, and wrecking became an industry."

"Ship*wrecked*, *wreck*ing…" Ruth made a sour face. "Thanks for putting my mind at ease about Brett."

"Don't worry. Nothing's in the forecast about foul weather, and modern technology will steer them clear of any reefs." Auggie gave her an encouraging smile. "Besides, hurricane season doesn't begin until mid-August."

She tried to return his smile. "I'd feel better if he called. I haven't heard from him since Sunday."

"I'm sure Brett's having the time of his life," said Auggie as the waiter approached.

"Instead of separate meals," suggested Keya, "why don't we order appetizers and share?"

"Add peel-and-eat pink shrimp to our lunch," said Auggie, "and I'm in."

Setting down her menu, Ruth agreed, and fifteen

minutes later they were munching finger foods.

"You didn't finish the story about your Calusa-castaway heritage," said Auggie.

"I don't have many details, just that X generations ago"—Keya counted on her fingers—"my great-great-great-something-step-grandfather shipwrecked on one of the Key's islets. He met and married my Calusa great-something-grandmother and made his living wrecking."

Ruth let out an uneasy sigh. "I wish you'd stop using the word *wreck*."

"In this case"—Keya gave her a sympathetic smile—"it means salvaging the crew and goods."

Auggie tilted his head at a skeptical angle. "Nowadays, wrecking means marine salvage, but back then…" Shrugging, he let his words die off.

"Why? What did it imply in the past?" Ruth studied him as she peeled a shrimp.

"It *could've* meant saving crews, *or* tales abound of wreckers that were more pirate than salvager. They moved lights and lured ships onto reefs so they could steal the cargo." He helped himself to more deep-fried calamari. "Then they'd burn the grounded ship to destroy the evidence."

Pretending indignation, Keya straightened her spine, challenging him. "Are you calling my great-great-great-something-step-granddaddy a pirate?"

"Until Florida became a territory, the only rules were the 'Common Laws at Sea,' which *broadly interpreted* wrecking's ethics." His smile lines deepened around his eyes. "As for your great-something-grand*mother*, Florida's Indians were the first salvagers. The Spanish hired them to dive and reclaim what they could from the wrecks."

Keya gave a surprised laugh. "Maybe that's how she met my great-something-granddaddy."

"Ya never know." He shrugged. "Your salvager heritage goes back a lot further than mine. My father worked with Dan, and I've done some wrecking in my day, but *you*." He gave her an admiring smile. "Your family of wreckers goes *way* back."

"Again, thanks." Keya reached for the last shrimp as he did. "*I think*."

"Hey!" Mock sword fighting, he tapped her fork with his. "Quit being so shellfish!"

Snickering, she called over the waiter. "We need more shrimp to keep the peace." Then Keya's back straightened. "That's where we should take Ruth next— the Wreckage Museum."

"Must you use that word"—Ruth shuddered— "*wreck*?"

****

A costumed historian met them outside the wood-framed museum, its siding a weathered gray. "During the 1800s, over one hundred ships a day sailed into or past Key West," he said. "Because these waters are some of the most treacherous in the world, at least a ship a week ran aground its reefs."

Walking inside the museum was like boarding an ancient Spanish galleon. Ruth glanced about the recreated deck's hemp rigging, pulleys, railings, and sails, and whispered to Keya, "Have we stepped back in time?"

Colorful glass fishing floats and air-cured tobacco leaves hung suspended as if ready for use. Barrels and sea chests lined the wooden deck. Along the surrounding walls, glassed cases displayed recovered artifacts—from olive jars, muskets, and cannon balls to coins, pottery, antique maps, and nautical charts.

"Some wreckers patrolled the reef in their vessels," said their guide. "Others stood watch day and night, searching from observation towers. At the cry, 'Wreck ashore,' everyone scrambled to be the first to reach the stranded ship."

They scanned the artifacts, tried on a sponge-diver's metal helmet, and tested their strength against a salvaged sixty-four-pound silver bar.

Then before they exited, the guide pointed to the stairway. "Don't miss the observation tower. At sixty-five feet, it has the best views of Key West."

As they climbed the wooden stairs to the flag-festooned tower, Ruth snapped photos at each tier, capturing the changing views of the Gulf and Atlantic. A gigantic ship's bell topped the gallery's stairway, offering an irresistible photo op.

"Stand closer." Ruth waved them toward the massive bronze bell. "I want you both in the picture."

Auggie gave Keya a stiff smile as he took a step toward her.

Feet firmly planted, she tilted her head toward him, then pursed her lips in a closed-mouth smile as she faced the camera.

Ruth looked through the viewfinder. "No, *move* closer. Don't just lean your head."

Each took a half step toward the other, turned, and posed.

"No." Ruth scratched her head. "You're both so stilted. Move—"

The bell jangled behind them, startling Keya and

propelling her into his arms.

"That'll wake the dead." Auggie caught her in a protective embrace just before the child dashed behind them to clang the bell a second time.

The commotion offered an excuse to release their tension. Erupting in a paroxysm of laughter, they clung to each other. Then as the smiles subsided, their eyes homed in on each other, and their lips met in a kiss.

"Perfect!" Ruth snapped the picture.

When they left the museum's tower, Keya glanced at Auggie, her eyes seeming to glow with a violet-blue flame. "Where to next—Hemingway's house to check out that marble 'collateral'?"

A smile lit his face as he dimpled. Then with a groan, he glanced at his watch. "Sorry ladies, but I have a meeting."

"You're leaving?" Keya's smile drooped.

He blinked, seeming to process. "I could catch up with you afterward…that is, if you—"

"Great idea!" Keya's pupils dilated as a smile softened her features.

"Why don't I text you when the meeting ends?" Auggie leaned into her.

"Sure…" She inclined toward him.

As their body language mirrored each other, Ruth swallowed a smile.

"I'd skip the appointment if I could, but we're gearing up for Dan Miller Days."

"For *what*?" A slight V appeared between Keya's eyes as her tone rose.

"It's an annual celebration of finding the payload. This year the party starts Thursday and runs through Saturday."

"Thursday," Keya mumbled to herself, musing. "Is it open to the public, or—"

"Most events are…though the dinner's private." Then his face brightened as if getting an idea. "How would you two like to be my guests?"

"Sounds like fun!" Then as if an afterthought, Keya turned to Ruth. "Don't you think?"

"Sure, why not? Brett won't be back till Sunday, anyway." Tongue-in-cheek, she added, "I can always squeeze in my writing at night, while you two do the town."

Either ignoring her or not hearing, Keya stared at nothing, seeming to think aloud. "But we need to check on the house tomorrow." Her smile sagged. "And I have an appointment with my attorney about the lawsuit…"

A frown etched itself on Auggie's face.

"But we can come back Thursday." She grinned like a little girl. "Which just happens to be my birthday."

Ruth did a double take. "It is?"

At Keya's nod, Auggie brightened. "Perfect! This meeting shouldn't take long. I'll ping you when it ends, and we can decide where to meet."

Affirming with a nod, Keya caught his gaze. "Seize the day."

Auggie's face lit up as if he remembered something funny. "*Carpe diem,* or as Dan Miller used to say, 'Carp a D. M.' "

As their gazes locked, Keya gave him a warm, welcoming smile.

The unwitting interloper, Ruth looked away. *What have we here?*

Chapter 5

Six-toed Cats and Strutting Roosters

As Ruth and Keya approached Hemingway's two-storied Spanish Colonial house with its verandas and graceful wrought-iron railings, Earnestine hissed.

"Behave," whispered Keya, nodding toward the long-haired calico lounging in their path. "That cat's not bothering you." When Earnestine objected with a low growl, Keya shook her finger. "Shush."

A young man in a polo shirt introduced himself as their guide and began the tour in the foyer. "This is the only house in Key West with a basement. Excavating it, the builder blasted through fourteen feet of solid coral rock."

"Didn't they hit water?" asked one of the tour members.

The dark-haired guide shook his head. "At sixteen feet above sea level, this house stands on the island's second highest property, just two feet below the island's highest point—the cemetery, a five-minute walk from here. The builder mined the limestone, cutting blocks to construct the house, and then backfilled the hole, leaving a nine-foot basement."

Sharing Hemingway's legendary stories, the guide showed them the house's highlights.

Ruth gazed at the delicate Parisian chandeliers

lighting all but the children's room. Then she smirked at Earnestine's reaction to the six-toed cats sprawled everywhere, from the cordoned-off beds to the corners of the kitchen cupboards.

When the guide noticed polydactyl Earnestine, he rubbed her behind the ears. "Hemingway's original six-toed cat sired ninety kittens in his lifetime. His descendants are everywhere on the grounds and in the house, and they have complete run of the property. Though they tolerate being petted," he warned, "don't try to pick them up."

Next, he led them to the back balcony, overlooking the pool. "Even today, this is the biggest pool in Key West. Dug into solid coral rock, it's twenty-four feet wide, sixty feet long, ten feet deep at the south end, and five feet deep at the north. In a moment, I'll show you the Hemingway penny."

Wearing a confused frown, one of the tourists repeated, "Penny?"

"As the story goes, wife number two heard of his fling with a war correspondent during the Spanish Civil War. Out of spite, Pauline transformed his cherished boxing ring into a swimming pool. When he saw the changes, Hemingway threw down a penny. 'Pauline, you've spent all but my last penny, so you might as well have that!' Whether or not the story's true, the penny's mortared into the pool's edge."

"But wasn't he wealthy?" asked a tourist. "Why did he call that penny his last?"

"It might have been his last cent," said the guide. "When Hemingway and Pauline moved into this house, they had no money. Her uncle bought it for them, yet within nine years, Hemingway rose from obscurity to international fame."

Wanting to hear more, Ruth asked, "What was his secret?"

"Easy," sniffed a woman. "His writing."

Squinting, the guide shook his head. "Hemingway didn't write."

"Didn't write!" The woman stared down her long nose.

"He reported," said the guide. "From what I've heard, the only things he fictionalized were the names of actual people."

Hemingway reported? Ruth considered her own writing. *Technical writing—brochures and booklets—is 'reporting,' but if I'd ever find a true story to write about…maybe I could start a novel, too.*

"Don't misunderstand me." The guide pressed his lips together. "No matter how his writing is characterized—reporting or authoring—he had an unparalleled way of bending language to capture the experience. His narrative line unique, Hemingway was a master at articulating emotions and events through words. He invited the reader to experience the characters' every sensation and impression."

Ruth considered the guide's words as he led them down the backstairs.

As workers arranged chairs near a tented pavilion, Keya asked, "What's going on there?"

"This house is a destination venue for weddings." A sniff passed for the guide's laugh. "Ironic, isn't it?"

Keya canted her head. "What do you mean?"

"Plunging headlong from one stormy relationship into the next, Hemingway was married four times. Hadley, Pauline, Martha, and Mary. Plus, he had a whirling carrousel of mistresses."

"When you put it in those terms, his house does seem like an odd setting to begin a life together." Keya's forehead creasing, she shrugged. "On the other hand, getting married here might clear the negative energy."

"How so?"

"If the choppy water's already been crossed, maybe nothing's left but smooth sailing."

The guide seemed to laugh inwardly. "You have a romantic streak—like Hemingway. He was a skier, navigator, big-game hunter, boxer, soldier—all-around alpha-male stereotype—yet his letters to his wives were sentimental, even gushing. When 'Papa Hemingway' wrote love letters, he had pet names for his wives, calling them Wicky Poo, Kitty Kat, Picklepot, and Lovebug. His letters revealed another side of him, both personally and professionally. The pillow-talk tone of his love letters couldn't have been further from his terse writing style."

Writing style. The guide's words echoing in her mind, Ruth began to think about writing fiction. *Why not? If Hemingway could "report," why can't I?*

On their way out, Keya took a picture of Earnestine drinking from the garden's marble watering trough. "Just a minute." She wore a silly grin. "I want to text this to Auggie."

Ruth squinted. "What's so appealing about the fountain?"

"It's a urinal." She giggled, then tried to wipe the smile from her face. "Sorry. Something Auggie said. Guess you had to be there."

Ruth swallowed a smile. "Keya, you're crushing on

97

him."

"Who? Auggie?" She spoke slowly, stretching out each syllable. Her eyes wide from insulted innocence, she seemed shocked at the very idea. Then, she shook her head with a vehement "*No!*"

Five minutes later, they meandered among Passover Lane cemetery's disordered graves and misaligned headstones. Facing at unruly angles, the tombstones were barely organized into rows. Some monuments were cracked or black with age. Others were tilted or skewed where the ground had shifted.

Ruth read Gloria M. Russell's last words. " 'I'm just resting my eyes.' "

A few rows later, Keya read B.P. "Pearl" Roberts' epitaph. " 'I told you I was sick.' " Noting the birth and death dates, she winced. "She was just 50."

Then they discovered the above-ground family mausoleums with the clucking hens and multicolored roosters strutting about.

"These remind me of New Orleans' cemeteries," said Ruth, "except for the chickens."

"Gypsy chickens." Keya gave them an affectionate glance. "They're feral chickens but protected by law—just another example of Key West's offbeat charm. They're the perfect metaphor for the island—flashy, feral, vociferous, and sometimes frustrating."

The chickens scratched the soil for grubs, apparently unconcerned with Ruth's gaze.

"Have they always been free range?"

"Key West's always had chickens." Keya shrugged. "Some were set free when backyard coops became obsolete. Others were turned loose in the '70s when cock-fighting was outlawed."

As they continued their walk, they stopped by a concrete buoy at the corner of South and Whitehead Streets.

"The Southernmost Point," read Ruth.

"This is just a tourist attraction." Keya shook her head. "Fort Zach is the island's southernmost tip, or I should say it's the closest the public can get."

When they reached Higgs Beach, they strolled to the end of White Street Pier.

"Since the dock reaches so far into the Atlantic"— Keya's smile was lighthearted—"some call this 'the unfinished road to Cuba.' "

Brett's out there somewhere fishing. Her pulse quickening at the thought, Ruth stared across the waves before she sighed and dropped her gaze. *He's probably dozens of nautical miles out to sea.* Then shadows swimming alongside the pier grabbed her attention. "What kinds of fish are those?"

"Snook, redfish." Keya pointed. "And I think that one is a small tarpon."

Ruth strained to see through the sun's reflection on the water's surface. "You don't find these in freshwater lakes."

After retracing their steps to the beach, they crossed the street. "Here's what I wanted to show you—the wildlife center." Keya's smile was almost bashful. "I volunteer here, too."

Ruth nodded as she gazed at the surrounding greenery.

"This shelter's a refuge, smack in the middle of a high-end tourist town."

As they strolled the center's sidewalks, flocks of ibis approached them, fearless and curious. Feral chickens and iguanas roamed at will, seeming to enjoy the shaded, parklike setting. Then they passed a huge pen of brilliantly colored roosters, the birds' sunlit plumage captivating Ruth.

"Look at those fancy feathers—iridescent greens, golds, reds, oranges—even blues. Their coloring's magnificent."

"Most people think their feathers come in one color—white."

"Why are these roosters penned?"

"Feral chickens are protected on Key West," said Keya, "but to avoid any potential 'human-chicken conflict,' people borrow the center's humane traps and bring any troublesome roosters here."

"A poultry paradise for what you might call foul fowl?" Ruth gave her a crooked smile. "Then what happens to them?"

"The wildlife center relocates them to organic farms, where they control pests naturally," said Keya. "It's a win-win situation."

"I like the gypsy chickens strutting around town," said Ruth. "If you ask me, they're Key West's most colorful attraction."

"Couldn't agree more."

Keya's phone pinged. As she scanned the message, her face flushed.

"Let me guess. Is it Auggie?"

****

A half hour later, they met him in front of the Nautical Museum's cannons.

"Déjà vu," said Ruth.

"Isn't this where we came in this morning?" Then smiling to herself, Keya studied Auggie. "The similarity's *amazing*." She shook her head. "I don't know why I didn't see it right away."

"See what?" Auggie stared at her.

"The resemblance. You could be Jules'—" She bit her lip. "—brother."

"Just cousins." He pressed his lips into a tight line.

Glancing at her emerald wedding ring, she stifled a sigh before turning back toward him. "What's next on the itinerary?"

Auggie's gaze caught hers. "I thought we might stop in a ceviche bar at the seaport."

"What's ceviche?" Ruth squinted, trying to place the word.

"It's seafood 'cooked' in lime juice," said Auggie.

Ruth caught the wicked gleam in his eyes. "Something about the way you say 'cooked' has me worried."

"Okay, not cooked as much as cured. The citrus juice pickles the seafood. Then the chefs add herbs, chilis, and veggies."

"So, what you're telling me is, it's raw fish, right?"

****

Seated at an outdoor café along the waterfront, Ruth eyed the ceviche sampler before them. Each cocktail glass contained a different variety of seafood— shrimp with rococo pepper and *leche de tigre*; yellowtail snapper with *aji* chili and cilantro; grouper marinated in lime with Thai basil; queen conch with *ahi amarillo*; hogfish with sour orange, toasted corn kernels, and jalapeño; and scallops with mint, red onion, and agave nectar. Bowls of salty crackers, tostado wedges, and plantain chips accompanied the appetizers.

"These all look colorful and tempting, but the idea of eating raw fish is hard to stomach." Ruth winced. "Literally."

"Cured!" Auggie shook his head good-naturedly.

"Go on," Keya said. "Try it."

Ruth took a deep breath, dabbed a smidgeon of the snapper ceviche onto a thin plantain chip, and popped the morsel in her mouth. The lime juice puckered her lips. The *aji* chili nipped her tongue, but when she bit into it, the lime, chili, cilantro, and fish flavors melded together to create a unique flavor.

"Well?" asked Keya. "What do you think?"

"The snapper's so tender, it melts in my mouth." Ruth blinked. "It's delicious—"

"You mean, de-*fish*-ious." Auggie dimpled as he scooped his conch ceviche onto a cracker.

"I don't know why I didn't try ceviche sooner." Ruth spooned some of the grouper onto a chip while Keya helped herself to the scallop ceviche.

Savoring it, Keya groaned with delight.

Earnestine sniffed the fish, her little nose twitching, then patted Keya's cheek with her paw.

"You don't like citrus," said Keya.

Again, Earnestine tapped her face.

"All right. Here." Keya spooned a tiny sliver on a cocktail napkin.

The cat caught a whiff of the lime juice before tasting it and promptly wrinkled her nose.

"Told you."

While they polished off the ceviche samplers, the fishing charters returned to port and unloaded their day's haul.

"It's a hoot watching them fend off pelicans while

they clean the fish." Auggie glanced at the show.

His back to them, Keya checked out Auggie's physique instead of the charter boats.

Then turning around, he caught her staring, and his eyelids creased in a warm smile.

She smiled back, her violet-blue eyes flashing.

As if mesmerized, he stared into them. "I have an idea. Why don't we take a sunset cruise?"

"What a lovely idea." A smile softened Keya's features as her gaze locked onto his.

A beat later, he turned to Ruth. "What do you say? How does a harbor cruise sound?"

"I have a brochure to finish, but I'll be happy to babysit Earnestine and Diesel." She swallowed a smile. "Why don't you two go?"

****

After escorting Ruth and the critters back to the hotel, Auggie and Keya booked a champagne-catamaran cruise. As they undocked from the Historic Seaport, they climbed to the upper deck, viewing the harbor from above.

"Oh, look! There's the hotel," said Keya, waving. "And isn't that Ruth on the balcony?"

Auggie waved, but when he saw no response, shrugged. "Guess she can't see us."

Keya glanced at all the boat traffic crisscrossing the harbor and shrugged. "To her, we must be nothing but a blip on the radar." As the warm tropical breeze rustled through her hair, she breathed in the salt air. Then the catamaran rounded the bend, and Mallory Square came into view. "Was that only yesterday we watched the sunset from there?"

Auggie caught her eye. "Seems longer ago, doesn't

it?"

"Definitely." Champagne glass in hand, Keya turned toward him and gazed into his gleaming, amber-brown eyes. "It seems I've known you for years."

His eyes capturing the sun's reflection, he nodded. "I feel the same way, not as if we've just met, but as if we're old friends—"

"Yes!" Keya came to attention, recognizing the truth. "Catching up—"

"*Picking* up where we left off..." His words hanging, Auggie leaned toward her.

She hesitated, unsure as thoughts of Jules swept through her mind. *I haven't kissed anyone since...*Then peering into his eyes, she lost her train of thought, and impulse carried her into his arms. Reconnecting more than meeting as their lips touched, she caught her breath. Suddenly, she was whole, complete again, as if a jigsaw puzzle's missing piece had been pressed into place. *For the first time since...*

His arms around her, bracing her from the catamaran's sway and roll, he held her as Fort Zachary Taylor became a black silhouette against the orange-tinged sky.

They talked while the moon rose above the horizon, and the first stars glimmered overhead. She leaned her head into the crux of his shoulder, and they shared their thoughts without looking at each other in an interactive stream of consciousness—pillow talk in the dark.

Before she realized it, the ship was docking. "Two hours *already*?" Still in his arms, she turned to look at him.

He glanced at his watch. "Time flew—or I should

say flowed." He had a sense of longing or nostalgia about him, and his feeble attempt at humor failed. As his lips curled in a bittersweet smile, the effect was melancholy. "Keya...I don't want the evening to end. Do you feel like a drink or a bite to eat?"

She studied his wounded eyes and full, sensitive lips, trying to get a better sense of the man. "If you hadn't suggested it, I would."

****

They found a patio table near the water's edge. Lit by a single candle, the cozy light wrapped them in a warm romantic glow.

"After the champagne cruise," he asked, "want to stick with the bubbly or—"

"Champagne's perfect."

No longer speaking their thoughts anonymously in the dark, facing away from each other as they had on the cruise, they held each other's gaze, face to face, enveloped within the candle's intimate circle of light.

While they waited for the wine, Keya watched his eyes, trying to read his thoughts.

"What?" He gave a nervous laugh.

"Sorry. Didn't mean to stare." She took a deep breath. "Something's been nagging me, but I haven't..." She stifled a sigh. "I'm not sure how to broach it..."

He spread his hands. "Just do it."

"Your reaction to the smoke and commotion the other night...what was that all about?"

He shrugged. "Like I said, I was aboard the *USS Cole* when terrorists suicide bombed it."

"But so much seemed *unsaid*." Wincing, she paused. "I don't mean to pry, but when I left acting, I quit playing roles, stopped hiding behind masks—and I'd appreciate it if you would, too. So, what didn't you tell me?"

Rapid-fire, her words triggered snapshots of the past. "PTSD is something I haven't discussed with anyone—*at all*—at least, not until recently."

"Why's that?"

"Because I'm the strong, silent type." He scoffed, trying to pass off his reply as a joke. But as the memories gathered force, mobilizing, invading his peace of mind, he slouched in his chair. "They didn't diagnose my disorder as PTSD until fifteen years after the bombing. By then, I'd spent a decade and a half coping with it on my own."

Palm upturned, Keya reached for his hand.

He hesitated, unsure about accepting it, debating whether to trust her...and unwilling to mislead her. Then leaning across the table, he wrapped his hand around hers. "Before we go any further, I want you to know something. I was married before." He searched her face, looking for acceptance or criticism.

Keya squeezed his hand, as if encouraging him to continue. "What happened?"

"According to my ex-wife and her lawyer, I invested all my time and energy in my career; I gave the Navy all I had, leaving nothing for her. Two months after our honeymoon, she had our marriage annulled...which sent me spinning in a steep downward spiral."

"It sounds like you were shell-shocked in more ways than one." Keya's half smile was sympathetic. "Did you get any counseling?"

"After the annulment, yes—that's when they

106

diagnosed the PTSD—and psychologists *had* talked to us right after the bombing." He scowled. "But they were only interested in regrouping the crew, getting us back in action. Though they prescribed thirty-day furloughs, our R & R didn't start for another few weeks."

"Why was that?" Her spine stiffened.

"After the attack, the crew had to stay aboard the *Cole*, working night and day just to keep it afloat. If not for our actions, that ship would've sunk, but because we were stuck there at the scene of the blast…surrounded by the sights, *the smells*"—he glanced at her—"we relived the nightmare on a daily basis."

Wincing, Keya momentarily closed her eyes, as if shutting out the images. "How did you manage?"

"I flipped a switch—shut it out mentally—just like the day of the bombing. I had a job to do, even if it was hazardous."

"Emotionally, you mean?"

"Emotionally, *physically*—every way." Despite the balmy evening, a shudder slithered down his spine. "After the attack, the ship had no light, no ventilation, and no air conditioning. The heat was stifling. The ship's interior was so hot the food began to rot. Between the reeking perishables, the smoke, the acrid odor of leaking fuel oil, and the putrid stench of death…" Momentarily closing his eyes, he drew a cleansing breath. "It was bad."

She shook her head slowly as if commiserating.

"Not a day has passed without reliving those memories. They've robbed me of my peace of mind"—he caught her eye, assessing her reaction—"and robbed me of my marriage."

"I can identify. Though I haven't survived a suicide bombing or annulment, I have survived the death of a spouse, the loss of the person I love, and I can empathize. Healing takes time." She took a deep breath as if grounding herself. Then her eyes probed his. "Are you coming to terms with those flashbacks now?"

"I'm starting to—like a turtle peeking out its shell." He attempted a smile, trying to lighten the mood and give himself some mental space, but the ruse backfired. The memories crowded in on him. "I'm still bitter about the attack. I want justice, not only for those who lost their lives, but for those of us who *stopped living our lives* because of it." He searched her eyes.

Keya stifled a groan in her throat. "We've all been wounded and known loss, but I can't imagine the horrors you've experienced." As if donning a gasmask, she put on a smile. "Thank God it's behind you."

"That's the point. It wasn't then—and it isn't now." Still trying to gather his disjointed memories into a coherent story with a beginning, middle, and end, he struggled to find a redeeming pretext for the incidents. "A second shock hit us when we got home. Because the flight to the States took just a few hours, we had no time to decompress. Returning from deployment, *from war*—whether declared or not—we had no time to adjust, no transition from one life into the next.

"After we landed, I remember feeling so displaced in civilian life that just walking through the airport seemed surreal, like an out-of-body experience. Even on the taxi ride home, I remember trying to make sense of it, asking myself over and over, 'What the hell am I doing here?' " He stared at her. "Sometimes, I still wake, asking myself, *Why did I survive and not the others?*"

****

With the waves breaking on the rocky beach below, the gulls crying into the wind, and the sea breeze tousling her hair, Ruth lingered on the balcony, debating. *Play it safe and work inside, or stay on the terrace and risk being stalked?* She breathed in the salt air, filling her lungs with its briny bouquet. *We're paying for this gorgeous view. I might as well enjoy it—or at least try.*

Shaking off her cowardice, she set her laptop on the patio's tiny table. Then she took the precaution of angling her chair away from the room, so she could enjoy the view yet keep an eye on the staircase. As she gazed out to sea, her thoughts drifted to Brett, just a few miles out, yet apparently not within radio range.

The shrill ring of her cell slashed though the evening's hush.

Flinching, she reached for her phone as she checked caller ID. *Brett!* "Hey! How are you doing?"

"Great, though I've missed you."

The warmth came through his voice, and Ruth hugged herself, imagining his arms were around her. "I've missed you, too! How are you able to call?"

"*Finally*, we're within fifteen nautical miles of shore, so we're getting reception." He gave a frustrated laugh. "These guys are hard-core anglers who want to stay out at sea."

"I'm just glad to connect." She smiled, happy to hear his voice. "What have you been up to besides fishing?"

"Cleaning fish, cooking fish, eating fish, and

109

playing poker."

His enthusiasm coming through the phone, she imagined his smile. "Glad you have buddies for all those *fun* activities." Though happy for him, she made no attempt to hide her sarcasm.

He laughed. "What've you been doing?"

She caught him up on what had happened since their last call, adding, "And I think your uncle and my cousin hit it off."

"Is that a fact?" He hitched his breath. "What makes you think so?"

"What doesn't? Their body language, eye contact, and a certain frisson when they're near each other all shout infatuation. Their pheromones are flying fast and furious." Then she took a deep breath, preparing herself for his reaction to what she was about to say. "Something else, I've met a ghost—more like two."

"What?" He gave a hesitant laugh. "Is this the opening line to a joke?"

"I'm serious." She filled him in on the details.

He said something, but his words were garbled.

"What was that?" She strained to hear. "You're breaking up."

The crackling turned into static, and then the line went dead.

They must be out of range again. Opening her laptop with a sigh, she forced herself to concentrate on the brochure. *Wonder what he thinks of my new companions…*

****

Ruth and Keya left Key West early the next morning.

Yawning as she drove, Keya said, "Hope Auggie

and I didn't wake you when he picked up Diesel."

"I'm a sound sleeper." Not mentioning their prolonged goodnight kiss, Ruth deadpanned.

Either missing the irony or ignoring it, Keya glanced at her with bloodshot eyes. "That's good," she mumbled, before turning her gaze to the road.

"You and Auggie seem to get along."

"I guess." Though Keya stared straight ahead, her cheeks rose in a private grin.

Ruth swallowed a smile as she petted Earnestine on her lap. "What do you think about him?"

"He seems lighthearted and cracks corny jokes, but he has a serious side." Keya glanced at Ruth before focusing on the road. "He's a complex person."

"What makes you say that?"

"His reaction to the smoke and commotion the other night…and what he confided to me last night." As she drove, Keya became quiet, seeming to turn inward.

The speaker phone rang, jarring them both, and Keya took the call.

"Good morning." Detective Bell's crisp voice filled the air. "We've finished dusting the earrings for prints but found nothing."

"Did someone wipe them off?" asked Ruth.

"I doubt it." The detective's irritation came through the phone. "Fingerprints are little more than perspiration. The saltwater probably dissolved them. Stop by the station to sign the paperwork, and we'll release them to you."

Keya glanced at Ruth. "We're about forty minutes away. Would that timeframe work for you?"

"The earrings are at the front desk," he said. "No need to see me."

"Actually, I'd like to discuss something with you," said Keya. "My friends and I believe we've been followed and photographed for the past few days."

"In Marathon?"

"There," said Keya, "as well as Bahia Honda Park and Key West."

He paused. "Forty minutes, you said?"

Keya smirked as she stepped on the gas. "Maybe thirty-five."

****

After signing the paperwork, Keya absently handed Ruth the earrings as she described the two possible stalkers to Detective Bell.

The moment Ruth touched the earrings, Bartolomé appeared, removing his plumed, wide-brimmed hat and making a courtly bow.

Standing off to the side, Maita seemed oblivious of everything except the jewelry. She reached for the earrings, sobbing all the while.

Earnestine, in Keya's arms, hissed at the apparitions, her tail twitching and puffing up to twice its normal size.

"Hush." Keya tried to tell the detective the details, but the cat's growling only intensified. Frustrated, she turned to Ruth. "Here, you take her. Maybe she'll mind you."

Just as Maita's fingers grazed the earrings, Ruth dropped them in her pocket. By breaking physical contact with the jewelry, she broke the conduit for seeing the spirits. And as fast as Maita and Bartolomé had appeared, they vanished.

Keya passed her the cat, and with the specters gone, Earnestine began to relax.

"I don't know what's gotten into her today." Then Keya finished telling the detective about the man in the tan baseball cap and the woman in the oversized glasses.

Rather than wearing his usual impassive expression, he zeroed in on Keya, took out a pen and pad, and took notes. "The situations you mentioned all took place in public places. Did either of these people invade your solitude or seclusion?"

Ruth told him about the man photographing her on the hotel's balcony.

Detective Bell jotted down a note. "Intrusion upon seclusion is an invasion of privacy. Private investigators can tail but not pry."

Ruth blinked. "So these *were* private investigators?"

"Possibly." His shoulders jerked in a quick shrug.

"Something else happened." Keya shot Ruth a look before turning back to the detective.

"Concerning the private investigators?" He raised his pen poised to take notes.

"No, this happened prior to them." Keya shook her head. "In fact, it was the same night we found the earrings, but later, after you'd left." She described Earnestine's reactions to the purchasing manager when Gerry had introduced him, and how they had seen scratch marks on his arms.

"So?" The detective shrugged.

Keya shot Ruth another look. "We thought the scratches might be a clue to the young woman's drowning."

"Why would you think that?" Pokerfaced, he stifled a sigh.

"Earnestine recognized her scent on him."

"Earnestine…?" The muscles around his eyes tightened. "Your cat, right?"

Keya nodded.

"If you'll excuse me." He tucked his notebook in his pocket. "Another case requires my attention."

Watching him walk away, Keya said tongue-in-cheek, "That conversation went well, don't you think?"

Ruth snickered.

"Unfortunately, we took longer than I expected." As they left the station, Keya glanced at her watch. "The attorney's appointment is in less than an hour. Would you mind if I drop you and Earnestine off at the house?"

"Of course." Still holding the cat, Ruth added, "Earnestine and I are becoming fast friends. Besides, I should take some background photos for the brochure. Okay to use your beach as the setting?"

"Make yourself at home."

****

After unpacking, Ruth grabbed her camera and strolled along the white sand beach. Snapping pictures every few feet, she followed the contours of the narrow isthmus and crossed the bridge to the secluded island.

The turtle tracks in the sand reminded her of Keya's legal battle to save the nesting area. *This beach is a refuge—a paradise worth protecting.*

While admiring the key's natural beauty, she glimpsed the sand dune where they had found Maita's body. Instinctively, she touched the pocket holding her earrings. *Moment of truth—should I try to make contact?* Taking a deep breath of salt air, Ruth reached into her pocket and put on the silver earrings.

114

Bartolomé appeared, making his usual chivalrous bow.

Standing behind him, Maita gawked at the earrings. She again reached for them with her bloodied fingers, sobbing all the while.

"Stop that infernal blubbering!" Bartolomé pulled his hat over his ears.

Her eyes like a frightened doe's, her mouth snapped shut, and Maita stopped crying on his command.

"That's better." He heaved a great sigh before turning to Ruth. "Almost four hundred years of undisturbed silence, and this woman's caterwauling is driving me to drink." This time his sigh was nostalgic. "That is, *if* I could taste rum again."

Ruth gave him a sympathetic smile as she studied him. "It mustn't be easy feeling alive yet not being alive."

"Feeling…" As he gazed at the horizon, his eyes took on a faraway look. "To feel the splendid sensation of rum burning down my gullet or a forty-knot gale whipping against my face once more…" He broke off in a wistful sigh. "What I'd give to *feel* again."

His anguish was palpable. *Where do I begin?* Ruth asked, "If you're not happy here, why do you stay?"

Wheeling around to face her, he scowled. "I don't know." Then, he seemed to focus his attention inward. Though still visible, he mentally withdrew.

"What about you, Maita?" Ruth pounced on the opportunity to speak with the timid spirit. "Why are you here?"

The girl moved her mouth as if attempting to talk, but no words came out. Struggling, she uttered sounds that gradually resembled words. After a minute, she started speaking in halted phrases. "Can't...tell."

Ruth cocked her head. "Can't or won't tell?"

The girl frowned. "Can't tell."

It was Ruth's turn to frown. "You don't know, or you're not allowed to tell?"

"Can't tell." Maita stared at the earrings.

Ruth fingered one. "Are these yours?" At Maita's nod, Ruth took it off and gingerly held it in her hand, afraid of what would happen.

Maita warily reached for the earring with bloodied fingers. As her spectral hand passed through the metal and Ruth's flesh, the girl flinched. "What happened?"

"It seems you can't grasp objects on this plane." Shivering from the icy touch, Ruth took a deep breath to brace herself. Then as she put on the earring, Maita stared, never taking her gaze from it. "Yet you seem attached to these. Why?"

"He'..."

"He?" Ruth struggled to understand. "Bartolomé?"

Maita shook her head.

"Then who?"

"He'..." She made a guttural sound as she struggled to pronounce the word, as if she had a speech impediment. "He'...gave 'em to me."

Ruth tried to piece her clues together. "Okay, these earrings are a gift from someone, right? An admirer?"

A smile crossed Maita's face for the first time. She nodded.

"Who?"

"He'..." Again, her face clouded over.

Learning her story's going to take all afternoon at this rate. "Maita, did someone murder you?"

The girl's eyes filled with tears.

As Maita wept, the weight of her sadness smothered Ruth like a steam room's saturated air, taking away her breath.

"Not this caterwauling again," bellowed Bartolomé, coming out of his trance, his hands to his ears. Then rushing to Ruth's defense, he roared, "Cease and desist, woman!"

Sniffling and sobbing, Maita vanished.

"That's better." Seeming to regain his presence of mind, he turned to Ruth. "Are you all right, my dear?"

Ruth nodded as she caught her breath and smiled her thanks.

"Then I have a question for you. How can you see us?"

Ruth shrugged. "I can't tell you the scientific reason, Bartolomé—"

"Bart." He sported a roguish grin. "Call me Bart."

She swallowed a smile. "All right, *Bart*, if I touch an object, somehow I see a spirit associated with its history. It's happened to me several times now. In your case, you appear any time I touch part of the *Regala* treasure. In Maita's case, it's only when I touch her earrings—"

"That were made from the *Regala's* silver coins." He nodded. "But how do you do it?"

She shrugged. "For lack of a better term, let's call this ability a gift."

His good eye narrowed as it appraised her. "Witchcraft?"

She shook her head. "I think it's a gift from God—something to cherish—but I don't pretend to understand it."

"Does your gift have a name?"

"The closest I can find online is psychometry." Ruth grimaced. "To be honest, it scares me."

"Why?"

She gave an uncomfortable laugh. "I never know where it'll lead me."

"Afraid yet forging ahead into the unknown." The corner of his eye crinkled in an approving smile. "You're an adventuress."

"No." She shook her head. "I'm a writer."

His face lit up as if getting an idea. "An author?"

"Technical writer…a scribe."

"Akin." His hands resting at his sides, he paced back and forth, his coat open and his scabbard swinging beside him. At last, he stopped in front of her. "I have a situation for you."

Head canted, she squinted. "A situation?"

"A position, woman. A contract, a business proposition."

"A job?"

Nodding brusquely, he gestured to the sandy beach. "Sit down, my dear, I have something to discuss with you."

This should be interesting. Sitting cross-legged on the sand, she regarded him. "Can't say I've ever been hired by a ghost before."

"Let me come right to the point." He sighed. "I've been anxious to unburden my soul for almost four hundred years."

"If it's a confession, you need a priest, not a scribe."

"No." He shook his head. "Nothing of the sort. I wasn't a religious man. I was a sailor, a navigator."

"You were an explorer." She nodded.

"Precisely, my dear. Already, we're *sympatico*." He smiled his approval. "I'd like you to recreate my journeys through my journals."

Ruth blinked. "Weren't they lost at sea when the *Regala* sank?"

Closing his eye, he gave a solemn nod.

"Then how do you propose I recreate your journeys if I don't have your diaries?"

His smile returned. "After four hundred years, I have them memorized. I'll dictate as you record them."

Record them. She recalled the tour guide's words about Hemingway reporting events, not writing stories, and her idea resurfaced. *If I'd ever find a true story to write about…maybe I could start a novel.*

"Bart, would you mind if I adapted your memoirs into a book?"

As if surprised by her question, he hesitated, seeming to mull it over. Then with a smile, he shook his head while he studied her. "No, my dear, I wouldn't mind at all. I sense a strong temperamental consonance between us. We have an accord!"

****

Three hours later, Ruth sat engrossed at the patio table, listening to Bart as Earnestine napped on her lap.

"This must be one long brochure."

"*Yikes!*" Ruth spun her head toward the voice.

Keya peered over her shoulder, reading.

As Ruth's heartbeat slowed, she took a deep gulp of air to ground herself. "Next time, warn me before you sneak up on me." She glanced at the time. *Was that three hours ago Keya left?*

"I called you twice." Shrugging, Keya spread her

hands, palms up.

"Sorry, I was"—Ruth gave her a lopsided smirk, unsure how much to share—"captivated."

"What are you looking so smug about?" Keya studied her.

"I'm trying to capture Bart's every word."

"What?"

"Bartolomé's here."

Keya looked around.

"He's sitting across from me." Ruth pointed.

"Ghosts can sit?"

"You have a good point." Ruth turned toward Bart. "How can you sit on chairs while Maita can't touch the earrings?"

"I've existed on this plane for centuries, my dear." He tilted his head to survey her with his good eye. "Give me credit for learning a few skills over the years."

After Ruth shared his conversation, Keya shook her head as she gave a skeptical laugh. "Why's he sitting here?"

"Bart's telling me about his travels while I record it."

"For the brochure?" Keya squinted as if baffled.

"No." Ruth shook her head. "For the book I'm writing."

"What!"

"I'll tell you all about it in a bit." Smiling, she took out the earrings and dropped them in her pocket. Then with a wave to Bart, she saved her work, turned off the computer, and turned her full attention to Keya. "*First*, tell me what happened at the attorney's."

With a frustrated sigh, Keya pressed her fingers

into her temples. "We weren't paranoid this week." She gestured toward the neighboring property with her chin. "Gerald Granger has hired private investigators to follow me and check my background."

Ruth squinted. "Why?"

"It seems he wants this property so much, he's playing hardball to get it."

"How so?" Ruth struggled to connect the two thoughts. "We knew he wanted the land, but why do you say he's playing hardball?"

"Auggie was right about Gerald tracking down the Erskine family." Keya took a deep breath. "Gerald misled them into thinking they were the rightful owners of this property, and then assuming they'd win the case, he manufactured lawsuits, hoping to buy them out."

Her tone echoing her uncertainty, Ruth asked, "What does this have to do with the private investigators?"

"Not only has Gerald's corporation had my husband's and my financial records checked for the past seven years," Keya sneered, "but now, on behalf of the Erskine family, he's trying to have me declared mentally incompetent."

Ruth's jaw went slack. "What makes you say that?"

Keya pushed a thick stack of papers across the table. "Here's the transcription of everything 'incriminating' I've said during the past three days."

Her gaze clouding, Ruth stared at them without seeing. "What…?"

"These are supporting documents the petitioner—"

"The *who*?"

"Gerald's corporation, on behalf of the Erskine

family, has gathered evidence against me."

"Why would they—?"

"They want to use it in court to declare me mentally incompetent." Her chest heaved with an indignant sigh. "They're trying to prove I'm bonkers."

"What!"

Keya nodded. "They're accusing me of leaving the property to the turtles."

"Isn't that what you intend to do?"

"Indirectly, yes." Keya clenched her jaw. "I want to make a bequest to the Turtle Refuge. They're saying I want to leave the property to the turtles. *Directly* to the turtles, as if I've lost touch with reality and am incapable of being rational."

"That's ridiculous. They can't do that..." Ruth scowled. "Can they?"

Keya shoved the papers closer. "See for yourself."

Ruth rifled through the bound paperwork, noting the highlighted lines.

[Subject referring to personal conversation with turtle:] "I asked [the turtle] where he was going, and he said, 'To meet everyone.'

"To speed the process, I carried him around, greeting the people, one by one. When we reached a quiet woman named Ellen, he said, 'I love her. I lo-o-ove her!' I told her Flash's reaction, and though she took it in stride, several others in the group burst into giggles."

Ruth's jaw dropped. Glancing up from the transcription, she said, "Your words were taken out of context." Then she skimmed through the next line.

"Like I said, I want to leave [the property] to the turtles."

Shaking her head at the injustice, Ruth huffed. "I remember this conversation. You'd gone on to say how you intended to leave it to the Turtle Refuge. Half your remarks weren't even included."

"Just the 'incriminating' parts." Keya sneered. "Since the information supports the Erskine family's petition to have the Probate Court declare me incompetent, it conveniently leaves out anything vindicating me."

Ruth rolled her eyes. "We were chatting in the café when that 'gentleman' in the baseball cap eavesdropped on our private conversation."

"There's more," said Keya, tapping the file with her long fingernails. "Much more."

Again, Ruth rifled through the bound paperwork, noting the highlighted lines.

[Subject speaking to tour guide at aquarium:] "The sea cucumber in the touch tank is a bit sore from the handling. Could you remove her for the day?"

[Tour guide:] "What makes you say *her*? Visually, males are indistinguishable from females. Their sex organs are internal."

[Subject:] "She told me. The sea cucumber needs a break from the touch tank. She's sore."

[Associate Ruth Bernard:] "How do you know?"

[Subject:] "You mean, aside from her telling me?"

"This is ridiculous," said Ruth. "Not only were you not hurting anyone, you were trying to help that critter."

Flipping to a page near the front, Keya underlined a paragraph with her finger. "You missed the most incriminating 'evidence.' "

[Children asking subject question at Turtle Refuge:] "Can turtles talk?"

[Subject:] "As a matter of fact, they can."

[Children:] "Can we hear them?"

[Subject:] "Some of us can."

"Again, taken out of context." Glancing toward Gerald's house, Ruth uttered a disgusted growl. "That two-faced hypocrite plied us with limos and lunch. Then when that ploy didn't work, he pulls this."

"His investigators recorded every word I said, every conversation I had with Earnestine, every drink I ordered"—her chest heaved in another sigh—"and even each kiss I shared with Auggie. To read this report, I sound like an eccentric old fool."

Ruth surveyed her cousin's flowing trousers, canary-yellow blouson, and oversized citrine necklace. Framed in that context, she reconsidered Keya's flamboyant outfit.

Keya did a double take. "What?"

"Eccentric?" Ruth hunched her shoulders. "Maybe a tad, but that's just your dramatic flair. Old fool?" She shook her head. "You're a *long* way from being old." She gave her cousin a warm smile. "And you're the most mentally competent person as I know."

"Then they're making me sound like an irresponsible spendthrift, a...*a cash splasher*, who's trying to regain her youth."

"Cash splasher?" Ruth laughed inwardly at the phrase. "Trying to make a bequest of the property is anything but irresponsible."

Keya winced. "Better reserve judgment until after the next question."

"Uh-oh." Ruth steeled herself.

"My attorney wants you to testify as a character witness for me at the court hearing—"

"What's wrong with that?" Relaxing, Ruth spread her arms wide, her palms up. "I'm happy to help."

"Let me finish." Keya's smile was wry. "The hearing's next Friday…"

"And our flight leaves this Sunday…" Taking a deep breath, Ruth sat back in her chair.

Keya nodded. "I'll understand if you can't stay."

Ruth mentally listed a delay's complications— *longer separation from Brett, change fees, rebooked flights, missed work, cancelled appointments…*Then her cousin's bunched eyes and pursed lips came into view, and her qualms vanished.

"I've known you all my life. Who'd be a better character witness than me?" Ruth flashed her brightest smile. "Of course I'll stay. I would even if you weren't my favorite cousin."

Keya's relaxed smile and deep sigh reflected her relief, but she hesitated. "How will Brett take the news?"

"He'll understand." Ruth shrugged. "You need my help." Then she recalled Keya's earlier words. "Though *none* of this makes sense, I can't imagine why Gerald's corporation would check your financial records for the past seven years."

"My attorney called his investigation due diligence. Sounds like they hope to dig up some dirt with a business compliance asset search."

"Like what?"

"First and foremost," Keya counted on her fingers as she named the reasons, "real estate deeds and mortgage information, corporate filings, judgments, bankruptcies, and federal or state tax liens—anything they can find."

"So, when the asset search didn't uncover anything incriminating, they started waging this mental-incompetence attack against you." As the pieces fit, Ruth nodded to herself. Then another thought crossed her mind. "How long can this legal battle drag on?"

"Don't worry." The corners of Keya's mouth lifted in a sympathetic smile. "It can't last more than a week. Florida has a statute of limitations. My attorney said the time to contest a will is short, about ninety days from when he provided the 'Notice of Administration' three months ago."

"So, because of the time constraints, they're under pressure to get results, and now they're getting ugly. This is their last-ditch effort to gain control of your property."

"Exactly. Bad as this witch hunt is, the good news is, the court battle ends next week—one way or the other." Her eyes warmed in a smile. "I can't take advantage of your good nature beyond then."

"I'm just glad events worked out for me to be here for you." Then Ruth remembered the earrings. As she took them from her pocket, Maita and Bart appeared and then disappeared when she placed them on the patio table. "I almost forgot to return these."

Keya shook her head. "They're not mine to give." Tongue-in-cheek, she added, "Please keep them as a souvenir of this 'adventure.' "

Ruth's ears perked.

"What?"

"It reminds me of something Bart said. He called me an adventuress."

"Maybe you are." Keya's eyes glinted. "You're the only person I know on a first-name basis with ghosts."

She grimaced. "But I've been monopolizing the conversation. What were you doing when I came in?"

"Capturing Bart's stories about his travels and discoveries."

Keya frowned. "Why?"

"Because…" Ruth took a deep breath. "I've decided to write a novel based on his memoirs." *Whew!* Hearing her thoughts put into words, she laughed out loud as the adrenalin pumped through her veins. "Announcing my goal is a whole lot different than thinking it."

"A novel?"

Curbing a gleeful smile, Ruth nodded. "Life is stranger than fiction. When we visited the Hemingway House, something the guide said inspired me to consider writing a book. Then today, Bart offered me a job—"

"A job?" Lifting her chin, Keya scrutinized her.

"Yup." She gave a wry laugh. "You heard right, *a job*. He called it a situation, but he wants me to transcribe his memoirs. Basically, I'll be ghostwriting for a ghost. Since I can't acknowledge my source, I'll just change the names and present the facts as fiction."

Keya's eyes sparkled. "You're an adventurous adventuress."

"More like an armchair adventuress." Ruth glanced at the metal outdoor furniture. "Or in this case, a backyard buccaneer. Bart's tales are fascinating, but all I'm doing is recording them."

Keya fingered the jewelry. "All this because you and Auggie found these earrings."

Nodding, Ruth studied her cousin. "You'd said they weren't yours to give. Though the police didn't find prints, I'm sure they belonged to Maita. It's only fair to ask her permission to keep them."

Keya handed her the earrings. "Only one way to find out…"

Chapter 6

Found Treasure

The moment Ruth's fingers connected with the silver earrings, both spirits appeared.

Bartolomé asserted himself, standing front and center, taking charge, his legs planted wide apart, hands on hips, while Maita cowered on the sidelines, gazing down and wringing her hands.

From the girl's body language, Ruth guessed her inhibition and lack of self-confidence. "Bart, would you mind giving Maita some privacy?"

His spine stiffening, his bushy eyebrow rose indignantly.

"We'd like to ask her a personal question." Ruth appealed with a smile.

He nodded. Then with a chivalrous flourish, he bowed and disappeared.

Left alone on her spiritual plane, yet in the company of women on this level of existence, Maita visibly relaxed. No longer hunching, she lifted her head to meet Ruth's gaze. "What do you want to know?"

With Maita's speech impediment less noticeable, Ruth's expectations rose. *Maybe now I'll get some answers.* "Since you can't connect with objects on this physical plane anymore, would you have any objections if I wore your earrings?"

Maita stared at them in Ruth's hand for several moments. Then squeezing her eyes shut, she winced as she pressed her fists into her forehead. An agonized expression passed across her face before she covered it with her bloodied hands. Then she began making an eerie, wailing sound.

"Maita, I'm sorry. I didn't mean to upset you—"

"What's wrong?" asked Keya as Earnestine crept onto her lap, cringing, tail tucked between her legs.

"Maita's not crying as much as keening or grieving." Ruth blinked, processing. "It's almost as if she's mourning her own death." Trying again, Ruth said, "If you don't want me to wear the earrings, Maita, I won't, but to see you and Bart, I'll need to touch them. Would that be all right?"

Still moaning and rocking on her toes, the girl shook her head.

Ruth grimaced as her options dwindled. "Okay, but without seeing you or talking to you, how can I help you?"

Maita's ears perked up, and she stopped her lament. "You'd…you'll help me?"

"Of course.

"In 'at case, you can touch 'em." Maita's speech impairment was more noticeable with certain words and sounds.

"These earrings obviously mean a lot to you. Why?"

"He'…"

Ruth struggled to understand.

"He'…" Maita struggled to pronounce the words. "He'…gave 'em to me."

Ruth tried to piece together her information. "Who

gave you these earrings? Who's *he*? An admirer?"

Maita nodded.

"Who?"

"He'…" Her face contorted as if she was about to start wailing again.

Ruth glanced at Keya and shook her head. "I don't know if Maita's speech impediment prevents her from answering me, or if she can't tell me for some other reason." She sighed.

"I'm trying to tell you." A deep V wedged itself between Maita's eyes. "Watch my mout'." She placed the tip of her tongue against the back of her upper teeth, but no sound came out. "I can't pronounce dental fricatives."

"Dental fricatives," repeated Ruth, turning on the computer and searching the phrase on the internet. When she read the definition, she sat back, smiling at Keya. "Maita has trouble making 'th' sounds." Ruth gave a relieved sigh. "I believe we've 'broken the code.'"

"Yes." Though Maita had disappeared when Ruth set down the earrings, she reappeared, nodding as Ruth touched them. "Ask me 'ose questions again."

Ruth tested her theory, linking the sounds. "Th…ose. Ask you *those* questions again." She breathed a sigh of relief, glad they had cracked the code. "Okay, who gave you the earrings?"

"He'…"

"He…th." As Ruth combined the sounds, she caught her breath. "Heath?"

"Yes!" Maita's eyes lit up.

Ruth looked from Maita to Keya and back. "The same Heath Hawkins who works for Gerald Granger next door?"

"Yes," said Maita, "his purchasing manager."

Ruth took a deep breath before asking, "Maita, was your drowning accidental, or were you killed?"

The girl's eyes filled with tears as she began sobbing.

Again, the weight of Maita's sadness overcame Ruth, this time like thick smoke, forcing the air from her lungs and suffocating her. Her heart pounding, she broke out in a cold sweat. Panting, she struggled to breathe.

"What's happening?" Keya shook Ruth's shoulders as if shaking her awake.

Unable to catch her breath, Ruth hyperventilated. Panicking, she flung the earrings on the table, and as the apparition vanished, the oppressive atmosphere lifted.

Keya let go her shoulders. "You seemed in a trance."

"It was so real." Ruth's torso rose with each gasping breath. "I couldn't breathe."

The muscles around Keya's eyes bunched together. "Have you experienced this sensation before?"

Ruth nodded, recalling Maita's reaction when asked if she had been murdered. "But this was more than a sensation. It was a *force* that affected my breathing."

Keya winced. "That doesn't sound safe."

"No, it doesn't." Ruth filled her lungs with a deep, cleansing breath.

Earnestine's piercing snarl drew their attention. Then her ears back, she hissed.

"Knock, knock," said a man's voice.

Ruth and Keya pivoted toward the sound.

"I trust I'm not intruding." Heath picked his way through the firethorn separating Gerry and Keya's properties. Bare-chested, wearing just sandals and swimming trunks, he graced them with a self-assured smile.

A glossy folder in hand, he strode toward them with the confidence of a man who knew his attractive, well-defined features turned heads. He seemed accustomed to being welcomed into women's company. "How are you ladies doing this fine afternoon?"

Yowling as her tail whipped back and forth, Earnestine arched her back and flattened her ears, warning him off.

"What do you want?"

He missed a step at Keya's no-nonsense tone, combined with Earnestine's caterwauling. Then flashing a practiced smile, he continued toward them. "I wanted to follow up on the information Gerry and I'd given you ladies earlier. Have you had time to look it over?" His gaze direct, he homed in on Keya. "Got any questions?"

Ruth studied his lean, muscular frame. His arms, chest, and back were covered with half-healed scratches and fresh abrasions. "What have you been doing?" she asked. "Fighting a losing battle with the firethorn?"

His smile drooped momentarily, then he seemed to recover his composure with a dry laugh. "Not firethorn, fire *coral*." He shook his head. "I brushed against some skin-diving at the John Pennekamp Coral Reef State Park."

Frowning, Keya glanced at Ruth and shook her head. "Those look like scratches to me, not fire coral stings."

Shrugging, he offered her the glossy folder. "Do you have any questions about the portfolio?"

"Nope." She added a popping sound on her final P as she ignored the packet.

Apparently unfazed, he used the folder's pen to scribble on his business card. "If you think of any, here's my cell number. Feel free to call any time." He gave Keya an arresting smile. "Day or night."

Ruth rolled her eyes.

Again, he offered Keya the folder, but she made no move to accept it. Instead, Earnestine hissed as her paw thwacked it with two right jabs, knocking it from his hands. He retrieved the packet, set on the table, and gave a parting nod. "Ladies."

"Actually—" Ruth's tone made him pause. "—I do have a question."

"Yes?"

"Did you know Maita?"

His smile wavering, he shrugged. "Sure, I did. She worked for Gerry."

"I mean, personally?"

He drew in his breath before answering. "We might've gone out for coffee a time or two." Dropping his smile, he scoured her face. "Why?"

She gestured toward the silver earrings on the table. "Did these belong to Maita?"

"They might have." He raised his shoulders in a casual shrug.

"The police analyzed them for fingerprints."

His face paled beneath his tan, but his expression remained indifferent.

She tried to mirror his poker face. "You wouldn't

have any reason for your prints to be on them, would you?"

"Are you saying they were?"

"Why?" Ruth searched his face. "Were they?"

"Who knows?" He worked his jaw as he chose his words. "She wore them a lot."

Ruth picked up the earrings, and Maita appeared.

"He'…gave 'em to me for my bir'day."

Ruth held them out to Heath. "Didn't you give these to Maita for her birthday?"

His jaw dropped. "Who told you that?"

"Did you, or didn't you?"

"I might've…I don't remember."

"Don't remember?" Maita's voice rose in pitch. "How could you forget!" Using her fingernail, she seemed to write on his arm as she struggled to speak. " 'at was 'e night you told me you loved me."

An angry, red welt surfaced on his arm as the word LOVE appeared. Then the wound began bleeding, resembling a vampire font. Heath looked at the scratch, gasped, and turned toward Ruth. "What did you do?"

"Nothing"—Ruth shook her head as she set down the earrings—"though *someone* wants to communicate. Wonder who…?"

Bug-eyed, he gazed around the patio as he backed away. Then he turned and ran through the pyracantha hedge, yelping as the thorns tore at his flesh.

Keya gave a disbelieving snort. "You don't see that every day."

"Did you see all his scratches?" asked Ruth.

"You mean the skin writing?"

Ruth shook her head. "Beneath that."

"I couldn't take my eyes off the skin writing.

135

Though I've read about it, this is the first time I've ever seen it." Keya shook off a chill. "Creepy."

"Heath had layers of fresh scratches on top of earlier, half-healed scratches."

"He didn't get those from fire coral. Uhn-uh." Keya shook her head. "Their stings leave a blotchy, burning rash—not individual scratch marks."

"I can't believe today's message was Maita's first." Thinking aloud, Ruth tapped her index finger against her upper lip. Then she raised her finger as a new thought struck. "What if she's been *contacting* him ever since she drowned?"

"What makes you think so?"

"Aside from her fingernails always being bloody, his arms, back, and chest were *covered* with scratches, all at various levels of healing." Ruth squinted as she pieced it together. "My guess is the welts leave scratch marks after the swelling goes down. The scratches we glimpsed were the remains of not one, but multiple messages she's written over the past few days."

Keya laughed wryly. "What reason would Maita have to haunt him?"

"Let's ask her," Ruth said as she touched the earrings.

The spirit appeared surly and sullen, her eyes red and ominous.

The suffocating memory was still raw. Ruth struggled to catch her breath, and she dropped the jewelry in her pocket. "Now's maybe not the best time. Instead, how 'bout a walk to the island?"

"Good idea." Keya's mouth rose in a wistful smile. "I haven't seen it in a few days, and I've missed it."

"You have?" Ruth glanced at her as they strolled

along the white sand beach. "Why's that? I mean, aside from its obvious beauty and serenity?"

Keya took a deep breath. "I've spent a lot of time there."

"Since Jules's death?"

Crossing the footbridge, Keya shook her head. "It started fourteen months before then, following his stroke, when he went into the coma." Pausing, she took a deep breath as if gathering her thoughts, her strength. "My husband was alive, yet not among the living. I was married but in spirit only. Alone, afraid of the future, and with no one to confide in, I spent a lot of time thinking, looking inward." As she resumed their walk, she glanced around the island. "This key became my refuge. Then when the sea turtles nested, I realized this beach was *their* refuge. They just loaned it to me a while."

Reaching out, Ruth lightly stroked Keya's forearm. "Is that why you're so compelled to make it a sanctuary?"

Keya's eyes misted, and she nodded. "I've cried so many tears here—spent so many hours, worrying about Jules, praying for him, asking for guidance, and searching for direction. When the idea came to me, it wasn't a random thought. It was inspired. Leaving this property to the Turtle Refuge…" She sneered. "Leaving it to *the turtles* became my mission."

Ruth pressed her lips together. "It's what you feel you're meant to do?"

Keya glanced at her. "Yes, it'll be Jules's and my legacy. Since we never had children, we can leave this land for posterity."

"So, not just a refuge for the turtles, it'll also be a

tribute to Jules's memory."

Her head bowed, Keya gave a shy nod. When she looked up, tears were in her eyes. "I'll always love him. That hasn't and won't ever change." She caught Ruth's eye. "But he's been 'gone' much longer than the three months since he passed away—nearly a year and a half."

Putting her arm around her cousin's shoulders, Ruth hugged her as she tried to find a parallel. Jack darted through her mind, but the ache of missing Brett pushed that dim memory aside. "I don't like being apart from Brett a week. I can't imagine the pain of being separated for the rest of your life."

Keya pulled away from the hug. "And I'm keeping you here till next week—"

"No!" Ruth shook her head. "That's not my point! I'm just trying to grasp your loss by scaling things back to a perspective I can understand." She met Keya's gaze. "I'm happy to help. Don't give that another thought because staying isn't an issue." She waved it away. "I'm just beginning to realize the extent of your grief."

Giving her a crooked, inscrutable smile, Keya drew a deep breath. "Then this might make what I'm about to say easier."

Ruth inclined her head. "What do you mean?"

Keya hesitated, seeming to choose her words. "So much has happened this past week. Ever since you arrived, my life's been nonstop chaos. Between finding Maita's body, being stalked by peeping toms and private investigators, interrogated by the police, and indicted by sundry cousins and corporate attorneys, you'd think I'd be depressed, discouraged."

Ruth gave her a sympathetic half smile. "I don't know how you've managed to hold up under the pressure."

"It's just the opposite." Keya gave her a mischievous smile.

"Wait a minute." Blinking, Ruth did a double take. "Did I miss something in the past thirty seconds? Weren't you just bemoaning all the recent events?"

"Not *all* the recent events." Keya's smile widened.

Ruth squinted at her, puzzled. "What are you leaving out?"

"Despite all the incidents, the negatives, one thing trumps the rest." Her eyes dancing, Keya said, "Auggie!"

Ruth's eyelids flew open.

"This can't come as a surprise to you." Keya scoffed.

"I knew you two hit it off." At a loss for what to say, Ruth hunched her shoulders. "Guess I didn't realize how serious you are."

"I know! I just met him, yet I feel like I've known him for years, and he reminds me so much of Jules." Keya stifled a sigh. "Even his name."

Ruth squinted at her. "How does Auggie's name remind you of Jules?"

"Auggie, August, Augustus"—her upturned face radiated her joy—"Jules, July, Julius. Summer months, Roman emperors, their names are connected, just like I feel a connection to each of them, and I feel it's time to get on with life—move *past* this—*move on*."

"You do?" Beyond surprised by her cousin's swift turnaround, Ruth's first impulse was to caution her. *Slow down.* But Keya's glow kept her thoughts from becoming words.

Keya nodded. "If I didn't know better, I'd say Jules had a hand in your introducing me to Auggie."

Ruth scratched her head. "That's bothered me since you two met. If Jules and Auggie had spent summers together—were 'two peas in a pod' as Auggie put it—how come Jules never introduced you?"

"Long story…" She scowled. "Jules said besides him and Auggie spending their summers here when they were boys, their families celebrated their holidays together. Then one Thanksgiving, their mothers had a falling out with Aunt Libby."

Keya gave an uneasy laugh. "I've just heard vague allusions with very few details, but this quarrel seems to have caused a rift between their mothers, too. Shared family holidays became a thing of the past. Even summer vacations with their aunt ended when Jules' mother remarried, and they moved to New York."

Keya shrugged. "For a while, Jules and Auggie wrote to each other, but life happened, and over time, they lost touch. Auggie's name didn't resurface until their Aunt Libby left them the property."

"The inheritance is another thing," said Ruth. "Why did Auggie disclaim it?"

"You heard him. He said he and Diesel were content living as they do. They have everything they need on his houseboat." Keya shrugged. "If he has other motives, I don't know what they are."

"I'm guessing their mothers' quarrel was over something trivial, like most family spats. What a shame." Ruth shook her head. "A family squabble ended what sounds like a solid friendship between Auggie and Jules. Wonder what it was about?"

"We should ask him when we see him Thursday. And speaking of asking questions, weren't we going to ask Maita if she'd written any other messages on Heath's arms?"

"Hope she's in a better frame of mind." Ruth drew a deep breath as she dug in her pocket for the earrings.

Maita appeared. No longer threatening, she seemed attentive, her eyes gleaming as she gazed at Keya.

"Maita, had you writ—"

"I heard her crying on her patio one day," said Maita, "and I followed her here."

When Ruth shared the information, Keya blinked in surprise. "I never knew. I never noticed her or met her."

Maita nodded. "It's true. After overhearing her prayers, I didn't want to intrude. I was too embarrassed, so I hid until she left."

When Ruth relayed her words, Keya asked, "Why did she...*Where is she?*"

"Maita's standing to your left," Ruth said.

Turning, Keya asked the air, "Why did you follow me in the first place?"

"You sounded so upset." Maita grimaced. "I was afraid you'd do some'ing...*foolish.*" She drew closer to Keya. "But you were strong, bot' in spirit and in your beliefs. You inspired me."

After Ruth repeated it, Keya shook her head. "You heard me at my lowest ebb. I can't imagine having been inspirational."

"But you were! *You*, not your words, touched me. *Your example* made me do what's right—no matter what 'e results." Maita lightly rested her hand on her arm.

Keya flinched. "Did she just touch me?"

Nodding, Ruth repeated Maita's words.

Keya squinted. "How did I encourage you to do anything when I was drowning in self-pity?"

"You rose above it. You showed me how to believe in more 'an"—her mouth twisted in a bitter sneer—"*man.* You called on a higher force, and that lifted you, gave you direction." Then Maita's face relaxed into a wistful smile as she gestured toward the beach and the marked turtle nest. "Hearing your words and seeing how important 'is beach is to nesting turtles, I wanted to help."

When Ruth repeated her words, Keya tilted her head and paused. "Help with what?"

"Keeping your property for 'e turtles."

As a thought occurred, Ruth said, "You were Gerald's bookkeeper. Did you know about the lawsuit?"

Slouching, Maita nodded.

"And about his corporation's plans to purchase this land from the relatives if they won the lawsuit?"

"He'…"

"Heath?" Ruth raised her brow.

Nodding, Maita frowned, seeming to mentally withdraw as if looking inward, remembering something.

Ruth spoke up, hoping to rouse the girl. "What did Heath have to do with the inheritance lawsuit?"

"It"—Maita paused, as if distracted—"was his idea."

"Of course," said Ruth, the pieces fitting together. "As the purchasing manager, Heath would have overseen the land acquisition." She glanced at Maita, whose interest seemed to be drifting. "You'd said you wanted to help protect the property. What did you do?"

She shrugged. "I tried to talk him—"

"Who? Gerald?"

Maita shook her head. "He'…I tried to talk him out of hiring a CPRES."

After translating for Keya, Ruth asked Maita, "What's a 'sea press'?"

"A Certified Probate Real Estate Specialist." Blinking, seeming to collect her thoughts, she began to speak with more confidence. "Parts of 'e story had been fading, but now it's coming back. He' hired a CPRES and a legal firm, specializing in probate law." She grimaced. "He wanted 'is *particular* property, no matter what."

"Why?" Ruth asked. "Other than the fact it's adjacent to Gerald's property and has this fabulous beachfront?"

Maita's eyes darkened as she seemed to look through Ruth. Her attention drifted as she focused on the horizon.

Ruth tried again. "Why did Heath want Keya's property?"

Maita lifted her shoulder in a shrug.

"You don't know?" asked Ruth.

"Maybe…" Maita's thoughts seemed to taper off.

Stifling an irritated sigh, Ruth glanced at Keya. "She seems to have withdrawn into her shell." She turned toward the girl and asked once more. "Why is Keya's property so important to Heath?"

Maita grimaced.

"*Maita!*" Ruth tried to get the girl's attention. "Is it something besides the land—besides this beach? Is it something *on* the property?"

Her face contorting into a malicious smirk, Maita trained her dark eyes on her.

Immediately, the weight of the girl's pain pressed down on her, as if pushing her, *holding* her underwater. As Maita's pain engulfed her, the force intensified, like hydrostatic pressure driving her deeper and deeper, squeezing her lungs. Desperate for air, she hyperventilated.

"Ruth," cried Keya, shaking her shoulders, *"what's wrong?"*

Keya's voice broke Maita's emotional grip, ending the trance. Ruth dropped the earrings, and Maita vanished. As the oppressive atmosphere lifted, Ruth gasped, filling her lungs with air.

"What just happened?" asked Keya.

"Something I said must've set her off." Still gulping air, Ruth leaned over to retrieve the earrings, lifting them with a tissue to avoid touching them. "Maybe I triggered a memory."

"All you asked was whether it's something on the property." Keya scowled. "What could be so important? The house?"

"I don't know. I hoped she'd tell us." Breathing deeply but no longer fighting for each breath, Ruth tossed the earrings in her pocket, wanting no connection with them or the girl.

****

As Ruth undressed for bed, the earrings fell out of her pocket. She hesitated, debating whether to touch them again or reach out to Maita after the previous encounter. With a sigh, she retrieved them, intending to set them on the dresser and be done.

"I'm sorry." Maita appeared, wringing her hands and moaning. "I don't know why my anger does 'at."

Ruth grimaced, silent and still ticked. "Don't you know the effect you have on me?"

The girl shook her head. "I've never affected anyone in my life." She began sobbing, her chest rising and falling. "Only you can see me now, but even before I died, no one ever noticed me…except He'…"

Though wary of the girl's temper, Ruth was intrigued. "How did you and Heath meet?"

Maita's focus changed. Her sobbing stopped, and her eyes took on a faraway look. "I was working in 'e office next door, when he walked in, his hair glistening, still damp from diving." Her eyes lighting up, she smiled at Ruth. "He loves to dive, especially for artifacts."

"Artifacts," mused Ruth. "Has he ever found any?"

The glow left Maita's eyes, and her smile vanished as she withdrew into her shell. "Maybe."

Ruth quickly rephrased the question before Maita retreated. "Has he ever found anything of value?"

"Historical value." She inspected Ruth. "Fragments of ships' timber, an occasional scrap of iron, some ballast—all close to shore."

"What's ballast?"

"Heavy stones 'ey used to stabilize old ships." Her smile returned. "In fact, 'at's how he found the site. He followed 'e ballast from 'e *shore* out into deeper water, freediving—"

"Freediving?" Ruth asked as she pulled back her head.

"Diving wi'out a tank. When 'e water became too deep for 'at, he rented a boat and dove off 'e side. 'at's 'e reason for our first date." Maita's eyes shimmered and shone. "When he learned I sailed, he suggested we team up. I'd pilot 'e boat, while he'd dive." Her cheeks rose in a shy smile.

"Did you have many of these sail-dive dates with him?"

Wearing a gentle smile as if reliving a fond memory, Maita nodded. "We'd meet every weekend. Sometimes, I'd pack a picnic lunch. Sometimes, he'd take us to dinner."

Recalling Heath's earlier response, Ruth asked, "So you met for more than just coffee…" She studied the girl as she left the question hanging.

Surveying her through distrusting, suspicious eyes, Maita withdrew into her shell.

"Why wouldn't Heath mention all the times you two had gone on these expeditions?"

Fidgeting, Maita mumbled.

"You said he'd given you these earrings for your birthday." Ruth tried the question from another angle. "Did he ever give you anything he found on his dives?"

Maita shook her head. "It's illegal to keep sunken treasure."

"It is?" Ruth assessed her. "Why?"

"You need salvage permits."

"So it's not a case of finders-keepers, huh?" Ruth gave her an ironic smile.

"Not since 1982"—she glanced at Ruth—"but 'ere is one exception."

"What's that?"

"'ough you can't keep sunken treasure, you can keep buried treasure—*if* you find it on your own land."

Your own land. Ruth blinked. "Did Heath ever

mention where he'd picked up the trail of the ballast rocks?"

Maita frowned as if concentrating. "Not exactly, 'ough I know where we anchored."

"Where?" Ruth leaned forward, studying her. "Anywhere nearby?"

Nodding, she pointed out the window toward the key's shallows. "About a hundred feet due east of 'ere."

"Off Keya's island…" A vicarious thrill set Ruth's imagination tingling. *If he stumbled on buried treasure, the land grab's making sense.* "Is this the real reason Heath wants Keya's property?"

Maita's eyes became almost as big around as the coin earrings. Then she stared out the window as if thinking or remembering. "He told me 'is land is for 'e hotel complex." Turning toward Ruth, she added, "He' doesn't have enough money to buy 'is land."

"No, but Gerald does." Ruth grimaced. "Has this been their plan all along?"

Maita shook her head. "I don't remember him talking to Gerald about 'e treasure. He'…only discussed it wit' me…" Tears shone in her eyes. "It was our secret, what bound us toge'er."

Is that all she knows, or is she still covering for him? Ruth chewed her lip. "Did Heath tell you he planned to dig for treasure on this property?"

"No!" Maita's spine stiffened. "He only talked sunken treasure wit' me, not buried treasure. He dove to connect wit' history, not steal it."

Ruth studied the girl, convinced Maita believed him. *But what about Heath's and Gerald's motives…?*

****

The next morning over breakfast, Ruth told Keya

about the exchange with Maita. "Something bothered me last night."

"What's that?" Keya studied her as she sipped her coffee.

"Have you ever heard of any buried treasure here?"

Keya shook her head. "Nothing other than what Auggie told us he found, but Florida's Keys are littered with sunken ships and scattered treasure. Who's to say some hasn't washed ashore…" She broke off, grimacing.

"Like Maita's body," Ruth finished for her. "That thought crossed my mind, too. The currents, tropical storms, and hurricanes all could've carried treasure ashore."

"Then sand could have buried the coins over the centuries." Keya set down her cup as Earnestine jumped on her lap.

"Do you know anything about Florida's laws for finding treasure?"

"No." Keya's eyes lit up. "But I know someone who probably knows them inside out."

Ruth snickered. "Let me guess. Auggie?"

Her finger already pressing the speed-dial number, Keya asked, "Why don't I give him a call?"

****

Auggie and Diesel arrived in time for dinner on the patio. Over grilled chicken breasts glazed with honey and fresh tarragon and zucchini, bell pepper, and red onion shish kebabs, he said, "The Antiquities Act of 1906 is the grandfather of all land laws, but since then, Florida's enacted its own laws about public lands."

"We're not talking about public land." Ruth shook her head. "What about digging for treasure on private land—your own land?"

"My, my, what a leading question." Auggie gave Keya a sly smile. "As long as you own the land and the DHR—"

"DHR?" She gave him a puzzled look.

"The Division of Historical Resources. If it hasn't designated the property an archeological site, nothing can prevent you from digging for treasure."

"So, *in theory*, if we found treasure here, we could keep it, right?" asked Ruth. "I mean, legally."

Swallowing a smile, Auggie nodded. "Minus taxes and the twenty percent the U.S. District Court in South Florida would take into custody."

"You said the DHR could designate private land as an archeological site?" Keya studied him. "How?"

"All they need is the landowners' written permission. Once that's given, even the owners themselves would need a permit to dig on their own land."

"*Any* land—even a beach?"

He nodded. "Sure."

"So—*as a last resort*—could designating this property an archeological site protect it from being excavated for a hotel?"

He shrugged. "Probably."

Keya mumbled, "That might be a backup plan to consider…"

"Consider for what?" He scrutinized her. "Why are you asking all these questions?"

Ruth told him about Maita's conversation.

"In case the hearing goes south Friday, and I lose the property," said Keya, "maybe the DHR could label this beach an archeological site."

Auggie nodded slowly. "It'd be a way to protect the nesting area from development since it would mean no one—"

"Not even a future owner?" Keya's gaze bored into his.

"*No one* could dig for treasure on this property, but filing the paperwork takes time…maybe more time than you have…*and* if you win the lawsuit, it'd mean you couldn't dig on your own property."

Keya chewed her lip, seeming to digest that information. Then her face brightened as if she had an idea. "Has anyone ever found treasure here?"

He shook his head. "Nothing other than what Jules and I found—a few rusty nails, bottle caps, and quarters." Then he paused. "Although…"

"What?" Her head tilted to the side, Keya watched him.

Squinting, he worked his jaw as if thinking. "I remember hearing rumors…" He met her gaze. "No evidence or death-bed confessions, but family gossip said Aunt Libby built this house with money from antique coins she found."

"Really?" Ruth watched him.

He nodded as his gaze swept the building. "Until the mid-eighties, this had been a little two-bedroom bungalow."

"Out of curiosity," said Ruth, "about what time of year did your aunt build it?"

He took a deep breath, as if inhaling the past. "It was near the holidays, I believe, finished just in time for Thanksgiving."

"Thanksgiving!" Ruth almost jumped out of her patio chair.

"Why? What's the connection?"

"Wasn't that about the time your mother and Jules's quarreled?"

He slowly nodded. "Now that you mention it, it was that same year, but it wasn't just our mothers. Neither ever spoke to Aunt Libby again. All three sisters had a falling out."

"Did they ever say why?" asked Keya.

"Nope." He shook his head. "I overheard whispers, but the topic was strictly taboo."

Ruth studied him. "You don't suppose that's the reason your Aunt Libby left you and Jules the property, do you?"

Auggie shot her a puzzled look. "I don't follow."

"What if she'd found buried treasure, used it to build this house, and then—after it caused a rift with her sisters—felt guilty? Maybe leaving you and Jules the property was her way of righting things with the family."

"Anything's possible." He shrugged. "Like I said, all I heard were rumors."

"But Jules said you and he were the only ones to keep in touch with your aunt."

Auggie grimaced. "And I didn't do a very good job of that. After the rift, the families never kept in contact. Though I lived just fifty miles from her, it might have been five thousand. It wasn't until a few years before her death that a friend mentioned she'd been placed in a care facility. I started visiting her weekends, bringing her flowers or fresh fruit, but by the time I reconnected with her, age had taken its toll."

"Did she remember anything from the past?"

"Just events from the time before she built this

house. Her Alzheimer's progressed rapidly." He looked at the structure. "She talked about her little bungalow as if it still stood here." A warm smile lit his face. "She seemed happiest remembering the summer days when Jules and I stayed with her."

"That's something else that's nagged at me," said Ruth. "Brett's mother, Barbara, is your sister, yet your aunt never mentioned her in her will."

Auggie nodded. "I'd wondered about that, too. While Aunt Libby was in the nursing home, I talked to her about my sister, but she had no recollection of her. Then I realized Barbara had already married and moved to Wisconsin before the rift. After the quarrel, they had no contact. Compounded by Aunt Libby's failing memory, it was as if they'd never met."

"How sad." Keya grimaced. "The only thing wealth caused was division...both when your Aunt Libby built this house and again when she left it to you and Jules." Then brightening, she glanced at Ruth. "But one good thing about the lawsuit—Ruth's staying into next week."

"Great!" Auggie smiled at her. "I'm glad you're staying longer, but why this change of plans?"

"I'll be Keya's character witness at the probate hearing."

His smile fading, he turned toward Keya. "Why do you need a character witness?"

Her eyes gave off a cold glint like ice at twilight. "To prove I'm a character."

"I'm serious." Despite the wry half smile tugging at his lips, a V formed between his eyes. "Why?"

"To stop the Erskine family from assassinating my character."

"*What!*"

"On their behalf, Gerald's corporation has gathered evidence to have me declared mentally incompetent." Keya's chest heaved. "They're trying to prove I'm nuts."

"Makes me ashamed to be an Erskine." Reaching over to squeeze her hand, he stared into her eyes. "Maybe we can't direct the wind, but we can adjust our sails. Want any moral support at the hearing?"

"Yes…" As if surprised by his offer, Keya's eyelids fluttered. "I'd appreciate it."

"I'll be there. Count on it." Giving her hand another reassuring squeeze, he sat back. "When is it?"

"Friday. Is it the twentieth? Let me check." She scrolled to her phone's calendar app. "No, *the twenty-first* at the Key West courthouse."

Glancing at the whimsical turtle motif on her cellphone's case, he gave a dry laugh. "You do like turtles, don't you?"

Keya nodded. "Always have."

Rousing her head from a nap on Keya's lap, Earnestine objected with a meow.

"And cats," Keya added with a wink.

Auggie traced along the turtle's design with his finger. "Long before phone apps or online calendars, did you know Indians used turtle shells to track time?"

Keya shook her head. "No."

"Basing their calculations on the lunar calendar, they—as well as the Incas, Egyptians, Druids, Polynesians, Chinese, and others—all tracked time on turtle shells."

Keya studied him. "How?"

"The moon orbits the earth about every 28 days, so

365 days divided by 28 equals 13 moons and an extra day." He gave them a playful grin. "Remember, they based time on the lunar calendar, not an atomic clock."

Ruth rolled her eyes. "Okay, but how do turtle shells fit into this?"

"This is a stylized drawing"—he pointed to the phone's motif—"but a turtle's shell has 13 large, inner scutes surrounded by 28 smaller, outer scutes. This pattern gave the ancients a way to keep time. Thirteen 'months' surrounded by 28 'days.' "

"I'd never heard that before," said Keya, "and I thought I knew turtles." As she pulled up an image of a turtle's shell on her phone, they counted the scutes.

Ruth's sniff passed for a laugh. "Look at that, 13 and 28! Who'd a'thunk?"

Then Auggie glanced at the sun slipping into the horizon. He set Diesel on the patio, stood, and stretched. "We've still got a few minutes before sunset." A mischievous gleam in his eyes, he smiled like an alligator. "My metal detector is in the car. What with all your questions earlier about digging for buried treasure on private land, I might be reading between the lines, but is anyone up for a treasure hunt?"

****

Ten minutes later, they were walking along an isolated stretch of the island's beach when Auggie glanced at the marked-off area. "Is that what I think it is?"

"Yup, a loggerhead turtle nest." Keya nodded. "The eggs should hatch in the next week or so."

"How do you know?" He glanced at her.

"The day I found the fresh nest, I taped off the area and jotted down the date—May first, about ten weeks ago." Smiling, she pointed to the sign.

Sweeping his metal detector above the sandy beach, he said, "I'm glad you cordoned off the area."

"Why?" Keya glanced at him.

"Listen to this." Auggie removed his headphones and turned on the detector's external speakers. A series of high-pitched beeps assaulted their ears. "If you hadn't marked off this area and I hadn't known about the nest, I would've used my beach scoop and bucket to shovel through the sand—"

"And disturbed—possibly destroyed the eggs." Pressing her lips together, she shook her head. "They're so fragile, so vulnerable."

"Let me know when they hatch." He studied the surrounding terrain. "These readings are interesting. When the nest is empty, I'd like to come back and explore this area."

"Sure," said Keya. "I'll leave the barricade tape, so you can find it again."

"That's all right. I'll use the knoll as my landmark." He pointed to the rocky hill nearby as he resumed his sweep of the beach.

"What do those different sounds mean?" asked Keya.

"Different metals make different noises," he said. "Ferrous metals make dull beeps, while gold and silver make shrill beeps."

"Last time, we'd searched just a few minutes before you found the earrings," said Ruth. "Yet you said as a kid you'd swept the area often and found very little. How come you're getting all these readings now?"

"Compared to the metal detector Jules and I used

decades ago, this is lightyears ahead." He lifted the wand. "Today's detectors are lighter-weight, deeper-seeking, and far more discriminating between mineralized sand and metal." He shook his head. "No wonder Jules and I found only junk."

"So, technology's made metal detecting a science," Ruth asked, "not a child's game?"

"It's a hobby for me." He gave a dry laugh. "But I've met people who do this for a living."

Keya's gaze probed. "What *do* you do for a living? You don't seem tied to any routine."

"Between my naval pension and investments"—he shrugged—"I'm semi-retired." He gave her a warm smile. "I take occasional consulting jobs, but let's say I have a lot of hobbies to keep me busy."

"Do you travel a lot?" Holding her head back, she studied him. "Is that why you live on a houseboat?"

"That's part of it, but like I said the day we met, the sea's where my heart is." He gave her an enigmatic smile. "At least, where it's been…"

Keya did a double take. "Where's your—"

The metal detector's alarm sounded, its raucous beeping intensifying as he drew the wand across one particular spot.

"Something's buried here." Auggie pulled out his beach scoop and bucket, shoveling through the sand. As the grains sifted away, three coins remained. "Would you look at this…?"

"What kind of coins are they?" Ruth asked.

Turning them over in his hand, he wiped away the last of the grit. "I need to check when I get home, but these sure look like Spanish copper coins to me."

"How old are they?" asked Keya. "Can you see a

date?"

After buffing the coins against his jeans, he studied them. "Sixteen forty-one. If you don't mind my borrowing one to research their history tonight, here's your first buried treasure, ladies." Auggie handed them each a coin.

"It was minted too late to be part of the *Regala's* 1622 stash," said Ruth as she fingered the copper coin, "which explains why Bart's not materializing."

"They're definitely colonial-era." Auggie ran his finger over the imprint. "Their detail's respectable, and they're in good circulated condition."

"Especially considering they've been underground or underwater for several hundred years." Nodding, Ruth scanned the area, as if expecting to see a brimming treasure chest full of gold doubloons and silver *reales*. "Could more coins be here?"

"Maybe." He shrugged. "These could've been scattered and swept in by a storm, or they could be the clue to a buried cache nearby. You never know. The unlimited possibilities—the suspense—the *thrill* of discovering something is what keeps treasure hunters going. Dan Miller searched for almost sixteen years before finding the payload. He always said, 'Just do it. Carp a D. M.' "

"Seize the day," Keya muttered, "but in this case, isn't *tomorrow* 'the day'?" She fluttered her lashes.

"Huh?" Auggie gave her a puzzled stare.

She searched his eyes as if looking for more than the hour of their appointment. "What time should we meet you tomorrow for Dan Miller Days?"

Chapter 7

Dan Miller Days

They met Auggie and Diesel in front of the Treasure Trove gift shop.

He held up three tickets and greeted them with warm hugs. "We're all set for the conservation lab's three o'clock tour." Then he glanced at his watch. "Which still leaves us a few minutes. Want to see the street fair while we wait?"

The streets were lined with pop-up tents, kids' games, a dunk tank, and vendors selling food, drinks, and crafts. Bands played live music onstage while buskers worked the crowd.

A sign read, *Close to Perfect—Far From Normal*.

Ruth swallowed a smile. "Sure."

Acting as their guide, Auggie said, "Dan Miller Days started back in 1998."

"Why do they hold it?" asked Keya as she perused the vendors' displays.

"Couple reasons. It celebrates finding the payload. It gives back to the community, and most of all, it's a tribute to a Key West hero. Dan was a dreamer, a legend, *and* arguably the world's best-known treasure hunter. Finding the payload ended not only *his* quest, but a 400-year international search for the *Regala*."

"Wouldn't finding it have been exciting?"

Squirming, Ruth gave a self-conscious smile. "Yesterday, when you uncovered those copper coins, I think the treasure bug bit me." She sighed. "Too bad those days are over."

"They're *far* from over." Auggie shook his head.

"What do you mean?"

"They've located just a fraction of the *Regala's* treasure. Millions—billions more—are still waiting to be discovered."

"Are you serious?" Anticipating a joke, Ruth watched his expression for a telltale smile.

"Yup." His nod reaffirmed his conviction. "They're recovering coins, silver bars, pearls, and emeralds every day." He paused, glancing from her to Keya. "Even the public can join the search."

"Really?" Hope merged with skepticism in Ruth's dry chuckle. "How?"

"Certified divers can join a *Regala* Adventure trip and dive the site."

"But if you don't dive…?" Keya's lips curled in a sarcastic smile.

His eyes glimmered. "Then you can sift for emeralds at the Leprechaun site."

"Leprechaun?" Keya scoffed. "Where's that, at the end of the rainbow?"

"Something like that…" His eyes crinkling at the corners, he snickered as if getting an idea.

"What are you plotting?" Her lips pouting, Keya appraised him.

"How 'bout I keep it a surprise till tomorrow?" He caught her eye. "All I'm saying is wear your swimsuits under your clothes."

"This isn't Thanksgiving," taunted a dunk tank

clown's booming voice. "So why am I staring at a turkey?" Heckling the crowd while perched precariously above a dunk tank, the man drew their attention as he mocked the onlookers. "You couldn't hit the broad side of a cruise ship." When he caught Auggie watching, he called, "And *you* couldn't hit the water if you fell off a boat."

Auggie laughed. "Is that so?" Turning toward Ruth, he asked, "Can you hold Diesel a minute?"

"Sure."

Exchanging a twenty for three balls, Auggie took aim and threw high.

"A one-eyed pirate has a better aim than you," the man called, goading Auggie.

He took aim again and threw a smidge low.

"That's okay," the man jeered. "If I get bored, I can always start fishing."

Auggie swallowed a smile as he took aim, concentrating.

Just as he was about to pitch, the man shouted, "Keep missing, and I'll have to jump in to cool off."

Interrupted mid-pitch, Auggie laughed good-naturedly, again took careful aim, and pitched his last ball. As it connected with the dunk tank's arm, the man's platform gave way, and he plunged into the water, drenching the onlookers.

The crowd cheered as the clown emerged, unscathed though sputtering and dripping.

But instead of joining in the party atmosphere, Ruth visualized Maita and Bart floundering beneath the waves, and she shuddered as the imagery flooded her mind.

Amid the crowd's applause and laughter, Auggie

tipped an imaginary hat toward the clown and the onlookers. Then he reached for Diesel.

Still shaken, Ruth handed him the dog, trailing behind them as they explored the street fair.

A man on stilts walked past them, juggling rolls of toilet tissue. Another man performed acrobatics while walking on his hands. A puppeteer did double-duty as a one-man band.

Gradually the images of Maita and Bart receded while Ruth gawked at the entertainers and inhaled the air, rife with the tantalizing aromas of mahi-mahi burritos, conch fritters, and key lime pie on-a-stick.

Just before three, they joined the VIP tour at the museum, where people dressed in pirates' costumes took their tickets.

"Welcome to the Miller family's private conservation laboratory," said their guide. "This is where the magic happens. When the divers uncover 400-year-old coins, they don't look like this." He held up a shiny piece of eight. In his other hand, he held up a blackened, oxidized disk. "This is what silver coins look like when they arrive, and this lab is where we transform them from tarnished to treasured.

"When the salvage ships bring in their finds, we catalogue every item. Then, just like in a hospital emergency room, we do a triage."

Ruth shuddered as the words conjured more unwelcome imagery.

"We decide which artifacts need immediate attention and which can be stored in water for later treatment. Every material requires a specific treatment to become stable."

"Stable," called a member of the group. "What do

you mean?"

"Protected from further deterioration. Treatments are as simple as soaking the artifacts in fresh water to desalinate them, to using electrolytic reduction to remove the chloride. Then, we photograph, measure, and weigh them for the online database.

"Our collection contains over a hundred thousand artifacts, some inorganic, like coins and jewels, and others organic, like wood and leather." The guide showed them the tanks of water and chemical solutions containing the various materials.

At the tour's conclusion, he asked, "How many of you have taken the Treasure Hunting Boat Tour today?"

Half the group raised their hands.

"If you haven't been yet, go. The crew's giving tours of the *Intrepid*, Dan Miller's salvage vessel. You can see the equipment they use and how they map wreck sites. Then they'll show you the wheelhouse, so you'll get a feel for what it's like to work aboard an actual treasure hunting ship. The best part? The crew giving the tours are the same divers that find the sunken treasure, and they have amazing stories to share. Don't miss the chance to meet them."

"Want to go?" Auggie asked.

Keya nodded. "Definitely."

"The ship's docked at the Historic Seaport, not far from here, but first"—Auggie gave them a mysterious smile—"I want you to see something."

Her eyes wary, Keya studied him. "What're you up to?"

"You'll see." He led them into the gift shop and caught the saleswoman's gaze.

Nodding, she brought out a blue velvet gift box

from beneath the counter and handed it to Auggie. "All ready for you."

"Thanks." Then he turned toward Keya. "In honor of your birthday—"

She gave a small, surprised cry. "No one mentioned it today. I'd thought you'd forgotten."

Auggie shook his head as he presented the box. "I hope you like it, but if you don't"—he shrugged— "that's why we're here. Just choose something you do like."

As Keya handed Earnestine to Ruth, Keya's bare hands came into view.

When did she stop wearing her wedding ring? Ruth blinked.

Her fingers tentative, Keya shyly accepted the velvet box. "Without even opening it, I'm already impressed you remembered."

His cheeks turned pink. "Better reserve judgment till after you see it."

Smiling like a little girl at her birthday party, Keya opened its lid. Inside was a *Regala* silver coin made into a sea-turtle pendant. With a gasp, she reached up and hugged him. "It's perfect! A piece of history *and* mounted as a sea turtle. I love it! Thank you *so much*." Her smile built until it lit her face.

"Glad you like it." He took a deep breath as if relieved.

"It's an authentic, grade one, four *reales* coin," said the saleswoman. "It's mounted in fourteen karat gold, minted in Potosi during the reign of Philip III, *and,*" she added in a stage whisper, "he spent over an hour picking it out for you."

Auggie gave an embarrassed laugh. "Do you have

163

to share all my secrets?"

"I love it." Keya pressed the pendant against her chest as she caught his gaze.

Lingering a beat too long, he said, "Now pick out a chain, and you're all set."

"Oh, no." Keya shook her head. "You've already been too generous."

"I insist. This is meant to be worn, not hidden in a box." He turned to the saleswoman. "What do you have in gold chains?"

Ten minutes later, chin high and shoulders back, Keya beamed as they left the shop. "Where to next?"

"On to the Historic Seaport to tour the *Intrepid*."

Still holding Earnestine, Ruth turned toward them. "Guys, this is where I bow out."

"What?" Keya turned toward her. "Don't you feel well?"

"I feel just fine, but since I didn't have time to shop for a gift, I'm giving you babysitting coupons.' " As Keya pursed her lips, her usual prelude to an argument, Ruth swallowed a smile. "Hear me out. I'll babysit Earnestine and Diesel, while you two celebrate your birthday…in private."

Keya glanced at Auggie then turned back to Ruth with a hug. "It's a thoughtful gift, but what would you do tonight?"

"I have a date with Bart."

"What!"

Ruth laughed. "I brought my laptop and Maita's earrings. I figure, if Bart makes an appearance, this will give me time to capture his stories."

"Be kind to him," said Auggie, his expression wounded and reserved.

Ruth held back her head to better observe him. "Why do you say that?"

"I've been thinking about it, and I can relate to his situation. I know what it's like to feel displaced. When the *USS Cole* was attacked, we all thought we were going down." Looking at his feet, Auggie muttered, "Almost did."

Then he stared at Ruth, his eyes cold and haunted. "I duct-taped an American flag to my friend's body bag, but *I survived*. I know what it's like to question why you're here, and they're not. I know what it's like to wonder what the hell happened. Bart's been dealing with PTSD for four hundred years. Be gentle with him. Kindness makes a difference—helps you move on."

Nodding, Ruth considered his words. *Move on…*

****

Lingering at the door, Keya did an about face. "*Are you sure* you don't want to join us? Because—"

"Positive!" Ruth gave her a playful push, whooshing her out the hotel room. "Now scoot, you two! Have fun!" She closed the door behind them, her voice muffled as she called, "Happy birthday!"

Keya deadpanned. "Seems she's made up her mind."

"She wants you to enjoy your day." Auggie took her hand in his. "And I intend to see you do!"

Keya linked fingers with him, happy at the turn life was taking. "What's first?"

"How 'bout we tour the boat and then head out to dinner?"

"Perfect."

After a short stroll along the Historic Seaport's harbor walk, they spotted the *Intrepid*.

"This is the Millers' 90-foot treasure-hunting boat," said Auggie. "It's over sixty years old and still in use."

She glanced at the dented hull with its thick buildup of paint. "Looks like it's seen its fair share of service."

"It has." He nodded as they boarded. "Let me show you the wheelhouse, so you'll get a feel for what it's like to work aboard."

"Auggie?" A man with a craggy, gray-bristled face approached them.

"Bruce, you old son of a gun." Auggie clapped him on the back as they shook hands. Then turning to Keya, he said, "I'd like to introduce you to Bruce Daily, one of the golden crew. He was onboard with Dan and my father back in eighty-five, when they found the payload. Bruce, this is Keya Erskine"—he hesitated—"my friend."

Bruce's eyes sparkled. "Pleased to meet you Keya—Auggie's *friend*. What are you doing hanging out with this old seadog?"

She laughed, tickled by his gruff sense of humor. "Celebrating my birthday."

"Your twenty-first, no doubt."

"*Right…*" Snickering, she rolled her eyes.

"Well, you're in good hands. I've known this deckhand since he was, what?" Bruce turned toward him. "Ten?"

"Seven." A pink flush crept up Auggie's neck into his cheeks.

"He's a good man." Then responding to a handwave from across the wheelhouse, Bruce called, "Sam! Wait up!" Slapping Auggie on the back, he said,

"I want to catch him before he runs off, but next time you're in Orlando, look me up. We'll have a beer or three." Turning to Keya, he gave her a quick bearhug. Then as he strode away, he called over his shoulder, "She's a keeper, Auggie. Don't let this one get away."

Groaning, Auggie shook his head. "Bruce is a character. Hope he didn't embarrass you."

"Me?" She blinked. "You're the one who's blushing, though I don't know why. He seems to think highly of you."

"He's known me longer than just about anyone— was like a second father to me." Auggie smiled as if recalling a fond memory. "Bruce is a good guy."

*He's not the only one…*Keya eyed Auggie from his nose to his toes and back again.

After they toured the ship, Auggie tugged her hand. "It's still a little early for dinner. How 'bout a drink here on the wharf first?"

"Sure."

They found an open-air bar with a small balcony, overlooking the seaport.

Without glancing at the menu, he said, "This place has the freshest oysters in town. Want to get a dozen on the half shell?"

Her interest piqued, she upped the ante. "How about pairing them with Prosecco?"

"Prosecco?" He wrinkled his nose.

"Yup, the wine's crispness cuts through the oysters' creaminess, and the bubbles offset their texture." At ease with him and in her element, she leaned across the table, smiling and baiting him. "Are you game?"

"*Okay…*I'll try anything once." Returning her

smile, he called over their waitress.

While they waited for their order, Keya stole sidelong glances at him as they watched the big ships, schooners, sunset cruisers, fishing charters, and glass-bottom boats sail past.

A couple leaving the restaurant waved goodbye to Auggie. Another group stopped by to exchange a few words on the way to their table.

After the waitress poured their wine, Keya surveyed him. "Do you know *everyone* in Key West?"

He shook his head. "It's just a small town at heart. Without the tourists, everybody knows everybody."

"I'll drink to that." She lifted her glass to his as the waitress brought out the fresh-shucked oysters. Arranged on a platter of cracked ice with quartered lemons and Mignonette Sauce, the oysters shimmered in their own liquor.

He slid the platter closer. "Ladies first."

"I always like the first one naked." Keya gave him a mischievous grin. "No lemon, no sauce, so I can taste the full flavor." With a practiced hand, she tipped an oyster shell to her lips; sucked out its contents; chewed the meat, savoring its flavor; swallowed; and washed it down with Prosecco. Then leaning toward him, she dared him. "Your turn. Happy slurping!"

A glimmer in his eyes, he met her challenge.

Laughing, they toasted with more Prosecco, polished off the oysters, and watched the sun dip toward the coppery sea.

At dusk, they walked to a cozy restaurant with a wrap-around porch. Twinkling lights and yellow trumpet vines dangled from the eaves, wrapping them in a gossamer canopy.

The owner welcomed Auggie with a hug and an inquiry about Diesel before leading them to an intimate table lit with a flickering votive candle.

"Are you *sure* you don't know everyone in Key West?" Keya whispered, tongue-in-cheek.

Auggie shook his head. "Hardly."

"It seems everyone knows *you*." Protected within his circle of friends, any lingering inhibitions diffusing, she dropped her guard. *His social network will catch me if I fall.*

He shrugged as if unsure how to respond. "Would you like to start with the trio appetizer?" He picked up a menu and gave it his full attention. "Grilled pink shrimp with lime chutney, tuna watermelon ceviche, and Florida lobster macaroni and cheese."

"Sure, sample it all, try a little of everything…just the way I like it…" She left her words hanging, willing him to look up.

Apparently oblivious to any unspoken invitation, he kept his eyes glued to the menu.

She studied him, debating whether to pursue her train of thought. *We've just met…yet…*Reaching across the table, she gently lowered the menu to look into his eyes. "You know, food's a lot like life—full of choices. I'd like to taste all I can…while I can."

His expression turning serious, he closed the menu and set it aside. "Sounds like you're talking about more than hors d'oeuvres."

She fixed her gaze on him. "When Jules passed away, I was devastated, but *he* was the one who died. *Not me*. I survived."

"Survivor's remorse." He nodded. "I'm familiar with that myself."

Gazing inward, she stared at the candle without seeing. "Though I'll never stop loving him, I don't want to wear sackcloth and ashes for the rest of my life." Then she glanced at her fuchsia ensemble, her sniff passing for a laugh. "Not that I do now, but *my point is*, I'm alive, and I want to start living life again, not…" Her words fading, she looked into his eyes, wanting to say more, but uncertain if she had already said too much, too soon.

"Of course, you want to enjoy life, Keya." He reached for her hand. "You're a vibrant woman."

"But I've been floating in a limbo of memories these past seventeen months." Her eyes sought his. "I want to move past this inertia, *move on*, get on with life."

His eyes meeting hers, he squeezed her hand. "I understand gridlock. You call your limbo *memories*. I call mine *fear*."

She searched his face. "Of what?"

He took a deep breath, as if to bolster himself. "Of making the same mistakes twice."

She squinted, trying to guess. "What kind of mistakes?"

"Not trusting, being detached…bungling another relationship." His shoulders drooped as he pressed his lips together.

It was her turn to squeeze his hand. "Your 'mistakes' sound like PTSD symptoms to me."

"I can't blame it for everything. My marriage didn't work because"—he let go of her hand to count off on his fingers—"according to my ex-wife's attorney, I was always too busy with my career to pay attention. I didn't listen. I didn't let myself get close. I always kept her at arm's length." His chest heaved in a silent sigh. "We were disconnected, like two ships adrift."

"We all have regrets." She grimaced. "What's important is we learn from our mistakes."

"What can I get you folks?" Their waiter stood, pen and pad in hand.

Auggie caught Keya's eye before answering. "Does the trio appetizer work for you?"

"Isn't this where we came in?" Nodding, she gave him a warm smile. "And maybe another bottle of Prosecco? I'm in a talkative mood tonight."

"You heard the boss." He gave their waiter a pensive, lopsided smile.

As the man left, Keya again reached for Auggie's hand. "Owning up to mistakes is the first step to moving on."

"If it were only that simple." He sucked in his breath. "My gridlock boils down to fear of repeating history, botching another relationship—"

"So one relationship didn't work out. Maybe it wasn't a good fit to begin with."

He pressed his lips together. "My ex-wife left me, which *left me* dealing with trust issues."

"Don't mistrust everyone in the future based on the past. Just because one person let you down doesn't mean you shouldn't trust others."

"Once burned, twice shy…" His smile pinched, he seemed to look inward. "Or is it once bitten, twice shy?" Turning toward her, he tugged her hand. "But we *had* been talking about *you*, Birthday Girl. How did we get started talking about me?" Then his brow puckering, he sat up straight. "That's weird."

"What is?"

"I *never* talk about myself…open up." He caught her gaze. "You're the—"

"Would you like to test the wine, sir?" After showing Auggie the bottle's label, the waiter uncorked the bottle and poured a sample.

Auggie let go her hand to carry out the ritual, his lips pinched as if annoyed at the interruption.

Stifling an impatient sigh, Keya waited for the server to finally finish and leave. Then she lifted her glass in a toast. "May you have the hindsight to know where you've been, the foresight to know where you're going"—she gave a self-effacing laugh—"and the insight to know whether you've gone too far."

"I'll drink to that." Leaning toward her, he gazed into her eyes as he clinked his glass against hers.

The piped music selection changed, its sound barely wafting to them on the outer fringes of the restaurant's porch. Despite the muffled lyrics, the driving beat of the music entered her psyche, marshalling her awareness. Her head angling as her ears followed the sound, she gradually came to attention. Listening to Jules's and her love song, the music permeated her senses, and she set down her glass.

As *their* song played in the background, she studied Auggie. More than a family resemblance, he had Jules's mannerisms—his slow smile, his dimples, and the way he inclined his head.

After a minute, Auggie asked, "Is anything wr—?"

"*No!*" she snapped, resurfacing from her thoughts. "Why do you ask?"

"You seemed to react to something…" He hunched his shoulders. Then swallowing hard, he asked, "Is it anything I've said? Done?" He let out a defeated sigh. "The fact that I was married or have PTSD?"

Comparing the man before her to her husband, she caught her breath. *What am I doing? Trying to replace Jules with a look-alike?*

His raised his brow. "Okay, now you're staring at me. What's going on? What's changed in the last sixty seconds?"

She pressed her fingers into the bridge of her nose, staving off a sudden headache. "Remember how I said you reminded me of someone, and then I realized it was Jules?"

Wearing a stiff smile, he bobbed his head.

"Maybe it's no coincidence I'm attracted to you."

He blinked. "You're—"

"The attraction *has* to be obvious. I might as well admit it." She ran her hand through her hair, sweeping it behind an ear. "But maybe I'm not attracted to *you* so much as who you remind me of, look like…"

In the background, the song ended as the playlist changed.

He crossed his arms and sat back. "So now you think you're dating Jules's double?"

"Hearing you phrase it that way"—she scrunched her nose—"the idea sounds ridiculous, but everything's happened so fast. I can't help but wonder…" She shrugged off a sudden chill.

"As first cousins, Jules and I shared similar features…probably even some personality traits." His smile was nostalgic. "Aunt Libby called us the Bobbsey twins. Since we spent so much time together, it's understandable you'd see similarities in our expressions or mannerisms." He reached for her hand, gently tugging at her fingertips. "But I'm not Jules."

She looked deep into his amber-brown eyes.

Wearing an empathetic smile, he stared back—his eyes honest, open, and receptive.

The windows to the soul. Their color was almost the same as Jules's, but the person behind the eyes was not her husband. *Emphatically not.* She blinked.

"You say it's all happened fast. Considering we've spent almost every waking minute together since we met, that adds up to a month of Sundays." He gave her a lopsided grin. "That's thirty dinner dates. Who says it's a whirlwind romance?"

Giving in to a self-conscious giggle, she ducked her head to hide a smile.

"You're not the only one to sense the connection. It's as if we're old friends, catching up—"

"*Picking* up where we left off..." Remembering his words from their catamaran cruise, she lifted her head in a begrudging smile. Then with a flutter in her belly, she recalled the warmth of his arms around her when they watched the sunset and their embrace as the moon rose.

"And trust me, *you* don't remind me of anyone." He shook his head as a wry half smile played at his lips. "You're your own inimitable brand of you."

She tried to hide the smile tickling her lips.

"So how do we know if we're moving too fast?" Posing the question, he drew in his breath slowly as though gathering his thoughts. Finally, he nodded as if the answer had come. "A rudder and a sail."

She squinted. "I'm not following."

"To navigate the sea—*or a new relationship*—you need both. Keep one hand on the tiller to steer a steady course, but let the wind catch your sails, too." He caught her gaze. "Combined, a rudder and a sail are your sea legs. One foot's solidly planted in reality and the other's planted where dreams can take root and soar."

"It *sounds* good." She sat back, thinking over his words. "But *what if* we're moving too fast?"

"Then we'll have to keep out a weather eye."

Nodding, she reaffirmed in her own words. "You mean, go into this with our eyes wide open?"

****

After Keya and Auggie left, Ruth ordered dinner through room service. She ate on the balcony, facing the sea and stairway, alert for prying eyes.

Asserting dominance, Earnestine sat on her lap, aloof, grooming her coat, as Diesel sat at Ruth's feet, watching with big, sad eyes.

"Sibling rivalry," she told them. "You two should learn to get along. If Keya and Auggie marry…" She stopped mid-sentence. *What am I saying?* Then she mentally rewound the past few days. The facts that Keya removed her wedding ring and Auggie went of his way to remember her birthday spoke volumes. *They seem to have a bond, but I hope they're not plunging into a relationship before they're ready.*

As Ruth finished dinner, she looked past the marina to the sea, thinking of Brett. On a whim, she took out her cell phone and speed-dialed his number.

"Hello, stranger."

"Brett! Is that really you?" She gave a disbelieving laugh. "I figured the odds were a million to one I'd reach you, but—"

"I was just about to call you," he said, a surprised

175

tone in his voice. "To save the battery, I'd turned off my cell, but I had a sudden urge to hear your voice. On the outside chance we were within calling range, I'd *just* turned on my cell phone."

"Kismet! It's so good to hear you," she said with a sigh. "I really don't like being separated this long. I miss you." Then not wanting to waste time whining, she changed the subject. "What've you been doing?"

"Fishing wreck reefs for yellowtail snapper, fishing deep water for blue marlin, and trolling for mahi-mahi." His smile came through the line. "We've been eating, sleeping, and angling our way through the Dry Tortugas fishing grounds."

She grimaced. "Gee, that sounds like fun…"

"Yeah, I hear the enthusiasm in your voice." He laughed. "What've you been up to?"

She updated him, adding, "Earnestine and Diesel are keeping me company, and if I get lucky, maybe Bart will stop by."

"What?" The line crackled. "What?"

The cell signal deteriorated as she tried to clarify her 'date with Bart.' *He must be moving out of range.* "Can you hear me?"

"You're breaking up," he said. "We'd better…" Static drowned out his words.

"What?"

She tried again a time or two before the call dropped. Then with a sigh, she brought out the laptop and put on the silver earrings.

As both spirits appeared, Earnestine's tail puffed, and the hackles rose on Diesel's neck.

"Will you *stop* that incessant blubbering, woman," shouted Bart.

Earnestine yowled as Diesel barked.

Ruth shushed them, but the critters' objections got louder until she put them inside. Then returning to the balcony, she tried again.

Maita sobbed in the background as she covered her face with her hands, her fingernails still bloody and jagged.

Bart paced. "This woman is driving me mad with her infernal whimpering. *Stop it!*"

The moment he shouted, Diesel began barking.

"Please keep your voice down," said Ruth. "You're upsetting the dog"—she glanced at the cowering girl—"and Maita."

"If the woman would exert some *self-control*." His voice rose at the end of the sentence, starting Diesel off on another round of barking.

Ruth sighed. "It would help if *you'd* exert a little self-control, yourself." Unsure what else to do, she added, "Maita, would you mind giving Bart and me a little privacy?"

Slowly removing her hands from in front of her face, the girl peeked at her with gloomy, puppy-dog eyes. With one last sniff, she vanished.

"Thanks be to God for the peace and quiet!" His form leaned against the balcony. "Her relentless sniveling is infuriating."

"Hasn't any other spirit annoyed you in the past?"

He paused a moment, as if thinking. "I believe she's the only one."

"You mean no one's disturbed you in four hundred years?"

He shook his head. "Never."

"No other spirits are on your level of existence?"

She gave him a sympathetic smile. "Haven't you minded being alone?"

"I've interacted with the living on occasion, but she's the first to intrude from this spiritual plane."

She studied him. "You've said two things tonight that seem out of character."

He gave her a puzzled frown. "What do you mean?"

"You mentioned God and now a spiritual plane," said Ruth, musing. "I don't recall you referring to the divine before."

He shrugged. "I must have."

"No, you haven't." She shook her head. "At least, not till now. What's changed?"

"An excellent question, my dear." Tenting his fingers, he seemed to ponder her query. "As you know, I'd been anxious to unburden my soul for almost four centuries. Since you've begun recording my memories, two things are happening. I forget the incidents I've told you—"

"You mean, once you tell me, they're erased from your memory?"

"I think so." Giving a slow, introspective nod, he added, "Yes, that's a good analogy. As you pen my memories onto paper, it's as if they're blotted from my mind." He paused, blinking, as if processing new concepts.

"You said two things." She considered him. "What's the other?"

"As my mind empties of memories, other thoughts fill the void."

"That makes sense. What kind of thoughts?"

"Thoughts of the hereafter, thoughts of my future,

but…" He glanced at her. "Once I let go these shadows of my life, what will I have? What will I cling to?"

"Your memoirs will live on in literature. After your experiences are captured in the written word, you'll exist on the literary plane." She gave him a half smile. "In a way, you'll live forever."

He seemed to ponder her words. "But that's just it, my dear. I don't live. I haven't lived for four centuries. As my memories of life diminish, does it mean my 'life,' such as it is, will fade away, as well?"

Where do I start? Ruth took a deep breath. "You just mentioned thinking of the hereafter and the future. The hereafter *is* your future." She appraised him as she recalled Auggie's words. "After you release these memories, maybe you won't need to cling to anything. Maybe you can just *let go*, move on."

"Move on where?"

"The afterworld. Eternity." Unable to think of any other neutral terms, she said, "Heaven."

"Or hell." His face darkened. "I told you I wasn't a religious man. I was a sailor, a navigator—"

"An explorer." She nodded, recalling their conversation.

"Neither alive nor dead, I've existed in a kind of limbo between worlds." Then his eyes lit up as if he had an idea. Straightening his spine, he stood at his full height. "It's time I approached this like a man, not a smooth-chinned cabin boy. My dear, if you're ready to continue, let's finish recording my experiences and see where it leads."

"Ready when you are." Ruth smiled at him. "I'm glad you're moving ahead. Maybe it will help you *move on*." She gave him an encouraging smile. "Just think, after four centuries, you'll be exploring again."

"Charting unfamiliar territory once more…"

****

Waking when Keya came in, Ruth glanced at the alarm clock—three o'clock. After Auggie left with Diesel, she turned over and went back to sleep.

At eight, Earnestine jumped on the bed, tickling Ruth's face with her whiskers. Trying to ignore her, Ruth rolled over, but Keya's off-key singing in the shower put the idea to rest. She stumbled out of bed, yawning, and started a pot of coffee.

"Glad you're awake." Wrapped in a hotel robe, Keya towel-dried her hair. "Auggie's meeting us downstairs in forty-five minutes."

****

An hour later, they sat on the café's patio, overlooking the harbor, enjoying breakfast al fresco. Now hooked on any foods containing the word *ceviche*, Ruth tried the "Breakfast Ceviche" of fresh mango, pineapple, banana, strawberry, tangerine, and dried cranberries on plantain chips. Keya ordered the lobster omelet with avocado, and Auggie wolfed down the "El Cubano Breakfast Panini" of grilled swiss cheese, shaved ham, and fried egg on Cuban bread.

With the pair of binoculars provided at each table, they took turns watching the seagulls and pelicans while they discussed their plans.

As a seagull swooped overhead, Auggie said, "Good thing the sea's out there and not a bay."

"Why?" asked Ruth.

"Because if it was a bay, that bird would've been a 'bagel'."

Groaning, Keya smiled at him. "Okay, now what's

this surprise you've kept from us?"

A slight dimple appeared as he returned her smile. "Both of you've been hinting about treasure hunting, so I pulled in a few favors and got us passage to the Leprechaun wreck site."

"What?" Keya glanced at Ruth and, blinking, turned back toward him. "Isn't that where you said we could look for emeralds?"

"Yup." He smiled magnanimously. "Just about everyone's dreamt of finding sunken treasure at one time or another. Here's your chance."

"How did you manage it?" asked Ruth.

"Every few months, the shareholders get to hunt for Muzo emeralds from the *Regala*." He shrugged. "I happen to be a shareholder."

"What if we stumble on one?" Keya's eyes glinted mischievously. "Could we keep it?"

"Absolutely." Auggie nodded. "Finders keepers."

Then Keya peered through bunched, cautious eyes. "But you're *sure* we don't have to dive for them, *right?*"

"You wouldn't even have to get wet." He shook his head. "You sift for emeralds topside, so non-divers can share the adventure."

"What do you mean, 'sift'?"

"The crew dredges up sediment from the ocean floor—sand, pebbles, small shells, and an occasional emerald—and pumps it onboard through a big hose," he said. "Then you sort through it with gloves and paddles."

Except for the smile lines around her eyes, Keya's face relaxed.

"Have you ever found an emerald?" asked Ruth.

"A small one once," he said, "but last season, they found over forty. To give you a sense of scale, they've recovered not carats, not ounces, but six *pounds* of uncut Columbian emeralds." He arched his brow. "So far…"

Ruth gave a low whistle.

"And not one of them was listed on the *Regala's* manifest…"

Ruth wracked her brain trying to grasp his point. "Meaning what?"

"Meaning the emeralds had been smuggled aboard. Since no records exist, no one knows how many gems there were—*or are*—still waiting to be discovered."

Ruth smiled. "Maybe we'll get lucky."

"Carp a D. M." He fluttered his eyebrows Groucho Marx-style.

****

They boarded the *Intrepid* after breakfast and, peeling down to their swimsuits, sat in the sun, working on their tans. As they chatted, seabirds glided overhead, and a pod of dolphins surfaced and frolicked alongside.

When the captain shouted an order, a crewmember responded, "Aye, aye, sir."

"Why do they always repeat themselves?" asked Ruth. "Why don't they just say 'Aye'?"

"It's a naval tradition going back to the sixteenth century, meaning yes, I heard, and yes, I'll do it." Auggie smiled. "It's a lot like our aeronautical terms, roger and wilco."

"Don't those mean the same thing?" Ruth frowned. "Like over and out?"

Auggie shook his head. "Roger means I received your transmission, or I heard. Wilco means I will comply."

Ruth gave a surprised laugh. "Never knew that."

When the captain cut the engines, Auggie slipped into his diving gear. "This is where I leave you ladies to your adventure." Just before he pulled on his mask, he beamed. "Happy hunting!" With that, he did a reverse roll off the side of the boat, plunging tank first into the water.

His splash made them pull back in unison.

"Now what?" asked Keya.

"Welcome to the Leprechaun," said a voice over the loudspeaker. "I'm Captain Pete, and I want to know how many of you are here today to find emeralds?"

The small troupe of investors cheered like a boisterous crowd.

"That's the spirit! Carp a D. M." A smile came through his voice. "Now, a little background. We weren't looking for emeralds when we found this site. Two divers were airlifting sediment, when suddenly, the sand and pebbles moving through the aluminum tube sounded different. The divers looked up to see green stones streaming out the top, bathing them in a green shower. So many emeralds sprinkled down, they filled a pint jar."

Ruth glanced at Keya's glowing eyes and ear-to-ear smile. "Do I look anywhere as excited as you?"

"You're beaming." Then Keya glanced at Earnestine and laughed. The cat chose that moment to yawn, stretch, curl up in the sun, and close her eyes. "A little social commentary."

Ruth petted Diesel, who still stared over the side of the ship, watching where Auggie had splashed down. "He's coming back, boy. Don't worry." Deadpanning, she glanced at Keya. "Note the difference between cats and dogs."

Keya laughed out loud while Earnestine twitched her whiskers, as if turning up her nose in disdain, and Diesel continued watching like a rigid sentry.

"Here's how it works, folks," said the captain's soft-spoken voice. "The divers took a large hose down to the seabed. In a minute, the vacuum will pump soggy sand over several screens in this sluice box—like goldminers use to pan gold."

A crewmember handed out red gloves and what looked like stubby dustpans or spackle trowels.

Captain Pete said, "Next, the sediment will spill onto this grated platform and slide along as you work it for emeralds. It's not high-tech, but hey, it works."

Crewmembers demonstrated as the captain coached their group. "Pull on your gloves and line up along this sifting table on both sides. Then using a pan in each hand, sift through the sand for anything that's green or hexagonal. Remember, finding an emerald on the tray is just as exciting as finding it underwater."

The raucous pumps started, and watery sand gushed onto the table.

People flew into action, using their plastic pans as pincers, pulling and pushing the sediment with the pans' edges while they sifted through it.

Swallowing a smile, Ruth shouted to Keya over the pumps' roar. "We look like a line of lobsters waving our red claws."

Nodding, Keya laughed as they worked alongside the investors and crew, keeping out a sharp eye for emeralds.

Ruth glanced at the critters.

Diesel still stared over the ship's side, watching for Auggie, while Earnestine curled up in the sun, napping.

After half an hour, Ruth's arms started to ache from going through the same repetitive motions. She glanced at the others. Judging from their expressions and the lag in conversation, interest seemed to be waning.

The person on Keya's right dropped out of line. "I need a breather," he said, plopping on a bench.

Then Keya lurched, losing her balance. As she bumped into Ruth, she apologized. "Did the boat just rock? Either that, or I need to develop sea legs."

Ruth laughed while they moved up the sluice line, closer to the front.

Seconds later, Keya screeched as she rubbed the sand from an object with her red gloves. "I found one!" After admiring its color and clarity in the sunlight, she held it out in her hand for everyone to see.

"Would you look at that!" Ruth took off her glove and ran her finger over the angular, green stone.

Instantly, Bart appeared, wearing a devilish grin. "At your service, Madam." He made a deep, chivalrous bow.

Remembering Keya's stumble, she raised her brow. *Was that you?* She mouthed the words, so no one heard. *Why?*

"I don't know." He shrugged. "Something about her looks familiar. She reminds me of someone…"

She took her finger from the stone, and Bart's image dissolved. "Congratulations, Keya! What a fabulous find—a belated birthday gift!"

The other sifters' interest now piqued, they congratulated her as they resumed their task with renewed gusto. The overall mood changed from one of fading attention to friendly competition.

Ignoring the ache in her arms, Ruth patted and prodded the elastic sediment with her paddles. First, she *sliced* it with the pans' edges, sifting through it in one direction, and then she *diced* it in the other. Like the other sifters, she became absorbed in what was no longer a task but a quest.

After another half hour of focused attention, her plastic paddle hit something hard. Not convinced she had found an emerald, Ruth picked up the object, and its angular ridges etched into her thick, spongy gloves. Wiping away the clinging sand, she squealed. "I found one!" Then she took off her gloves and fingered the green stone.

Bart appeared, grinning ear-to-ear. "In payment for your transcribing skills, my dear."

Acknowledging him with a delighted nod, she showed her gem to the team before taking it to be catalogued. When she returned minutes later, Auggie had come aboard and was talking with Keya.

"Let's have a look," he said.

Still not believing her good fortune, Ruth showed him the little plastic bag containing the emerald. "We really can keep these?"

Auggie smiled as he nodded. "It's all arranged."

"Thanks to you." Ruth hugged him and then turned toward Keya. "What are you going to do with yours?"

Keya glanced at Auggie before answering. "I haven't decided." As she caught his gaze, she gave him another sidelong smile. "Let's see what develops."

Watching her, Ruth swallowed a smile.

The noise level ended abruptly as the crew turned

off the pumps, and the watery sand stopped gushing onto the sifting table.

"Last call to find an emerald," said Captain Pete, "before we head back to Key West."

Ruth glanced at the sand pile collected at the foot of the sifting table. "What'll they do with that sediment?"

"The crew will shovel it onto the table one last time," said Auggie, "just to be sure no emeralds slipped through."

Captain Pete turned the boat around, announcing, "Party time, folks. The bar's now open!"

Its engines throttled wide open, the *Intrepid* overtook a rusting boat with a string of plastic oil cans girdling its hull. What resembled a mast at first glance proved to be a wind-turbine serving double-duty as a laundry pole supporting a wash line of wet clothes.

As the trio chatted over beer and munchies, Keya lowered her sunglasses and stared. "Is *that* a houseboat?"

Watching the watercraft bob in their wake, Auggie shook his head. "More like a converted scow, but apparently someone's home."

"I didn't know houseboats were so—" She paused, seeming to search for a word. "—*rustic*. I thought they'd be more elegant."

"They can be…" Auggie shrugged.

"The idea of roving about with all the comforts of home holds a certain charm. Like a turtle in its shell, the wanderer has the best of both worlds. But living aboard that vessel looks like roughing it, which *doesn't* appeal to me." When she glanced away from the watercraft, Keya's eyes glistened as she caught his gaze. "Maybe if the boat were finished with a bit more finesse…"

Maintaining the eye contact, he rubbed his chin. "Is that so?"

Her white teeth gleamed in a broad smile. "Living at sea a year or two might prove an adventure."

"Before flying back to your *nest*, right?" He learned toward her.

"You remembered." She clinked her bottle against his before taking a sip. "I like to balance flitting about with regrouping in my nest."

He watched her. "Just not concurrently as I recall."

"It's always been one or the other in a yin-yang tradeoff…at least, to date. I love exploring unfamiliar places, trying new things, and *tasting new foods*." Her smile lines deepening, she winked. "But then I need to recharge at home. I could be a vagabond only half the time, unless"—peering through her lashes, she caught his gaze—"I discovered a way to roam while living at home."

"Why not try it?" Auggie glanced from Keya to Ruth. "How would you like to be my guests tomorrow?"

"I'd love it," said Ruth. "A day on your houseboat would give me a taste of Brett's lifestyle this week."

Her eyes dancing, Keya gave him a playful smile. "What say we discuss it over dinner tonight?"

"I know just the place," he said. "It has the best hogfish in Key West."

As the sparks began to fly, Ruth said, "Think I'll babysit again. Besides, I've got another date tonight with Bart and my laptop."

****

Ruth researched Bart's history online before she touched the emerald.

"Good evening, Madam." He appeared with a graceful bow.

"I've been reading about you—"

"A book's been written about me?"

"When I searched your name, I got almost thirty-four thousand hits—"

"Hits?" Wearing a perplexed frown, he inspected her with his good eye.

Ruth tried to explain without going into detail. "An online library mentions Bartolomé García de Castillo at least thirty-four thousand times."

"It does?" At her nod, he pulled himself to his full height. "I'm honored." Then scowling, he added, "But if everyone's read of me, what's left for me to tell?"

"*Your* story, a firsthand account."

"Dead men tell no tales…" Musing, he looked away, seeming to withdraw into himself.

"Isn't telling tales what you want?" Ruth tried to bring him back. "What you *need* to move on?"

Blinking, he did a double take. "What was that, my dear?"

"After you release your memories, maybe you won't have to cling to them anymore. Maybe you can just *let go* and move on."

He sighed. "I can't let go of one 'memory' because I never experienced it."

"What?" Squinting, Ruth shook her head, thinking she had misheard.

"Instead of a memory, it was a yearning or a regret." A sigh escaped his lips. "The last time I held my wife, she was pregnant with our child. I never set eyes on the baby. I remember my wife's excitement and recall her growing belly, but I never met our child. That's a 'memory' I can't let go because I never experienced it."

"I understand." Realizing they shared a bond, Ruth nodded. "I had a twin sister who was stillborn. I also miss the sister I never met."

"I *knew* we were sympatico, my dear. Now I know why." Bart's gaze verged on melancholy. "But if releasing my memories is required to leave this plane, and I can't let that one go…" His mouth turning down at the corners, he ended with a stifled sigh.

"Release what you can." Ruth reassured him with a smile. "Maybe that'll be enough."

"I hope so, or I may be bound to the *Regala* till Doomsday."

"Let's think positively." She tried changing the subject. "I read you lost your eye while boarding an English man-of-war."

The corners of his mouth upturning in a smile, he warmed to a war story. "I sustained three wounds that day, one of which cost me my right eye, but when King Philip III heard of my actions, he rewarded me with the ship I'd captured."

"You were quite the swashbuckler, weren't you?"

Seeming to regain his swagger, he sat up straight and alert as he related the details of that skirmish and several others.

Ruth recorded them, but after listening to an hour of bloody battles at sea, she said, "How about a change of pace? Tell me how you met your wife."

He inhaled deeply, as if breathing in past pleasures. "I went to sea when I was sixteen. The adventure was pay enough for a young lad, and for four years, the sea was my sole mistress. Then I was one of the first to board and capture a merchantman. In payment, Philip III made me Count of Castrillo."

"You were a count?" She jerked her head back, looking at him with renewed interest.

"Why does that surprise you?"

She shrugged. "I knew you were a sailor and explorer, but I never knew you were a nobleman, too."

With a subtle grin, he feigned a humble bow. "Just one of my many admirable traits, Madam."

Ruth smiled at his sense of humor. "So how did you meet your wife?"

"I was wintering at Cartagena, where I met a woman…" His voice faltered.

"Your wife?"

"I'm getting to that part!"

"Sorry." She rolled her eyes, muttering, "Touchy."

"What did you say?" His good eye stared her down as he jutted out his chin.

"Please continue."

After adjusting his cloak, he seemed to gather his dignity about him. "She was a captivating woman, unlike anyone I'd ever met—charming and dynamic. By spring, we were engaged, but then the Captain General appointed me the commander of three galleons in a convoy to New Spain. By the time I returned the following winter, she had married another man"—his face hardened—"a duke and grandee."

Ruth tried to grasp his point. "Do those titles outrank a count?"

Scowling at her interruption, he stifled a sigh. "By several magnitudes."

Not knowing what to say, she simply nodded her empathy.

"It was a seaman's lot." He shrugged. "I'd been gone on a long voyage, while he was accessible, better landed, and better titled…" His voice faded as he seemed to gaze inward.

"So how did you meet—"

"Madam, do you or do you *not* want to hear this story?" Irritated, he glared at her with his good eye.

"Sorry." With a shrug, Ruth held up her hands as if fending him off.

"For another two years, I jumped from one voyage into the next, never stopping to think, rarely going ashore. Then on one expedition, I met a native woman, who knew a few words of Spanish—"

"Spanish?" Thinking aloud, she mumbled, "Of course, you spoke Spanish." She turned toward him. "But I don't speak Spanish, so how come I understand you?"

His good eye glaring, his jawline hard, and his chin jutting out, his impatience was obvious. "You hear me with your mind, Madam, not your ears. You sense my thoughts, not hear my words."

"Of course." His explanation made sense. "That's why only I 'hear' you." Ruth gave him an apologetic nod. "Please continue with your story."

"Intrigued by this woman, I learned through interpreters that a padre had converted her family years before."

"Here in the Keys?"

Though he gave her a stern glance, he nodded. "The naval assignment kept me nearby, patrolling the straits through the winter. As a result, I spent a great deal of time with her. We fell in love and were married in April. Though I planned to stay in New Spain and build a hacienda, I needed to go back to Spain one last time to resign my commission and make the arrangements."

"So you sailed on the *Regala* in September?"

"Yes, I knew my pregnant wife would give birth before I returned in the spring." Biting his lip, he paused as if looking inward. "But when I said goodbye, I had no idea that would be the last time I'd ever see her, hold her, or talk to her."

"How sad"—she thought of the twin sister she had lost—"never to have met your child."

He nodded absently, seeming to withdraw into himself.

"Bart." As he mentally retreated, she tried again. "Bart!"

He acknowledged her with a half-hearted grunt.

"Thanks again for the emerald."

He nodded, but his gaze was inward.

She slipped the emerald in the pouch, and as Bart dissolved, she sat staring into the void. *Whatever became of his family?*

Chapter 8

Boat Rides, Tan Lines, and Good Times

After breakfast the next morning, they met Auggie and Diesel at the pier. He helped them aboard his skiff and then sped to his houseboat.

As they approached, Ruth gave a low whistle. "How big is this boat, anyway?"

"It's a nineteen by one hundred WB," said Auggie, maneuvering the motorboat alongside.

"WB?"

"Wide body." He cut the engines and gave them a hand aboard the houseboat. Then, taking their bags, he asked, "Would you like a tour?"

"Definitely!" Carrying Earnestine, Keya glanced at Ruth.

He held the cabin door for them as they entered. "This is the main salon."

Ruth took in the custom-built cabinets and hardwood floors. One wall was a solid bank of screened windows. Overstuffed sofas, chairs, and ottomans added a sense of luxurious comfort to the nautical theme. "Why is that wall glass?"

"It's a loadbearing wall," he said. "The glass supports the upper deck as it visually separates the salon from the galley, yet it gives the space an open feeling." Turning, he gestured toward the room's right side, where stemmed wineglasses hung from custom-fitted wine racks. "The starboard wall has a wet bar."

"All the comforts of home," said Keya, "and then some."

Auggie led them into the next room. "The galley has a side-by-side refrigerator, stove, oven, microwave, and dishwasher."

"This is a kitchen—not a kitchenette." Ruth turned 360 degrees to see the expansive room. "I thought a galley would be *cramped*, but it even has a central island."

"I'm impressed." Smiling her approval, Keya lightly ran her fingers over the granite countertops while Earnestine jumped down to explore with Diesel.

Auggie guided them through a wood-paneled hall that housed built-in cabinets tucked behind glass doors. "This Z-hallway starts on the port side and crosses midship to starboard." Then he slid open a pocket door. "This is the first of four staterooms."

"Staterooms." Keya gave him a quizzical smile. "You mean bedrooms?"

Auggie gave her a sheepish grin. "Guess I revert to nautical terms when I'm aboard ship."

"Is this bed queen-sized?" asked Ruth, not trusting her perspective. At his nod, she added, "I expected single beds or bunk beds. This room's so spacious."

"Is it the master bedroom?" asked Keya.

He shook his head. "That's at the end of the hall. This is a guestroom." He led them farther down the corridor, where he slid open two more pocket doors and set down their bags. "These rooms connect, sharing a head with a built-in vanity and shower. Why don't you use these as changing rooms while you're onboard?"

They poked their heads in the doorways, scanning each room's walk-around queen-sized bed with built-in nightstands and storage units.

Continuing down the hallway, he led them to a suite with a king-sized bed, built-in nightstands, and a double granite-topped vanity. "The master stateroom and head." He slid open another door, showing a whirlpool tub and stand-up shower. Then, turning, he pushed open an exterior door, leading them outside. "And a private entrance to the deck."

Outside, something hung from the roof above, jutting out over the water.

"What's that?" Angling her neck, Ruth stared.

His eyes glimmered in the sunlight. "That's a water slide connected from the party top."

"Party top?" Ruth glanced at Keya and back to Auggie.

"Want to see?" Anticipating their answer, he led them up a stairway to the next deck, where he pointed out the features. "A wet bar with a small galley in the stern, a built-in stereo with four speakers, and here's the water slide."

"Party top?" Ruth laughed as she looked around. "It's a party boat."

"Not really." With a self-effacing chuckle, he began the tour. "Though this end has a grill and a table for eight, and the stern has room for more seating with a dance floor…I'm not the partying type."

"So *this* is a houseboat." Keya turned in a circle to take in the deck's amenities. "It's more like a floating hotel."

"What did you expect?" Auggie's eyes tracked her. "A shanty boat with laundry hanging from a clothesline?"

"I didn't know what to think. This is the first time I've been aboard a houseboat." She shrugged. "I thought it would be *tiny*—more like the boat we saw than this floating palace."

"What do you think now?" He watched her closely, seeming to study her every nuance.

"It's obvious why you want to live here. It's a mansion on rudders." She winked. "You're at home while you travel—as self-sufficient as a turtle with his house on his back."

"Glad you approve." He deadpanned before turning toward Ruth. "What's first on the morning's agenda? Want to fish? Snorkel? Sunbathe?"

"What about snorkeling?" said Ruth.

"Sure, I've got extra fins, masks, and snorkels. We can even slide into the water if you want."

After changing into their swimsuits, they met at the waterslide, where Auggie had laid out snorkels and masks.

"The best reefs and snorkeling are at the Dry Tortugas," he said, "but we can see a respectable variety of fish right here, alongside the boat." He glanced at Keya, his gaze lingering a beat too long. "Maybe we can save the Tortugas for another day…"

Wearing a mysterious smile, she shrugged. "Maybe."

After they shared a private smile, he studied her back. "Did you scrape against something?"

"No, why?"

"Your shoulder looks grazed."

"Oh, that." Shrugging, Keya tried to peer over her right shoulder. "It's just a birthmark."

Ruth finished putting on her gear and looked over the slide's edge. Then, hopping on, she called, "Last one in's a rotten egg!" as she slid down and splashed into the warm aquamarine water.

Keya followed and then Auggie. Within minutes, an assortment of multicolored fish surrounded them.

"What are these rainbow-looking fish?" asked Ruth.

"Parrotfish." His voice sounded hollow as he spoke through his snorkel, and his words were stilted, like a ventriloquist's who didn't move his lips. "Their teeth are fused, making their mouths look like parrots' beaks."

"What about these gold and royal-blue fish?" asked Keya. "What are they?"

"Damselfish."

They snorkeled until Auggie asked, "Anyone want to catch lunch?"

"Sure." Ruth gave a wry laugh. "Normally, I'm not fond of fishing, but this will give me a feel for what Brett's been doing all week."

They climbed aboard, slipped on swimsuit covers, and met back at the stern, where Auggie had outfitted three poles and reels.

"We'll just surface fish," he said, "maybe catch a barracuda, bonito, or mackerel." As they cast out, he said, "Work the jig."

"What's a jig?" asked Keya.

"It's a kind of fishing lure," he said.

"What do you mean, *work it*?" Keya squinted.

"Roll your wrist when you reel in the line, like this"—he demonstrated—"and then cast again."

After a few minutes of casting and trolling,

something tugged at Ruth's line. As the fish took the bait and ran, the rod bent under the strain, nearly doubling over.

"You've got one," said Auggie. "Reel it in slowly."

When she brought the fish closer, its silver streak flashed in the water below.

Auggie grabbed a net and stood alongside her. Just as she lifted the fish from the water, he scooped it in his net. "You've caught a bonito. Good job!"

"I've reeled in perch and bluegills in lakes, but this is the first saltwater fish I've ever caught. Compared to those freshwater fish, this one's *huge*. Wait till I tell Brett." His name had not left her lips when her cell phone rang. "What the…?" Snickering at the irony, she read caller ID. "It's Brett."

"I'll take care of the fish." Auggie reached for her pole. "Take your call and tell him hi."

Nodding, she stepped away to answer. "Your timing's impeccable. I just caught a bonito."

"You did?" asked Brett. "Where?"

"From Auggie's houseboat."

"Which explains why I was able to get through. You're on the water."

Ruth told him about the past days' adventures, even going into detail about Bart and Maita. "What've *you* been doing?"

"Fishing, though I've had my fill for a while." He laughed. "I'm looking forward to being a landlubber again."

Glad to connect by phone, she hugged herself but wished the arms around her were his. "Can't wait to see you tomorrow. It's been a long week—in more ways than one. What time will you get into Key West?"

"Should be there by noon. I'll call you when we dock." Brett said something else, but interference made his words unintelligible.

"What?" She strained to hear.

He spoke again, but the line crackled.

"You're breaking up." Static, and then the line went dead. Stifling a frustrated groan, she reminded herself, *I'll see him tomorrow.*

When she rejoined her friends, Auggie was teaching Keya how to cast. Standing close behind her, he controlled her arm as they cast the line together.

"That's it." The wind carried his voice. "You're getting the hang of it."

Ruth called, "I'm going to read a while." When they did not respond, she shouted against the wind. "I'm going to read."

"Sorry, what did you say?" Auggie turned toward her. "Are you through fishing?"

She nodded. "I've caught my lunch. Now it's your turn." Smiling, she pointed toward the chairs at the bow. "I'm going to read."

"Have fun," called Keya with a wave.

Ruth swallowed her smile as she observed them, their heads close together and bodies almost, but not quite, touching. Ruth walked to the bow when a stiff sea breeze caught her by surprise. With a shiver, she jammed her hands in her pockets, and her fingers touched something metallic.

The earrings! I'd forgotten I'd left them here.

Instantly, Bart and Maita appeared.

"Not this caterwauling again," bellowed Bart, putting his hands to his ears. "Cease and desist, woman!"

With a loud sniffle, Maita vanished from sight.

"Much better." He took a deep breath. Regaining his presence of mind, Bart turned to Ruth. "Can you do anything to stop this woman's infernal blubbering?"

"I'm trying, but…" Ruth raised a shoulder in a half shrug. "At this point, she hasn't told me her story. If she'd identify her murderer, maybe I could help bring the person to justice."

"So she's been murdered, has she?"

"The police think so."

Bart shook his head. "The poor woman, God rest her soul." He made the sign of the cross.

Ruth blinked. "I didn't know you were religious."

"I wasn't. I was a sailor, a navigator—"

"An explorer, yes, I recall our conversations." She rolled her eyes. "Do you realize you're repeating yourself?"

Wearing a surprised, dazed look, his good eye stared at her. "No, I'm not."

"That's the third time you've told me those same words." Piecing it together, she nodded. "You repeat yourself as if you're at a loss for new experiences to share. And your habits are changing. For instance, I've never seen you make the sign of the cross before."

"Certainly, I have"—he shrugged—"plenty of times."

"I've never seen you do it."

"You just weren't watching."

She rolled her eyes. "I won't argue, but I do notice subtle changes in you."

"What do you mean?"

"Like saying 'God rest her soul' or—"

"Madam, I'm not doing anything different now

than before!"

"One thing that hasn't changed is your temper." She scowled.

"Confound it, woman! Why must you always disagree with me?"

"Methinks the captain doth protest too much…"

His good eye opened in surprise. "You know Shakespeare, Madam?"

"Sure." She tried to remember when the playwright lived. *The late sixteenth century?* "Of course you'd recognize Shakespeare."

"You're an educated woman, a perfect scribe, which reminds me. When are you going to record my memories again?"

"I didn't bring my laptop."

He gave her a stern look. "Madam, once you sit, you'll have your lap."

She swallowed a smile. "I didn't bring my writing equipment."

"Then listen and remember."

She recalled her cell's voice memo function. Though Bart had said she heard him only in her mind, she scrolled through the menu, clicked *record*, and smiled. "Please state your name."

"Bartolomé García de Castillo."

She played back the recording, but the soundtrack was blank. "I'll have to repeat your words, but it's a way to capture your stories for later."

Seagulls swooped overhead, their cackles seeming to mock them. Ruth watched until the birds flew out of sight, still laughing at them.

When she turned back to Bart, he asked, "Did I tell you about the parrot earrings?"

She shook her head as she repeated his words into her phone.

"For our wedding, I gave my wife a pair of parrot earrings." His expression softened. "Parrots mate for life, you know."

Ruth nodded, grasping the wedding/parrot connection. "Can you describe the earrings?"

"They were enameled gold, inset with emeralds and pearls." His good eye misting over, he suppressed a sigh at the memory. "She wore them every day—at least, until I set sail in September." He swallowed. "I wonder what happened to them…"

****

Following a leisurely lunch of fish brochettes grilled with hickory-smoked bacon, pearl onions, and cherry tomatoes, they sipped rum punch while Earnestine and Diesel played on deck. First Diesel chased the cat. Then they reversed roles, and Earnestine chased the dog.

After watching the pursuer become the pursued and reverse again, Keya chuckled. "You'd think they were actors the way they switch roles."

Auggie studied her. "Hadn't you mentioned before you'd been an actress?"

"Oh, yes." Her cheekbones lifting in a smirk, Keya fluttered her eyelashes. "After graduation, I left for the bright lights of Broadway. I made it to off-Broadway—close—yet *ever so far* from the brightest lights."

"She always was a ham." Smiling fondly, Ruth raised her glass in a mock toast.

"True, I was young when the acting bug bit me." Keya sat back, seeming to relive the memory. "Like Ruth said, we *always* put on skits as kids."

"What made you choose New York and theater?" he asked. "Why not LA and film?"

"The summer my mother took me to Manhattan, I fell in love with Broadway."

"How old were you?"

"Sweet sixteen"—Keya smiled—"and very impressionable. After I attended a Broadway musical, I was hooked. From that moment, I read every book written about acting, from Stanislavsky's *An Actor Prepares* to Uta Hagen's *Respect for Acting*. I took every course available on drama, theater, and public speaking, and I landed several roles in school plays." She laughed at herself. "At eighteen, I was ready for the big time, so a few days after my birthday, I set off for the Great White Way."

"Was it anything like you'd planned?" Leaning forward in his chair, he seemed to hang on her every word.

"It was culture shock—*shell shock*—to fly from a quaint midwestern town to mid-town Manhattan. After a short flight and a long cab ride into town, I might as well have landed in Oz. I was *so* unprepared." Scoffing, she shook her head, as if unable to comprehend how or why she had attempted such a thing.

"I can relate." Auggie nodded. "Did it take long to adjust to that lifestyle?"

"Adjust?" Keya took a long breath as if gathering her thoughts. "I don't think I ever acclimated to that life, but I spun enough spider threads to weave them into a safety net."

He squinted. "What do you mean 'spider threads'?"

"It's what I call those fine filaments that let you

explore but then lead you back—like breadcrumb trails. I found my way around town. I learned how to use the subway. I took a part-time job to leave my mornings open for making the rounds. I figured out how to audition at open calls, and I got a voice teacher. Then I knitted all those tiny threads into a web."

"When you were eighteen?"

Keya nodded.

"You must've grown up fast."

She grimaced. "Let's say I learned self-reliance."

"Being on your own at that age must've been hard."

"In Manhattan, especially," added Ruth, "but as I recall, you appeared in several plays and even a movie or two, didn't you?"

Keya nodded. "I landed chorus roles and extra parts—even a few bit parts—but nothing memorable, no starring roles." She chuckled before speaking with an affected Shakespearean accent. "There are no small roles, just small actors."

Auggie smiled as he topped off their drinks. "If acting gigs were so few and far between, how did you support yourself?"

"Mostly through modeling jobs in the garment district, which is only a few blocks from the theater district—a short subway ride. The jobs were close enough to audition in midtown and then return to work." Gazing at nothing, she took a deep breath as if reliving the past. "Then one day, I was offered a lead role. The only problem was, the play was a showcase…" She left the words hanging.

Auggie shared a blank stare with Ruth. "Which meant…?"

Chin high, Keya wore an enigmatic smile. "Which meant rehearsals and the off-Broadway debut didn't pay a cent, *but*"—she raised an index finger—"the musical was slated for an out-of-town tryout in Boston, followed by a month-long tour to attract backers, and *finally* a Broadway opening."

"I gather the tryout, tour, and debut *would* have paid," said Ruth.

"That's how they hooked me." Keya's smile was cynical. "I quit my modeling job and spent my days in rehearsal, gambling the risk would pay off in a Broadway role."

"Did it?" asked Auggie.

Keya took a deep breath. "Depends on how you define 'pay off.' "

"Your tone's not encouraging." Auggie's half smile was sympathetic. "What happened?"

"What you'd expect. During rehearsals, I lived on my savings and dreams." Keya scanned the sea's horizon, seeming to look beyond. "On opening night, we received excellent reviews—even a congratulatory telegram from the President of the Screen Actors Guild."

Impressed, Ruth lifted her brow as she gave an admiring nod. "Sounds like they had big plans for that showcase."

"Oh, they did…" A distant glint in her eyes, Keya paused as if reexperiencing the memory.

"But…" prompted Auggie.

"Though we finished the week-long showcase"— she turned toward him with a cynical smile—"neither the out-of-town tryout nor the tour developed. The backers backed out, and the curtains never did rise on

Broadway. My gamble didn't pay off. Instead of becoming the next Broadway star, I became just another out-of-work actor."

"What did you do?"

"With my savings almost gone, I had no choice but to hit the pavement, and I took a part-time job at a communications firm, specializing in the entertainment field."

"Did that showcase end your stage career?" he asked.

"I landed a few bit parts in films, and I understudied a couple off-Broadway roles, but the part-time job developed into a full-time position, and I found myself with less time *or* inclination to audition. Then Jules joined the firm, and a year later, we were married."

Auggie wore a sad smile. "Do you miss the theater?"

Keya shook her head. "I was drawn to the stage, *captivated* by it as a young adult"—she shrugged—"but I feel no attraction to that life anymore. The only way I express my dramatic flair now is through my wardrobe." Chuckling at her former self, she turned toward him. "Which reminds me, don't we need to dress for the dock party? What time does it start?"

"Three." Auggie glanced at his watch and then drained his glass. "We probably should head back. Why don't you two shower and change while I start the engines?"

****

A half hour later, Ruth shared the vanity mirror with Keya as they applied makeup and added the finishing touches.

When Keya put on a pair of colorful dangle earrings, Ruth stared at them. "I've never seen those before."

"My grandmother gave them to me." Keya spoke through the mirror. "She said her grandmother had given her the earrings, and *her* grandmother had given them to *her*. I rarely wear them—just on special occasions."

Ruth was about to touch them, when Keya's words registered, and she pulled back. "Why is this a special occasion?"

Keya gave her a mystifying smile followed by a wink.

Ruth made a humming sound. "Maybe I'll learn more by observing. Can I see?"

"Sure." Holding back her hair, Keya leaned toward Ruth, so the earrings hung in plain view.

Ruth moved in for a closer look. "Are those…parrots?"

She nodded.

"Pearls, emeralds…and is that enameled gold?"

"Cloisonné"—Keya shrugged—"or so my grandmother told me."

"Really?" As the words sank in, Ruth caught her breath. "I've got a hunch."

She slipped on the silver earrings, and both apparitions appeared. While Maita stared at Ruth's earrings, Bart gazed at Keya's.

"Are those…" His words broke off as he tried to touch them.

Keya shuddered. "What was that?"

"Bart's taking a closer look at your earrings," said Ruth.

Then his gaze left the jewelry as he began studying Keya's face. He walked around to the other side of her, examining her from different angles. At last, he nodded. "I thought something about her was familiar. She looks like…" His words trailing off, his jaw dropped.

"Who?"

"Luciana," he said, the name sounding like a sigh.

"Who's Luciana?" asked Ruth.

"My wife."

Ruth blinked as she made the connection.

"What?" Keya watched her. "What's going on?"

"You said these earrings are heirlooms, right?"

Keya nodded. "Passed down from grandmother to granddaughter for generations."

"How many generations?"

Keya shrugged. "Supposedly, they go back to my Calusa great-great-something-grandmother."

"The one who'd married the count?"

At Keya's nod, Bart's shoulders slumped.

"What happened to him?"

"He sailed away." Keya's mouth turned down at the corners.

"You mean, he deserted her?"

"No." Keya shook her head. "He was lost at sea. In fact, that's how she met my great-great-something-step-grandfather. He was one of the wreck's few survivors."

Ruth glanced at him before asking, "Could Bart have been your ancestor?"

"I doubt it." Her mouth twisting sarcastically, Keya scoffed. "What are the odds?"

He came to attention, as if remembering something. "Ask her if she has a birthmark on her right shoulder blade."

After Ruth passed on his question, Keya let her loose-fitting blouson slip low on her shoulder, exposing her back. "You mean this strawberry mark on my wing bone?"

"Everyone in the Castillo family shares this birthmark." Regaining some of his swagger, Bart gave a self-satisfied nod. "She's my daughter."

"*Perhaps* she's your great-something-granddaughter." Ruth turned to Keya, adding, "You may be related to Bart—"

"Bartolomé García de Castillo," he corrected, his tone proud. "At last, I've met my child."

"Your child's descendent—*possibly*," said Ruth, "and in a way, maybe you've 'seen' Luciana once more."

After Ruth explained Bart's disappointment at never seeing his wife again or meeting his child, Keya sighed. "I sincerely doubt we're related, but I guess anything's possible."

His good eye blinking, Bart studied Keya. "She looks like my wife. If she's *of* my wife, in a way, it is like seeing her again."

"So if you *have* reconnected with your family, maybe now you'll have fewer regrets to bind you and more 'memories' to release. Perhaps now you can move on."

He sighed. "But I haven't finished telling you my story."

"Don't worry. We'll finish recording your memories this week." Ruth gave him an encouraging smile. "Then, after you release them, you can stop clinging to them and let them go." She shook her head, clarifying her thoughts. "No, let me rephrase that, let go *their hold on you.*"

His expression drooped. "But if I have nothing to cling to, what will I have?"

"You'll have peace."

"If I let go, where will I go?"

"The afterlife, maybe heaven."

"Or hell." His face darkened. "I wasn't a religious man. I was a sailor, a navigator—"

"An explorer." She stifled a sigh, recalling their previous conversations. "After four centuries of seeing and doing the same repetitive things, you can explore unknown territory again. Consider it an adventure."

Keya's eyes grew large. "Are you calling death an adventure?"

"In a way," said Ruth. "Everything in life's an adventure, so why not death? If Bart stops resisting it, denying it, if he embraces death, he might discover it's his most exciting journey yet."

"What you're saying is—" Keya paused, as if searching for the right words. "—you have to let go the life you've planned, so you can live the life that's waiting for you."

"In Bart's case, the *after*life that's waiting for him." Ruth gave her a half smile. "But I don't think you're talking about Bart." She studied Keya, remembering her earlier words. "You said you wear these earrings only on special occasions. What's so special about tonight?"

Her eyes sparkling, Keya's face lit up with a coy smile. Instead of answering, she shrugged.

"Okay, be evasive, but does it have anything to do with Auggie?"

"Maybe." Keya pursed her lips.

"Fine," said Ruth, "tell me when you're ready, but how do you feel about meeting your great-something-grandfather?"

"I haven't." Her smile shifting to a frown, Keya stared without blinking. "Even if he is related to me, *which I doubt*, you're the only one who can see him or talk with him. All I hear is what you tell me."

"You felt him touch your earring."

"Maybe a stray hair tickled my ear." Keya shrugged. "It's not like the hairs on my arms stood on end or chills ran down my spine."

"You don't believe he's here?"

"I believe you see and hear something, but I'm not convinced it's my long-lost, great-something grandpa." She gave Ruth a crooked smile. "Seriously, what are the odds?"

"Your great-something grandmother was Calusa, the original owner of these earrings, and she married a count." Ruth shared how Philip III had made Bart the Count of Castrillo. "And Bart recognized your birthmark. I'd say the evidence is more than circumstantial."

Keya lifted her shoulder in a shrug. "These are things he could've overheard or seen. For that matter, how do we know this entity isn't evil?"

"If Bart was evil, he wouldn't be able to mention God." Ruth glanced at him. "And he's spoken of God several times."

"So?"

"Evil and God are a contradiction."

Keya studied her, as if appraising her. "I don't want to argue. Let's just say you're more sensitive to spirits than I am."

"Only when I touch objects connected to them." Ruth tugged at an earring. "If I take these off, I can't see or hear anything out of the ordinary, either."

"Say what you will"—she made a face—"you're still more receptive to the *idea* of ghosts than I am."

"Nothing wrong with skepticism, but that mindset can go either way," said Ruth. "Even if I can't prove ghosts exist or Bart's your ancestor, neither can you dismiss the ideas."

Keya stifled a long-suffering sigh. "Like I said, I don't want to argue about Bart or anything else. I want tonight to be special."

Ruth recalled Keya's earlier words. "That's the second time you've referred to tonight as special. Why?"

****

After they docked, Auggie shuttled them to the annual dock party in his motorboat.

As they arrived at three-thirty, Keya gave him a playful smile. "So, we're fashionably late. I have a feeling this will be a night to remember."

He did a double take. Then Auggie's puzzled expression morphed into a conspiratorial smile. "The day's been terrific. Why not expect a banner evening?"

The dock was packed with partying people, most standing and mingling, while some clustered around tables beneath sun-umbrellas. A high-energy band and rum-laced drinks kept the mood dynamic.

From the crowd's expectant faces and lively body language, Ruth sensed the contagious currents. The atmosphere was charged with electricity, each person seeming to feed off the others' excitement. As she absorbed the ambience, Ruth flushed from her contact high's adrenalin rush.

"What are all these?" She glimpsed the various pop-up tents with signs reading *Lucky Cupcake Contest, 50/50 Raffle, Enter to Win Raffle, Silent Auction,* and *Live Auction.*

"They're lotteries to win cash and treasure prizes, with the proceeds benefiting the orphanage." Auggie pointed to the table of cupcakes, each decorated with a numbered gold-colored coin. "Besides a pastry, the lucky winner takes home an authentic *Regala* coin."

"Is that why so many people are here?" Ruth asked, puzzled. "Just to win prizes or donate to a charity?"

"Partly." He glanced at the crowd. "But most come here to relive the good old days and mingle with the current and past treasure-hunting crews—just enjoy themselves. It's first and foremost a party, one they've been holding since 1998—unofficially, since 1985."

Earnestine in one arm, Keya linked her other arm with Auggie's. "In that case, let's get rum punch and tickets for the silent auction, in that order."

Watching them, Ruth swallowed a smile. "How 'bout I give you two some privacy?"

"You can't be alone at a party." Keya's brows pulled in.

"When I'm wearing these"—Ruth laughed as she touched an earring—"I'm never alone. Bart and Maita keep me company."

"You mean, you really *do* see these spirits?" Tipping her head to the side, Keya gave a doubtful laugh. "They're not just in your mind's eye?"

"They're as solid as you and Auggie." She hunched her shoulder, shrugging. "Visually, anyway."

Keya studied her. "Are you sure these aren't just projections of your mind?"

Ruth shook her head as she shared a private smile with Bart.

Keya glanced at Auggie as if looking for support. "We'd worry about you wandering around with no one to keep you company."

"Don't give it another thought. Bart and Maita will keep me entertained while I give you two some space." With a wave, Ruth added, "I'll call you in a half hour. In the meantime, have fun!"

"Good," said Bart. "I'll tell you more about my battles at sea."

"No more war stories for a while." Ruth rolled her eyes. "Instead, why don't you tell me about Luciana while I record you?" As he spoke, she held her cellphone close to her mouth and softly repeated his words.

"What about *me?*" Maita clenched her arms, her bloody fingernails digging into her biceps. "No one ever pays any attention to *me*."

Ruth stifled a sigh. As if placating a spoiled child, she said, "Bart needs to finish telling me his tales so he can move on."

"What about *me?*" Her brow puckering, she pouted. "What about *my* stories?"

Ruth glanced at the time. "Okay, Bart will talk for ten minutes. Then you'll talk for ten minutes. How's that?"

Her lips poised to say no, Maita seemed to change her mind. Instead, she said, "Ten minutes," precisely enunciating each syllable and drawing out the final S in a hiss.

Bart resumed his story as Ruth repeated his words into her cellphone.

Nine minutes and forty-five seconds later, Maita said, "My turn!"

Stifling another sigh, Ruth struggled to be patient. "All right, Maita, I'm listening." After a few seconds of silence, she asked, "What do you want to say?"

Maita pursed her lips and hunched her shoulders. Then she began wringing her hands.

Ruth tried again. "Do you want to tell me what happened the night you drowned?"

Maita shook her head.

"Do you want to talk about Heath?"

Maita's eyes flashed, but then she looked at her feet and shook her head.

"Okay, what *do* you want to talk about?"

After a moment, Maita whispered. "I'll…I'll skip 'is turn."

Ruth bit her lip as she stifled an annoyed sigh. "Okay, Bart, why don't we pick up where you left—"

"I've changed my mind," said Maita. "'ere's some'ing you should know about him—some'ing I want to get off my chest. He' has an addiction."

Turning toward her, Ruth whispered, "What kind of addiction? Drugs? Alcohol?"

"Online gambling and horse racing." Maita shook her head. "He made me promise not to tell anyone about it, but it's a sickness, a disease."

"Why do you say that?"

"Once he starts gambling, he can't walk away. He gambles until he's spent his last dollar upping his bets, trying to win back his losses. 'en after he's spent his own money, he moves on to money 'at isn't his, 'borrowing' from 'e company accounts. I covered for him for as long as I could, but…"

"But what?" asked Ruth.

"All I did was enable him…not help him…and I destroyed myself in the process. I finally told him I wouldn't cover for him anymore, 'at he had to help himself."

"What did Heath have to say?"

"Not'ing." Again, Maita shook her head. "He denied any problem. He said 'e debt was no'ting he couldn't handle—no'ting he couldn't fix."

"Did he ever try to stop gambling or limit himself?"

"He promised to," Maita looked up, "*tried to* many times, but going cold turkey made him restless and anxious. He couldn't relax until he chased his losses, as he called it."

"What do you mean 'chased' his losses?"

"He'd try to break even by betting more and more money, and 'en double his bets, trying to win back what he'd lost."

"Sounds like a losing proposition," said Ruth. "With so much at stake, what was the attraction?"

"He said winning was 'e greatest 'rill he ever knew—his kick, his buzz, even his ecstasy." Maita pressed her lips together in a grimace.

"If winning was his ultimate thrill," asked Ruth, "wouldn't losing have been his deepest disappointment?"

Maita shook her head. "He said losing was 'e *second* highest 'rill he ever knew—not as big a rush as winning—but still exhilarating."

Ruth stared into the distance. "How could a person

ever climb out of that reversed reality?"

"He couldn't. He'd make promises, but whe'er he meant 'em or not, I finally realized 'ey were not'ing but lies—to me, to himself."

"What kind of promises?" Ruth remembered the copper coins they had discovered. "Did he promise to return the money he skimmed from Gerald's company?"

Maita nodded. "Always…well, up until…"

"Until what?"

Maita's face clouded over. "Until 'e end, 'e last night."

"What happened then?"

"He said he was in too deep, 'at he was going to make a fresh start of it."

"How?"

Maita's lips quivered. "He said he had no choice but to make a run for it, change his identity, and start over—'at is, unless someone took 'e blame for him—someone with access to the accounts."

"In other words, he wanted you to be the fall man for him"—Ruth shook her head—"or in this case, the fall *woman*."

"It's true." Tears starting in her eyes, Maita nodded. "He wanted me to cover for him, say I'd stolen 'e money."

"What? Where'd he get the nerve to ask such a thing?"

"He knew I'd do anyt'ing for him—"

"Even go to jail for him?" Ruth scowled at her. "Maita, what were you thinking?"

"Nobody ever loved me but him. He was 'e only one. I couldn't lose him, couldn't let him leave."

"He obviously didn't love you. He was just taking advantage of you, using your love and blind trust." Ruth frowned, thinking about the suspected homicide. "But if you'd already agreed to take the blame for him, why would he—"

Maita shrieked, the sound like a wounded animal.

Ruth flinched. "What!"

Intent, Maita stood rooted to the spot, glaring at Heath, his arm familiarly slung around a girl's slim shoulders. When he leaned over to nibble her ear, Maita rushed at him, clawing his exposed forearms.

He screeched in a combination of horror and rage as he gawked at the scratches. The words *Don't forget*...surfaced on his arm in angry, red welts. Then the words oozed blood like a scene from a B vampire movie.

The girl dropped her to-go cup while she backed away, slack-jawed.

Conversation ceased, and the crowd stepped back, giving him a wide berth as they watched in fascinated horror.

Heath gasped at the bleeding wound. Then searching the throng for the offender, he spotted Ruth. "You! You're connected to this, aren't you?" He charged her like a crazed bull, his eyes blazing.

Distracting him, Maita grabbed his other arm to complete her message...*your child's mother*.

"Leave me alone! Leave me alone," he cried, flailing his arms, striking at his unseen tormentor as the words rose on his flesh in stark relief.

His date escaped into the mass of people, glancing over her shoulder as she scurried away.

After shifting his gaze from her retreating figure to

his forearms, Heath glared at Ruth and then bolted, slamming into shoulders as he elbowed his way through the crowd.

Only Ruth saw Maita shadow him.

"What's going on?" asked Keya, approaching from the opposite direction.

"We were coming to get you," Auggie added, "when we heard shouting."

"You just missed your 'friend' Heath," said Ruth, describing the incident.

"We can't seem to avoid him," said Keya, "whether here or at home."

"And he can't seem to shake Maita," said Ruth.

"Is she haunting him?" At Ruth's nod, Auggie asked, "Why?"

Reluctant to start rumors, Ruth hesitated before sharing her thoughts. *But what else can it be?* "Maita was pregnant with his child."

"Why do you say that?"

"The message she wrote on his arms said not to forget his child's mother."

Keya raised her eyebrows as she glanced at Auggie. "That doesn't leave much room for misinterpretation, does it?"

He shook his head.

"I'd suggest telling Detective Bell," said Keya, "but my guess is he wouldn't believe us."

"He'd want proof," said Ruth, "and other than the short-lived welts on Heath's arms, we don't have any."

Auggie grimaced. "It's definitely something you've got to see to believe."

"*While* it's happening," added Keya, "not after the welts have faded into illegible scratches."

"Enough talk of spirits and spirit writing." Waving off Heath's dilemma, Auggie pulled three tickets from his pocket. "The Division Party dinner starts in ten minutes, and other than *high* spirits and *distilled* spirits, I say let's forget about any other spirits tonight."

Bart's shoulders slumped as the wind seemed to leave his sails.

Ruth glanced at his dejected posture and shook her head. "Bart was on a roll with his memoirs. It's important he share them so he can shed those memories, and the sooner, the better. I'm going back to the hotel."

"What?" Keya frowned. "You haven't had dinner."

"Something tells me this is a night for me to bow out early." She hugged her cousin. "Besides, it'll save time if I capture the notes directly on my laptop, rather than record them on my cellphone and transcribe them later."

Bart shot her a grateful smile.

"Why don't I take Earnestine and Diesel back to the room and get some work done while you two enjoy yourselves?"

****

Ordering dinner through room service, Ruth worked outside, documenting Bart's notes on the balcony while it was still light. After sunset, she continued recording his accounts inside, at the desk.

When the keycard clicked in the door, she glanced at the time. *Three o-clock? Already?*

Keya cracked the door and peeked inside.

"No need to tiptoe." Ruth chuckled. "I'm awake."

"Good!" Keya swung open the door for Auggie to join them. Gripping his hand, she pulled him into the room. Then, her face beaming, she turned to Ruth. "Guess what?"

Her cousin's glowing eyes and luminous smile spoke volumes, but Ruth hesitated to presume. "You have the look of love…"

Keya gave an approving nod. "Go on."

"Did Auggie—"

"We're getting married!"

"Congratulations!" Ruth stood and hugged them both. Then a thought struck. "You won't even have to change your name."

"That's right! I'll still be an Erskine." Keya glanced at Auggie. "I hadn't thought of that."

Palms uplifted, he spread his hands wide. "Just one more perk I provide."

"Let me see the ring." Ruth scanned her hands.

Auggie shook his head. "I wasn't sure about her taste in jewelry—"

"And we want to design the ring ourselves using the emerald I found yesterday," said Keya.

Bart nodded affirmatively as he took in the conversation.

"But the truth of the matter is…" Auggie's cheeks colored. "I wasn't sure if she'd have me, especially after such a whirlwind courtship."

Keya stared into his eyes. "I feel I've known you for months." She shook her head. "*Years*. It's more like we'd known each other sometime in the past, and now we've reconnected. Déjà vu."

Wearing a wistful smile, Bart looked on fondly.

"I felt the same way when I met Brett." Ruth smiled, remembering. "When's the wedding?"

Their smiles drooping, Keya and Auggie

exchanged a grimace.

"What's the problem?"

"Though we want to start our lives together as soon as possible…" Keya's words drifted off in thought.

"Yes…?"

"The hearing's Friday." Auggie slipped a supportive arm around Keya's waist. "Frankly, that's another reason I wasn't sure she'd accept my proposal."

Head angled, Ruth squinted at him. "What do you mean?"

"The name." His lips twisted in a mocking smile. "Erskine and lawsuit have become interchangeable cusswords. I'm surprised she's had anything to do with me."

Keya shook her head. "The lawsuit's the issue. I don't want to enter into marriage with that sword of Damocles hanging over our heads." Sighing, she exchanged a dejected smile with Auggie.

As the pause lengthened, the mood deteriorated.

"Hey, you've decided to marry. That's the important thing." Ruth tried for a festive tone. "Friday, at the hearing, you'll have a better idea of *when* to marry. For now, let's just enjoy the moment." She pressed the desk phone's button for room service. "Please send a bottle of champagne and three glasses to room 315—*and can you hurry?*"

Chapter 9

God's Acre

Sunday morning, Ruth woke to the sound of Keya singing offkey in the shower. Squinting, she glanced at the clock and groaned. *After getting to bed so late, last night's rest was closer to a catnap.*

Earnestine jumped on the bed. Her whiskers tickling Ruth's cheek, she meowed.

Half asleep, Ruth scratched the cat's head. "Looks like you're getting a brother soon."

Earnestine purred as she kneaded the covers.

Ruth's cellphone chimed, and she reached over to the nightstand to read Brett's text

—Should be back early afternoon. Call you when we dock. Love you.—

Then the separation hit her. *I miss him so much.* The excitement had kept her too busy to think, but now, lying here…She sighed as she mentally reviewed the week—discovering a body, seeing two spirits, being tracked by private investigators, finding an emerald—

As Keya's singing broke into her thoughts, Ruth smiled to herself. *Maybe that's why I miss Brett the most. Seeing how happy Auggie makes Keya.*

"The last service is at 10:30," said Keya, emerging from the bathroom. "Will you be ready in ten minutes?"

****

As they walked into the basilica, Ruth surveyed the delicate columns towering above. The sky-blue ceiling and high arches painted white with gold trim gave the church an ethereal feel. Despite no central air, the open doors lining both sides of the building created a cross draft, with overhead fans aiding the gentle island breeze.

Bart stood by the nearest doorway, hat in hand, poised to watch and listen, but he stayed outside the church proper.

When Ruth waved him over, he held back, shaking his head, and she stifled a sigh.

"What's wrong?" whispered Keya.

"Bart acts like he wants to come in yet won't…or can't." Ruth grimaced. "Whatever the reason, he's standing outside, looking in."

"Where?"

Ruth gestured toward the closest door. "Over there."

As the lector stepped to the lectern, she asked, "What will separate us from the love of Christ? A reading from the Letter of Saint Paul to the Romans. 'For I am certain of this—neither death nor life, nor angels, nor principalities, nothing already in existence and nothing still to come, nor any power, nor the heights nor the depths, nor any created thing whatever, will be able to come between us and the love of God.' "

When the priest began the homily, he asked, "Who remembers the Gerry Leiber/Mike Stoller song, 'Is That All There Is?' "

Half the congregation raised their hands.

Reminded of Bart, Ruth glimpsed him standing outside the door.

"Of all the fears that torment us, death is the most frightening. Nothing's certain except death and taxes, and though a smart person with a good lawyer can dodge taxes, no one escapes death. Whoever is born must die, so I ask you—*Is that all there is?* What happens when you die? Is death the end of your story? Is it the end of you?

"Saint Paul said we have nothing to fear. No matter how we die, or when, or where, no matter what our circumstances, God made us a promise that even death can't break."

Ruth glanced at Bart, leaning against the doorframe, seeming to hang on each word. Standing just outside the threshold, he strained forward, as if yearning to come inside the church, yet unable, somehow prevented from taking that first step.

"God gave us the Holy Spirit as a 'deposit,' as 'earnest money' on our future resurrection at the Last Judgement. Like buying a house, you put down a token amount that legally binds you to pay the balance later. That's what the Holy Spirit was—God's 'down payment' on our resurrection, 'money in the bank.'

"So what's your part of the bargain?" He stared out at the people. "*Believe.* Then when you die, death doesn't have the final word. God has more planned for you. In that faith—in that *confidence*—we have the courage to believe death isn't the end. Like Henry Wadsworth Longfellow said of consecrated ground—'This is the field and Acre of our God/This is the place where human harvests grow.' At resurrection, Christ will gather His 'harvest.' "

After church, as they walked back to the hotel, Keya turned toward Ruth. "What you said about Bart standing outside the church, looking in, made me think. He's dead, so why's he still here?"

Ruth opened her mouth to speak, but Keya pushed on.

"Then today's homily about death not being the end made me think." She pursed her lips. "I don't necessarily believe he's my great-something grandpa, but what if he is? Wouldn't I, at least, owe him a proper burial?"

"Good question." Ruth glanced at Bart, but before she could ask his opinion, he disappeared, and she turned back to Keya. "Why? What are you thinking?"

"I'm going to have a Mass said for him to put his soul at rest."

Ruth took a deep breath. "I think he'd like that." Then her phone chimed with a text from Brett.

—We're coming into port now. Will call when we dock. Love you.—

****

Racing ahead of Keya and Augie, Ruth sprinted the length of the pier, calling out to Brett. When he turned toward her, she did a double take at his tanned, rough-shaven face. Then she wrapped her arms around him, welcoming him back. When they finally broke apart, she whispered, "It's so good to see you, hold you, though I almost didn't recognize you with that beard."

"Good to see you, too. *Love you*," he whispered, his voice husky, as the others approached. Then he gave Keya a hug. "I hear congratulations are in order." Shaking hands with Auggie, he thumped him on the back. "How soon?"

Auggie shook his head. "Not soon enough for me—"

"Just as soon as we wrap up this lawsuit." Keya's smile faded. "Which reminds me, I'm sorry to keep your fiancée here till Friday."

Brett put his arm around Ruth's waist. "I'll miss her, but I'm glad she can help you at the hearing."

"She'll be a huge help as a character witness."

Turning toward Brett, Ruth deadpanned, "She needs me to prove she's a character."

Keya glanced at her brightly colored beach dress— gold, aqua, and violet silk threads spun together in a butterfly bodice that flowed into a graceful, ankle-length skirt. Then, she caught Auggie's eye. "That's true. I've always suffered from being such an introvert."

"*Right*." Leaning over, Auggie kissed her neck. "And I wouldn't have you any other way."

"And now that I'm back on *terra firma*"—Brett looked from face to face—"I could go for a landlubber's breakfast."

"What?" Auggie asked, tongue-in-cheek. "No seafood?"

Brett rolled his eyes in disbelief. "Never thought I'd tire of it, but after fish three times a day, every day for a week, I thought I'd OD on iodine. I'm ready for some pancakes and eggs!"

"I know just the place. Let's put your gear in my car." Auggie glanced at the luggage. "What's in this cooler?"

"Enough fish to last you three till Friday." With a wry smile, Brett shook his head. "I'm done with seafood…at least, for now, but I hope you'll enjoy it."

****

They found a table in the al fresco café's

cobblestoned courtyard. A breeze rustled through the sun-dappled palm, fig, and banana trees, while a triangular sail strung beneath their canopy created a second sunshade.

Onstage, a trio accompanied themselves on guitars and string base as gypsy chickens and six-toed cats roamed freely among the tables, lending the eatery a lively charm.

Ruth glanced at Brett and breathed deeply. Her jigsaw-puzzle self's missing piece restored, she smiled at the realization, glad to be near him. *He complements me, completes me.*

"What?" He squeezed her hand.

"It's just so good to see you, touch you. I didn't realize how much I've missed you…till now…" Stirred, she leaned into him, sneaking a kiss.

As her earrings grazed her cheek, Bart materialized, promptly breaking the mood. With an exasperated huff, she yanked them off and tossed them in her purse.

Brett gave her puzzled look. "Now what?"

"Privacy," she whispered, "or lack thereof. We have *one morning* together, just a few hours." She stifled a sigh. "I don't want to share you with anyone— or anything."

He drew her close in a side hug, their hips and shoulders brushing against each other as they sat side by side. His lips to her ear, he breathed, "Just a few more days till we're together. Then we can have all the privacy you want."

Despite their friends' presence and the jam-packed restaurant, Brett's proximity made their connection almost intimate, and she took another deep breath, grounding herself.

While they inhaled their pineapple pancakes and Eggs Benedict, Auggie and Keya hogged the conversation as they updated Brett on the week's events, apparently too infatuated to sense any strain.

Brett appeared unperturbed, listening as he wolfed down the "Rooster Special" of eggs, hash browns, sausage, and homemade banana bread. Then when he glanced at Ruth's breakfast choice, he did a double take. "Shrimp with grits?"

She smirked at his skeptical expression. "Just because *you've* eaten all the seafood you can doesn't mean I can't get my fill of Key West pink shrimp."

Auggie gave her a friendly pat on the back. "We'll make a Freshwater Conch out of her yet."

"A *what*?" Brett pulled back his head to glance at his uncle.

"A Key West newcomer," said Auggie.

Keya nodded her support. "She's showing a real knack for finding emeralds, too."

"Emeralds?" His nose wrinkling, Brett glanced from her to Ruth and back.

As Keya described their finds, Ruth showed him her green gem, handling only the tip of its plastic bag.

Brett studied it, shaking his head. "How did you ever find that?"

"Auggie arranged it."

Brett gave a low whistle as he handed back the gem. "Not bad wages for a day's work. Any more where that came from, or after all these years, has the treasure petered out?"

"Millions," said Auggie, "possibly billions of dollars' worth of treasure are still waiting to be recovered."

"Don't forget Bart's role in all this," said Ruth. "He orchestrated the find."

"What do you mean?" Brett's forehead wrinkled.

"He's responsible for us discovering the emeralds."

"Maybe you mentioned this event in one of our calls, but with the bad connections, I must've missed it. Sorry." Brett scratched at his whiskers. "How is Bart responsible?"

"Since he's linked to the *Regala's* treasure, he led us to the emeralds—or vice versa."

"Still not following," said Brett. "This Bart's a ghost, right? So how could he be linked to the *Regala* treasure?"

"For whatever reason, when he went down with the ship, his identity and memories were somehow bound up with the cargo. It's as if he's held on to his memories, waiting to share his stories before he moves on." Hunching her shoulders, Ruth held the bag by its edge, avoiding contact with the stone. "Anytime I touch something from the *Regala*, Bart appears, which is why I won't touch this stone now and why I took off the earrings earlier."

"Okay, I get his connection with the stones," said Brett, "but what's Bart got to do with you taking off your earrings?"

Ruth gave Brett a sheepish half smile. "Since they're from the *Regala*, they're also linked to him—and I didn't want Bart distracting me while you're here."

"Got it." Brett's eyes crinkled in a private smile.

As her eyes lingered a beat too long, Ruth became aware of their tablemates and glanced at her cousin.

"We also think he might be related to Keya."

"With no proof, it's a long shot." Keya's smile was skeptical.

"What about your birthmark?" asked Ruth.

Keya shrugged. "Coincidental."

"I don't believe in coincidences." Ruth shook her head. "And what about your parrot earrings?" She turned toward Brett. "They could be the same earrings Bart gave Keya's great-something grandmother on their wedding day."

"It's a romantic notion," Keya grimaced, "but nothing we can prove."

Auggie glanced at his watch and winced. "I hate to say it, but if you want to make your flight from Miami, we'd better get moving. Highway 1 backs up on Sundays."

"I still need to rent a car—"

"Nonsense," said Auggie. "I'm driving you. It'll give us time to catch up with each other."

"Rather than drive back to Key West, why don't you spend the night at my place?" Keya's smile was welcoming. "I've got an extra room, and it'd save you a couple hours on the road."

His eyes took on a faraway glaze as if glimpsing the past. "I haven't spent a night in that house since Jules and I were boys. I'd like that. It'd be like old times." His eyes connecting with hers, he gave her a warm smile. "Yet so different."

****

After they returned to Keya's house, Ruth changed clothes, and one of the earrings fell out of her pocket.

Apparently thinking the bauble was a toy, the cat batted it under the bed.

"Earnestine!" Getting down on her hands and knees, Ruth reached underneath, feeling around for the earring. When she came up emptyhanded, she got a flashlight. Earnestine had knocked the top off a plastic under-bed storage container and was crouching inside it "out of sight," her ears and eyes plainly visible over its narrow sides.

"News, cat—I see you." Groaning as she stretched her arm, Ruth could not reach the container with her fingertips. She wedged her shoulder under the low bedframe to get more leverage. Then, inching near enough to pull the container closer, she shook the container. "Earnestine, get out!"

The cat jumped out, indignantly whacking her hand with its paw.

Ruth pulled the container out from under the bed and found not just her earring, but an oil painting. "Keya!"

"What?" She stuck her head in the doorway.

"Who're these people in the painting? The woman looks like you wearing the parrot earrings and a 1930s-style floral dress."

Walking closer, Keya glanced at the picture. "Those are my grandparents' grandparents." As she lifted the portrait from the container, the painting partially fell away from the frame.

"Look at this." Ruth inspected the loose lining. "Something's behind this canvas board."

They lifted off the frame and top painting to reveal a second, older painting beneath, its oil surface crackled with age. There stood the exact likeness of Bart, wearing the same eye patch, his good eye peering out at them from 400 years in the past. Beside him was a remarkable likeness of Keya, wearing the parrot earrings and a seventeenth-century empire-waist gown. Her dark hair was long and done up in an elegant chignon, with the sides hanging in soft curls.

Keya stared at the portraits. After a few minutes, she lifted the front painting, studying it. "This was a permanent fixture in my grandmother's house. It hung in the hall for as long as I can remember. Everyone ignored the painting except to dust it, but Grandma told me she kept it for sentimental reasons. The portrait was of *her* grandparents on their wedding day."

"What about the frame?"

"Grandma said it was a family heirloom, handed down through the generations. She didn't know how many." Keya compared the back and front paintings. "The women in both portraits are wearing the same earrings."

"Your earrings," said Ruth. "Look on the paintings' backs. See if anything's written on them."

"The older one has a date." Holding it to the light, Keya read, "1622."

Ruth caught her breath. "Now do you believe Bart's your great-great-something grandfather?"

"Have to admit it's persuasive, but I'm still not convinced." Her brow creasing, Keya eyed the painting. "Can you ask Bart?"

"All right." Slipping on the silver earrings, Ruth paused as he materialized. "Is that your portrait?"

He nodded. "Luciana and I commissioned a traveling artist to do our wedding portrait." His one eye misty, he studied Keya. "I'd all but forgotten that portrait, but comparing Keya to my wife's likeness is almost like glimpsing Luciana through time."

When Ruth passed on his information, Keya gave a skeptical sniff. "Hard to believe, but I guess this proves Bart's my long-lost grandpa."

"If you had any doubt, look at his eye," said Ruth. "It's the same violet-blue shade as yours."

As Keya studied Bart's likeness, a slow smile spread across her face. "It is, isn't it?"

"I've heard of paintings being concealed behind other works," said Ruth. "But to be hidden in plain sight—forgotten by your family—how could that happen?"

Keya shrugged. "I guess one generation forgot to tell the next. Like I said, no one's given this painting a second glance in years—decades."

"Centuries…" Ruth pressed her lips together.

"I don't think my family had any hidden agenda. Time just forgot the portrait."

"Maybe they simply repurposed the frame, using the original canvas as the backing for the thinner canvas board that replaced it," said Ruth.

"Maybe, but even more than the painting." Keya gave an uncomfortable sigh. "What's hard for me to understand is how we lost the family *stories*, those fragile threads that connect the generations. Without knowing my family's legacy, without those invisible strands linking me to the past, I'll never know my identity."

"You said you'd heard rumors about your Calusa great-great-something grandmother marrying a nobleman."

Keya grimaced. "They were just fairytales, so unsubstantiated, I never believed them. Not really."

"You never had proof—till now." Ruth caught her

gaze.

"True…"

"Since I began recording Bart's tales, I've hoped he'd let go whatever's holding him here. Now maybe reading his stories will be as therapeutic for you as telling them is for him."

Keya's eyes glowed with a violet flame. "What secrets will I learn?"

Chapter 10

Bad Buoy

When Auggie returned from the airport, he suggested grilling some of Brett's catch for dinner.

"Good idea. It'd be like Brett's joining us." Ruth attempted a wry smile. "Almost."

Keya glanced at her, set down the paring knife and tomato she had been slicing, wiped her hands, and hugged her. "It's my fault you're not flying back with him."

"It's okay." Ruth forced a broader smile. "Friday will get here soon enough."

They carried the salad and sides to the patio while the fish grilled. Then after a leisurely dinner, as they sat around the table talking, a penetrating screech stopped them cold.

"What was *that*?" Keya's ears perked. "A seagull?"

They listened, straining to hear above the palm trees rustling in the ocean breeze and the persistent waves lapping against the shore.

Like a terrified woman's scream or an owl's screech, the high-pitched shriek pierced the twilight.

"I heard that sound again," said Keya. "Did it come from next door?"

"That time, I'm sure it did." Ruth shook off a sudden chill.

Sounding closer, the screeching became a loud series of shrieks and yelps.

Diesel barked as Auggie got to his feet to investigate.

Bare-chested and wearing nothing but chinos and shoes, Heath ran through the firethorn separating Gerald and Keya's properties. Skin writing covered his arms and upper body. "Make her stop! *Make her stop!*" Shadowboxing, he struck blindly at an invisible assailant.

Only Ruth saw Maita tormenting him.

"All right. *All right!*" he screamed as he kept moving, trying to escape Maita. "Call the police! *Now!*"

"I've got Detective Bell's number in my cell phone…"

"Call him! *Now!*"

As Keya dialed, Ruth spoke to Maita. "What's going on?"

Heath answered, apparently thinking the question was directed at him. "She won't leave me alone. She hasn't stopped since last night."

"Who?" asked Auggie.

His tone frustrated, Heath shouted, "*Maita!*"

Ruth recalled her chasing Heath through the crowd. "You mean, she's hounded you since then?"

"Look!" Heath spread his arms and turned around for them. Front and back, his skin was raw from layer upon layer of spirit writing. Some had faded into illegible scratches on his arms, chest, and back, but others were oozing red welts, the spirit writing still readable.

As they stared, Maita clawed his exposed chest. The word *Tell* rose on his flesh, standing in stark relief against the multi-layers of fading scratches.

His screech was a combination of fear and rage as he stared at the message. "*Make her stop! Call the police!*"

"I am," Keya snapped as she gave the dispatcher her contact information.

Sitting on Keya's lap, Earnestine hissed and arched her back at Heath, warning him away.

As if fascinated, Auggie shook his head in wonder. "This is *definitely* something you've got to see to believe."

Within minutes, Detective Bell and two uniformed officers wearing body cameras arrived on the scene.

Though Heath's latest wounds were still legible, Detective Bell asked, "What's this about?"

When Heath hesitated, Maita retraced the word *Tell* over a previous laceration.

Shrieking, he struck at his invisible assailant. To all appearances, his gyrations reopened the scratches and made them bleed.

Only Ruth saw Maita's hand write.

"All right!" Heath's chest and shoulders sagged. "I let it happen."

"Let what happen?" Detective Bell calmly took out a pen and pad.

"Let Maita drown."

Maita staggered and then slumped. "At last," she said, the words a cross between a hiss and a sigh.

"Maita Rogers?" At Heath's nod, the detective asked, "How'd she drown?"

"We were on a sailboat when the wind came up, capsizing the boat and throwing us overboard."

"Just a minute," said the detective, writing on his

scratchpad.

Heath paused as the detective took meticulous notes.

"Maybe you'd better start at the beginning," said Bell. "Whose sailboat was it? Miss Rogers'?"

Heath shook his head. "She rented the sloop from Sails Ahoy."

Pen poised midair, the detective assessed him. "The rental agent saw a man—fitting your description—carry her gear onboard and check her rigging, but the agent said he left the sloop. Can you explain that?"

Heath licked his lips.

The detective tried again. "He said you left the boat, yet you've admitted you were aboard when it capsized. How did you get onboard?"

"I swam out from the island." Heath glanced at Keya.

"What island?"

"This one." Heath pointed to the property's little key.

Keya's jaw went slack. "You were here? Trespassing?"

Heath's head dipped in a quick nod.

"You must be a strong swimmer," said the detective.

Shrugging, Heath half nodded. "Usually."

"What do you mean *usually*?"

"The wind was blowing twelve, fifteen knots that afternoon. The water was choppy, and I took longer to swim out than I'd planned. Maita came as close to shore as she could, but the water was too shallow. By the time I reached the boat, the sun was setting."

"So how did the boat capsize?"

"We sailed toward the bridge for a better view of the sunset, taking us over deeper water. On the way, we got into an ar—" He licked his lips. "—conversation and weren't paying attention to the weather. When the wind came up, Maita jibbed the boat away from it, but without warning, a rogue wave hit us broadside. She tried to turn the boat around, but it turtled."

"It *what?*" The detective looked up from his notes.

"It capsized, overturned." Heath gave an exaggerated sigh. "As the sloop keeled, Maita and I were thrown overboard."

An image of the dunk-tank clown plunging into the water swept through Ruth's mind. Picturing Maita being hurled into the sea, she shuddered.

"I searched for her as long as I could," said Heath, "but the waves were high, and it was nearly dark. I held on to the capsized hull and rode the keel toward shore, until I could swim the rest of the way."

"Why didn't you report the incident?" His gaze probing, Detective Bell watched him through skeptical eyes.

Heath's shoulders drooped. "I panicked. For the first days, I was in self-denial, hoping she'd somehow make it back. Then, when I came to grips with what happened, I…I asked the neighbors to call the police."

Maita shrieked like a crazed wildcat. She rushed at Heath, clawing his exposed chest as the word *Liar* appeared.

Diesel barked while Earnestine hissed.

To the others, Heath appeared to do a Saint Vitus dance, twisting away from and slapping at an unseen attacker.

Detective Bell shared a look of disbelief with the officers. "Are your body cams capturing this?" At their nods, he turned back to Heath. "Would you care to explain what just happened?"

"Can't you see?" His eyes darting left to right, Heath looked like a hunted animal. "She's haunting me."

His hand steady, Detective Bell jotted down a note. "Why do you say you're haunted?"

"Because…" Heath swallowed his words as he stared at his feet. "I…"

"You what?"

Shrieking like a banshee, Maita clawed his chest, reopening a previously written word—*Tell*.

Heath waved his arms in a terrorized frenzy as he struck at his invisible assailant. "*Make her stop!*" As he twisted and turned to prevent his tormentor from tracing over earlier scratches, more wounds reopened and bled. "All right. *All right!*" Taking a deep breath, he finally whispered, "I killed her."

Pen poised above his notepad, the detective stared at Heath. "How?"

Barely raising his voice, Heath looked him in the eye. "I pushed her."

The detective finished his notes before studying him. "Why'd you do it?"

"Because…" Heath chewed his lip. "She was going to tell Gerry—"

"Gerry?" The detective examined him. "Gerry who?"

"Granger."

"Gerald Granger?"

Heath nodded.

"What was she going to tell him?"

"That I'd—" Heath squirmed. "—*borrowed* against several of the hotel's accounts. For months, I'd skimmed off the top, while Maita cooked the books."

"Cooked the books…" The detective paused in his note taking. "How do you mean?"

"I overcharged customers, substituted inferior products, and then kept the difference." He shrugged. "Maita used 'funny money' to cover for me."

"So you stole the money. Why?"

"I didn't steal it! I was going to repay it!"

Earnestine hissed.

"Then why did you 'borrow' money that wasn't yours?" His eyes narrow slits, the detective searched his face.

"I…" Heath licked his lips. "I'm not sure—"

Maita rasped earlier scratches, and the word *Tell* reopened.

"Okay." Screaming, Heath jerked away his arm. "*Okay!*" He glanced at Keya and swallowed. "Treasure diving was always my hobby, but then I happened on an old wreck offshore, close to the island."

"What island? *This* island?" Auggie's ears perked. "I've never heard of any wrecks near here."

Heath gave a quick nod. "I found a trail of debris with a few coins mixed in leading from the island to a wreck's ballast."

"I don't suppose you applied for a salvager's license?" Auggie's tone was tongue-in-cheek.

"More of the wreck's buried offshore—just beyond wading distance. If I'm right—" Heath stifled a frustrated sigh. "—hotel excavation would've uncovered buried treasure."

Keya made a dubious growling sound in the back of her throat. "So *that's* why Gerald wanted this land for his hotel."

Heath shook his head. "He doesn't know about the treasure."

Keya blinked. "You're telling me this whole plot to get my property, *the lawsuit*, wasn't Gerald's idea?"

Again, Heath shook his head. "I just convinced him this was the best location to build. When you wouldn't sell—" He shrugged. "—I thought more 'cooperative' owners would."

"So you goaded my relatives into suing me." Keya slumped in her chair. "And all along, I'd blamed Gerald."

"What about the private investigators?" asked Auggie.

"They were Gerry's idea," said Heath.

Keya glanced at Ruth. "At least we know *that* piece of the puzzle."

"Speaking of puzzles…" Detective Bell gave Keya a sharp look before turning back to Heath. "You still haven't told us why Miss Rogers threatened to tell Gerald Granger."

Heath fidgeted.

Maita's chest rose and fell as she started sobbing and wringing her hands.

"Why?"

Finally, Heath looked the detective in the eye. "Maita believed me when I told her I'd pay back the money. She covered for me, kept a double set of books until I did. Then when I couldn't"—he shrugged—"*wouldn't* repay it, she threatened to tell Gerry…"

"Because…?" asked the detective.

Heath drew a deep breath. "Because the debt was exorbitant. On my commissions, I could never have repaid what I owed, but…"

"But *what*?"

"I kept getting in deeper. I kept losing yet doubling down—trying to win back my losses. I couldn't stop." He took a jagged breath. "Can't stop. It's an addiction, *I know*, but I thought, if I could just make a clean break of it, get a fake ID, and start over somewhere else, I'd be free."

Maita's chest shook with silent sobs.

"You'd be free…Who did you think would pay for your gambling debts?" When he did not answer, Ruth continued. "Since Maita juggled the numbers to buy you time, didn't it occur to you she'd be responsible for the missing funds?"

Heath stared at his shoes.

Detective Bell took up the line of questioning. "What'd you do? Try to coerce Miss Rogers into taking the blame for you?"

His jaw quivering, Heath focused on the ground.

"What went wrong with your plan? Miss Rogers wouldn't take the fall?" The detective's question was phrased a a statement. "Is that why you shoved Miss Rogers overboard and left her to drown, so she'd take the rap for you—dead or alive?"

Heath swallowed hard, his Adam's apple sliding up and down. At last, he gave a faint nod.

"Did you know she was pregnant?"

Her sobs increasing, Maita dropped to her knees.

"It was her own fault." Heath jerked his chin. "She wouldn't get an abortion. I tried to convince her. I offered to pay for it, but she refused."

"So you destroyed the evidence," said the detective. "You killed them both, making their deaths look like an accident."

His eyes red-rimmed, Heath faltered. "How'd you know she was pregnant?"

"The autopsy's reports came back."

Ruth recalled Maita's first written message—*Don't forget your child's mother*. Then she remembered Gerald's words about the auditors discovering her bookkeeping's inconsistencies. "Gee, I wonder who told the auditors about the second set of books? You wouldn't have any idea, would you…?"

Sullen, silent, Heath's lip curled in a sneer.

"Cuff him." The detective turned to the officers. "Take him to the hospital for his lacerations. Then book him."

After the officers read Heath his rights and escorted him out, Keya asked, "What about Maita? Will she have a funeral?"

The detective shrugged. "No one's claimed the body."

"Didn't she have a cousin?"

"According to her HR information, the nearest relative was in Saint Augustine, but that person has moved, disconnected the phone, and left no forwarding address."

"What'll happen if no one steps forward?" A deep V appeared between Keya's eyes.

He shrugged. "Social Services will have her body cremated and buried."

"By 'no one,' " Keya's eyes misting, she blinked. "Do you mean *anyone* could claim her body?"

"If no relatives are found, that's right." He nodded.

"Even me?"

The detective eyed her suspiciously. "Why would you want to claim Miss Rogers' body?"

Shrugging, Keya glanced at Ruth. "I'm having a funeral Mass said this week for…a relative. Why not have one said for them both?"

"You'd be willing to take on the costs of her cremation and interment?"

Keya nodded.

"For a stranger?" His eyes doubtful, he appraised her. "You said you'd never met her."

"I hadn't…*exactly*"—Keya glanced at Ruth—"but discovering her body, finding her *here* on my property, makes me feel responsible somehow." Then her eyes seemed to peer into the distance. "I want to do the right thing for the memory of someone I never had the chance to know."

Maita's sobbing subsided as she rose and stood beside Keya.

The detective nodded. "We'll have to ensure the bloodwork and tissue-sample results are all back from the labs." He shrugged. "Then if no relatives come forward, I'll have the station contact you about the paperwork and burial."

Keya swallowed. "Thank you."

After he left, Maita said in hushed tones, "I know how you can get in touch wi' my cousin Lil."

Ruth looked at her. "Do you have a phone number?"

Maita shook her head. "But her mot'er's name is Bela Naus, and she lives in Saint Augustine."

Ruth passed on the information to Keya.

"How do you spell the last name?" Taking out her

phone, Keya ran a search. "Maybe we can call her." But after a few minutes, she said, "No name listed under that spelling. Do you know the address?"

After Ruth translated, Maita said, "She lives on La Porte Court, but I forget 'e house number."

Keya ran another search but came up empty. "Nothing."

"I..." Maita faltered before looking at Ruth with eager eyes. "I know how to find 'e house even 'ough I don't remember its street number."

When Ruth relayed the information, Keya checked her phone's app. "Saint Augustine's over four hundred miles away."

Auggie grimaced. "Depending on traffic, one-way is a six-to-seven-hour drive."

Ruth glanced at Maita's woebegone expression. "Is finding your relatives that important to you?"

"It would mean a lot if my cousin Lil'"—she swallowed—"if *someone* from my family was 'ere."

"Were you close to your cousin?"

"We were as kids, but as we got older, we just sent birt'day and Christmas cards. 'en just Christmas cards. 'en..." As her words died off, her eyes bunched together. "I always liked her, even after we lost touch." She attempted a shy smile. "In fact, I named her as my beneficiary."

"You mean for your life insurance?" At her nod, Ruth passed on the information.

Auggie asked, "Would the policy have had a more current address listed for her?"

Maita shook her head. "It was 'e same address for my nearest-of-kin contact and insurance." Her eyes lit up hopefully. "But I could show you 'e way to my aunt's house. I remember how to get 'ere."

After Ruth shared the information, Keya glanced at Auggie. "If we left in the morning and stayed overnight, we'd be back by Tuesday afternoon."

Auggie shook his head. "Sorry, I can't join you. I have to finish a painting project, but why don't you two go?"

****

After breakfast, Ruth and Keya stopped by the police station to sign the initial paperwork for Maita's body. Then they took the Ronald Reagan Turnpike to I-95, arriving in Saint Augustine's western suburbs in the early afternoon.

Maita guided them through the neighborhoods to the Shady Whispers trailer park, where she pointed out a rundown home. "This is it." Laundry hung from its improvised trellis fence, and a satellite dish crowded the lot's gravel front.

They parked and climbed the warped planks that passed as steps. When the doorbell did not work, they knocked.

A disheveled woman in a housecoat cracked the skewed aluminum door. "What do you want?"

"That's my cousin Lil," said Maita.

Unsure where to begin, Ruth swallowed. "By any chance, are you related to Maita Rogers?"

"Who wants to know?" growled the woman.

Uneasy, Ruth gave a nervous laugh. "Sorry, my name's Ruth Bernard, and this is my cousin Keya Erskine."

The woman's eyes narrowed. "What do you want?"

As Ruth suppressed an annoyed sigh, Keya took

over. "We're trying to locate Maita Rogers' cousin. Are—?"

"About what?"

Keya took a deep breath and tried again. "About Maita Rogers. Are you her cousin?"

"You with Social Services?"

"No, we—"

"The police?"

Keya gave a frustrated sigh. "No, we're try—"

"You bill collectors?"

"No!" Keya bit her lip. "Are you her cousin Lil Naus or not?"

Scowling, the woman eyed them. "Yeah. Now what do you want?"

Ruth considered turning around and walking away. Then remembering the reason for their visit, she forced a sympathetic smile. *She probably hasn't heard.* "There's been an accident."

"Car wreck?" asked Lil.

"No," said Ruth, "she was in a boating accident, and—"

"She laid up in a hospital?"

Pressing her lips together and stifling another irritated sigh, Ruth shook her head. "Maita's in the morgue. The police tried to contact her closest relative, but—"

"So why are you telling me?" Squinting, she glared at them. "How's her death any of your business?"

Keya crossed her fingers. "We were neighbors…friends."

Maita gave her a grateful smile.

Lil smirked. "And now you're looking for someone to foot the bill for her funeral."

"No, we—"

"Why should we get stiffed with the tab? *Stiffed.*" Cackling at her joke, she glanced at the person on the couch. Then any trace of a smile gone, she turned back to Ruth. "We don't owe her nothing." Lil shrugged. "Let the county take care of it."

"She's your cousin, isn't she?"

Lil wrinkled her nose. "We weren't that close."

"Wait!" A couch squeaked in protest as a woman hoisted herself up. "Didn't she have an insurance policy made out to you?"

"Did she?" Lil's eyes took on a cold glitter. "Does she?"

"Oh! You mean use that fund for her burial." Ruth shook her head. "You don't—"

"No…" Cigarette in hand, an older woman shuffled into the room.

"She's my aunt Bela," said Maita.

"Lil's her beneficiary," said Bela. "She'll need the death certificate for the policy."

Incredulous as she caught on, Ruth stared at her. "You mean collect her insurance, but leave her burial to the county?"

Sneering, Lil said, "Thanks for the tip," and slammed the door in Ruth's face, forcing her to step back.

"Now, *just a minute!*" Keya hammered on the door. "We drove all the way from Marathon to talk to you."

"Never mind." Her shoulders sagging, Maita shook her head. "Tell Keya to stop."

When Ruth translated, Keya scowled. "Why?"

"'ey're not worth it." Maita's long face morphed

into a smile. "You've treated me more like family"—
she nodded toward the trailer—"'an my own family. If
you two come to my funeral, it'd be enough."

As Ruth repeated her words for Keya's benefit,
Bart appeared. "What about me?"

Maita ventured a shy smile. "I'd like that."

"Where have you been?" Ruth studied him.

He shrugged.

"Where to now?" asked Keya. "I don't feel like
turning around and driving another seven hours. Since
we're here, what do you want to see?"

"I've never been in Saint Augustine." Ruth
squinted, thinking. "Isn't Ponce de Leon's Fountain of
Youth here somewhere?"

Keya nodded. "It sure is."

A half hour later, they arrived at the Fountain of
Youth Archaeological Park. After exploring, Ruth and
Keya purchased souvenir bottles of its spring water.

Ruth took a sip and turned to Keya. "Do I look any
younger?"

"It's taken off at least ten years," she deadpanned.

"If I was four hundred years younger—" Bart wore
a rascally grin "—I'd cast an eye in your direction."

Laughing to herself, Ruth turned toward Maita and
did a double take at her hunched shoulders and pained
expression. "What's wrong?"

"I lived twenty-four years. My baby lived 'ree
mont's…inside me. Neit'er of us had 'e *luxury* of
aging."

Sobered, Ruth passed the news to Keya, then
turned back to Maita. "How can we help?"

She brought a shaky hand to her forehead. "Could
we go to 'e Mission of *Nombre de Dios?*"

"Why?" asked Ruth. "What's there?"

"'e Shrine of Our Lady of *La Leche*, Our Lady of 'e Milk. It's a pilgrimage for childless couples and wannabe mot'ers. It's where I prayed for"—Maita glanced at Bart, blushed, and looked away—"for special intentions. T'ings didn't work out like I'd hoped, but I'd like to pray 'ere again for my baby since…" She ducked her head as her voice faltered.

"Of course," said Keya after Ruth translated. "The shrine isn't far from here."

Her head still lowered, Maita peeked, shyly lifting her eyes to them. "I'd also like to pray for He'."

"Heath!" Ruth scowled at her. "After he shoved you overboard and left you to drown?" She scoffed. "Why?"

"At first, I enjoyed tormenting him—persecuting him. I hated him for using me and killing our baby, but now…" Maita's eyes glistened. "Now I know 'ere's more to life 'an *life*."

"More to life than life…" Tilting her head, Ruth struggled to understand. "What do you mean?"

"After I drowned, I couldn't move on because I wanted justice, *payback!*" Her agitation returning, Maita took a deep breath.

When she exhaled, her distress seemed to fall away in sheets. As if an electromagnet had been turned off and lost its current, her negativity's "metal filings" seemed to slip off, no longer magnetized.

The atmosphere lightened, lifted.

Did Maita's hatred attract the darkness? Ruth studied her. "Now how do you feel?"

"Now I understand life is temporary." When Maita looked at Ruth, she seemed to shimmer in the sunlight.

"My body may have died—who I t'ought I was died—but 'e *real me* lasts forever."

"I'll second that," said Bart.

Maita flinched.

"Sorry, I couldn't help overhearing." He grimaced. "Life's short, and everyone dies. Death doesn't need faith. It just happens, but what I hadn't expected—what I wasn't prepared for—is the endlessness of my soul."

"What do you mean?" Ruth examined him.

"When I was alive, I thought the only way I'd 'live on' was through my children's children. Deep down, I didn't believe my soul would exist beyond my last breath, but I've learned, whether you believe it or not, the soul's eternal." Spreading his arms, he looked at his form and gave a mirthless laugh. "I'm 'living' proof."

Maita nodded. "I'd t'ought, after I got revenge and forced He's confession, I could move on…" Her words drifting off, she stared at nothing, seeming deep in thought.

As the pause lengthened, Ruth prompted her. "And now?"

Maita jumped. "Now I realize 'at, not only does my soul persist…but life is fragile. All life is precious—even He's. No matter how much pain he's caused me, I must forgive him. Not just say 'e words or go 'rough 'e motions, I have to forgive him before I can move on."

Ruth stared at her. *At first, Maita seemed wrapped in a shroud of misery—always sobbing and crying. Now she's glowing.* "What's changed?"

Maita's radiant face burst into a smile. "I'm learning what makes me happy. Getting revenge didn't. Getting even didn't." The smile dimmed, became wistful. "Everyt'ing's allowed in our culture, but not'ing's forgiven or forgotten. Forgiveness seems to be 'e key."

Key. Her ears perking, Ruth latched onto the word. "Key to what?"

"Peace of mind," said Maita. "As I forgive He', my resentment fades, and I can let go."

Ruth studied her. "Of what?"

"Everyt'ing." Maita shrugged as she glanced about them. "Whatever's keeping me here and holding me back. It's loosening its grip, just as I'm losing my grip on it."

****

They parked near the Mission *Nombre de Dios* shrine, then strolled beneath a canopy of ancient cedars and live oaks dripping with Spanish moss.

"'is place is called 'America's Most Sacred Acre,' " said Maita. "Hallowed ground for almost five centuries."

When Ruth glimpsed the ivy-covered chapel, a sense of reverence gripped her. "I see why." She looked at a statue of St. Peter above the Spanish-styled chapel's entrance. The figure held the keys of the kingdom of heaven.

Keys—that word again. She paused, reflecting. *Keys of the kingdom, Florida Keys, offkey, low key, keyed up, Keya, key to your heart, skeleton key…*the *key.*

As they walked inside the sanctuary, Ruth absorbed its peaceful atmosphere. The furnishings were stark, minimal—sturdy oak pews and stools. The only adornments on the coquina walls were the stations of the cross. In a niche behind the altar, golden light bathed the two-foot-tall wooden statue of Mary holding

Jesus.

"Our Lady of La Leche," said Maita, wearing a serene smile. "Some say Crusaders found her in a fourt'-century grotto in Bet'lehem, brought her to Spain, and 'en explorers brought her here."

"Why are you so devoted?"

"People have asked for her intercession since 'e sixteenth century." Maita's dewy eyes swept the chapel. "Heaven knows how many children were conceived here in prayer. Doctors told my mot'er she'd never have children—but here I am!"

Ruth studied her. "Your mother asked for Our Lady's intercession for a baby?"

Maita nodded. "A lot of infertile couples conceive after praying here."

As Ruth retold the story to Keya, Maita stepped closer to the altar, crossed herself, and began to pray.

Bart observed her a moment. Then he removed his plumed, wide-brimmed hat and stood quietly beside her, his head bowed as if in prayer.

Ruth blinked. *Bart's inside the chapel. Whatever kept him outside must have released its hold.* Moved by his change as much as Maita's devotion, Ruth genuflected, knelt at a pew behind them, and prayed God would answer their prayers.

Both had missions to complete before moving on. *Maita needs to forgive Heath and let go her resentment. Bart needs to release the memories tying him here.* She groaned inwardly. *And I've only got a few days to finish recording his stories.*

As Ruth looked about the chapel, her gaze rested on Keya. *Friday, the Probate Court will decide the fate of her property—a sea-turtle refuge or a five-star hotel.*

Dan Miller's motto came to mind. *Carp a D. M., but will she seize the day?*

****

The next morning on the drive back to Marathon, Keya gave a loud gasp.

"What's wrong?" Ruth spun her head.

Keya glanced at the clock before turning toward Ruth, her eyes startled and panicked. "With all that's happened, I almost forgot. Today's my day to volunteer at the Turtle Refuge. I don't have time to drop you off. Would you mind coming along?"

"No, not at all." Ruth took a deep breath, grounding herself. "I'm just relieved you're all right." Then she recalled the brochure's loose ends she needed to tie up. "Besides, it'll give me a chance to take more pictures, maybe get a few more interviews to use as blurbs on the cover"—she smiled—"*and* see you in action."

When they arrived at the refuge, the veterinarian and her assistant were inside the operating room, prepping the first sea turtle.

"Hope I'm not late," said Keya from the glass viewing area, her turtle-coin necklace reflecting the overhead lights.

How appropriate. Ruth smiled.

"You're fine," said the veterinarian, her words muffled behind her surgical mask, but her eyes crinkling in a smile. "I'm just glad you're here."

Keya made introductions through the viewing window. "Vera, I'd like you to meet my cousin Ruth. Ruth, Vera." Then she gestured toward the green turtle. "What's the story on this one?"

"FP." Vera pointed to the growths covering the sea

turtle's flippers and face.

"What's FP?" asked Ruth.

"It's Fibropapillomatosis, a virus that causes these tumors," said Vera.

"Can they be removed?"

Vera nodded. "Most tumors are superficial, easily removed with lasers. The good news is they can't grow back, making the turtle immune to the virus."

Ruth squinted. "Then what's the problem?"

"Space, for one thing. Turtles take a year to recuperate."

"Which requires funding," added Keya.

Vera nodded. "Plus, FP can invade a turtle's internal system, making surgery risky. Since a turtle's heart beats only 20 times per hour, procedures are limited to an hour, max. *Time is critical.*"

Vera glanced at Keya as she lifted the turtle's flipper. "X-rays and an endoscopy didn't indicate anything internally, but before we anesthetize this turtle, I'd hoped you could communicate with it, *make sure* nothing's going on inside."

Ruth met Keya's gaze, realizing the importance of her cousin's gift.

"Of course." Keya turned her attention to the turtle. Homing in on it, she stared into its eyes as she took deep breaths, seeming to center herself. After several minutes, Keya frowned, as if straining to understand. "I'm getting an image of something flowing…swimming through the system. I'm sensing something in the bloodstream."

Vera turned to the assistant. "Run a blood sample." Then after taking off her surgical mask and rubber gloves, she joined them outside the operating room.

A few minutes later, the assistant returned with the results.

Vera read to herself until she came to one word. Grunting, she mumbled, "Spirorchiid."

"What's that?" asked Keya.

Vera looked up from the paperwork. "You were right about something in the circulatory system. This turtle has blood flukes."

"Can it be treated?" As Ruth swept back her hair, her hand grazed an earring, and Maita appeared, listening intently.

Vera nodded. "Drugs will kill the parasites, but if they'd gone undetected, they could've grown large enough to block an aorta and caused cardiac arrest."

Keya took a deep breath. "I'm just glad the turtle's imagery was clear."

Ruth glanced at her. "What do you mean?"

"Though not verbally, the turtle 'told' me what was wrong through mental pictures," said Keya. "When I communicate with animals, they 'talk' to me through images, visual impressions."

"How does she do 'at?" asked Maita, shaking her head. Ruth repeated her question.

"I start by quieting my mind." Keya shrugged. "Then I send a mental picture of the animal's body and ask what I can do to help. It's part empathy, part intuition, and part telepathy."

"It's a gift," whispered Maita.

"However you characterize it," said Vera, "your ability to communicate helps a lot of turtles."

"Just be careful of telling people I 'talk' to animals." Keya gave a dry laugh. "Friday, a Probate Court will decide whether I'm mentally competent enough to leave the property to the Turtle Refuge."

Her expression blank, Vera asked in an uncertain tone, "Isn't that what you intend to do?"

"Yes," said Keya, "but they're trying to prove I want to leave the land *directly to the turtles,* not to any organization. They want to demonstrate I'm so irrational, I've lost touch with reality."

Vera gave a disgusted groan. "That's utter nonsense!"

Maita tugged at Ruth's sleeve. "Ask her to be a character witness."

Nodding, Ruth turned toward her cousin. "What if Vera testifies in court Friday? Her credibility might help prove you're not leaving the land to the turtles, but to the nonprofit Turtle Refuge?"

"I'd be happy to help," said the veterinarian.

"Thank you, Vera." Arms outstretched, Keya took a step toward her, then stopping abruptly, gave her a warm smile. "I'd hug you if you weren't dressed for surgery. Instead, how 'bout I call my attorney to make the arrangements?"

Chapter 11

Voice of the Turtle

Auggie and Diesel arrived at Keya's house late that afternoon. "I had a brainstorm." Wearing a mysterious smile, he turned to Ruth. "Would you mind babysitting?"

She shook her head. "Not at all. In fact, this will give me time to transcribe Bart's tales. I want to finish them before I leave."

"Thanks." Then, grabbing Keya's hand, he asked, "Ready?"

"Sure, just let me fix my—"

"You look great." He glanced at the clock. "Besides, if we're not there in fifteen minutes, he'll close shop."

Flinching, Keya squinted. "What shop?"

"You'll see." Putting his arm around Keya's waist, he hustled her out the door as he waved to Ruth. "Back in a couple hours."

Ruth turned toward Earnestine and Diesel. "What's he up to?"

Diesel woofed at the door, apparently piqued at being left behind, as Earnestine groomed herself with cool indifference.

Chuckling at their different temperaments, Ruth got out her laptop. "How about we work on the patio?"

Ten minutes later, Earnestine was dozing on the outdoor table while Diesel lay at Ruth's feet.

Ready for the interview, she touched an earring, and both Bart and Maita appeared. "Maita, I'd like to finish transcribing Bart's stories. Would you mind giving us some privacy?"

Instead of sulking, Maita glanced toward the island. "All right. I have a few t'ings to t'ink over, anyway." With a nod, she disappeared.

Bart pushed back his plumed hat and rubbed his hands together. "Are you ready, my dear?"

Ruth blinked at his appearance. "Bart, you're not wearing your eyepatch."

"Oh, this." Smiling, he put his hand to his face. "I meant to tell you, but since you've already noticed—"

"Noticed? It's as plain as the…eyes…on your face." Intrigued, she stared at his violet-blue eyes. "You and Keya have a remarkable family resemblance—but I couldn't see your eyes until you removed your hat. What happened to your eye patch?"

"Yesterday was the first time I've prayed in centuries…" He gave a surprised laugh. "I sensed a warmth in my blind eye while we were in the chapel, then later, a trembling. When I took off my patch…it was as if scales fell away, and I could see."

Ruth shook her head. "It's amazing."

"It *is* amazing, but more so than you might think." He paused as if choosing his words. "I see—not just what's around me—but what's *ahead* of me."

"And what's that?"

He started to speak and then paused. "I need to finish what we've started. I've wasted enough time these past 400 years. Now I want to…" Wearing a look of astonishment, he stopped mid-sentence.

"What? Is anything wrong?"

Blinking, he slowly shook his head.

"What were you going to say?"

"I almost said I want to finish"—he swallowed—"*move on…*"

"That's wonderful!" Ruth smiled until his brow puckered. "Isn't it?"

"I don't know." He spoke in a monotone, and his shoulders slumped as if he was exhausted. "This is the first time I've thought of moving on—"

"Bart…" Pursing her lips, she stifled a sigh. "We've discussed this several times."

He shook his head. "You misunderstand, my dear. This is the first time *I've* thought of moving on. It's the first time I've believed I *could* move on. After 400 years of just existing, I'd thought that's all there was…is…"

"What's changed?"

"Pouring out my heart has freed my mind. Maybe it's helped free my soul." He gave her a faint smile. "I'm not as attached to my memories anymore."

"How so?"

"They're fading. I barely recall the earliest stories."

"Since your memoirs are recorded for posterity, maybe you don't need to cling to your memories, anymore. That's what the written word's for—chronicling."

"Maybe." Then he took a deep breath and exhaled. Slumping as his shoulders relaxed and his arms fell to his sides, he seemed to loosen his grip on the past. "What a liberating thought."

"I'm glad." Ruth smiled. "Think we can finish this

afternoon, while everyone's gone?"

****

Five hours later, Auggie and Keya returned, beaming ear-to-ear.

"Don't you look like the cats that swallowed the canaries." Ruth pulled back her head to better observe them. "What's up?"

Keya held out her left hand. On her ring finger, she wore the rough Muzo emerald in a freeform setting.

"It's gorgeous! I've never seen anything like it."

"That's because it's one of a kind," said Auggie.

His voice tinged with pride, Auggie stared at Keya, not the setting.

"Auggie's goldsmith friend helped us design it." Keya swiveled her hand to better show off the mounting. "See how he made the prongs look like strands of seaweed?"

"The setting goes perfectly with the raw stone—very natural looking. I commend you on your choice." Ruth glanced at Auggie. "And I don't mean just the ring."

Keya's gaze followed hers. "I call Auggie my diamond in the rough, so wearing a raw emerald for a wedding ring makes sense."

"Wedding?" Ruth's head spun as she looked from one to the other. "Did you two get—?"

"Nope"—Keya took Auggie's hand in hers—"but we did complete our marriage preparation course and get our marriage license." She took a deep breath. "No matter what happens Friday, we want to be together."

"So when's the big day?"

Auggie and Keya glanced at each other and then turned toward her, shrugging.

"We haven't decided, but soon," said Auggie.

"Soon?" Ruth tried to read their body language. "While I'm still—"

"Ru'! *Ru'!*" Her face shining with wonder, almost as if she'd had a religious awakening, Maita suddenly appeared. "Quick! Come see! 'e turtles are hatching!"

Ruth relayed the information, and they raced to the island.

As the hatchlings used their tiny flippers to dig their way out, they emerged from the sand and propelled themselves across the beach.

Keya sighed. "Look at all those little loggerheads."

"I'm glad we're here for this," said Auggie.

"Me, too." Ruth shook her head in wonder as the turtles continued to erupt from the sand like a terrapin volcano. "How many are in there?"

"I've read each nest contains one hundred to one hundred twenty-six eggs," said Maita.

"Wow." After Ruth relayed the message, she watched the surfacing turtles race to the sea. "Just look at them go."

Wearing a carefree smile, Maita giggled.

Like the baby turtles, Maita also seems to be "digging out" and "coming out of her shell."

Keya seemed captivated with the last loggerhead to surface. She stared as if connecting with its thoughts. Finally, the turtle broke eye contact, and turning, rushed toward the water.

"Were you talking to that hatchling?" asked Ruth.

Keya nodded. "When I asked if she was the last one, the image she gave me was of shiny turtles that don't move."

Her head tilted, Ruth pushed her hair from her

eyes. "What does 'shiny turtles that don't move' mean?"

Auggie stared at the nest's churned up sand. Then his face brightened as if he had the answer. "Coins?"

"Do you think so?" Ruth followed his gaze.

Reflecting the afternoon sun, something round and shiny lay in the loose sand. The three stepped slowly toward the nest, careful not to tread on any late-hatching turtles.

Keya picked up the coin and handed it to Auggie.

Two latecomers emerged, bringing up another coin as they climbed their way out.

Auggie pulled the second coin from the sand. "These are Spanish copper coins." After buffing them against his jeans, he studied them. "Minted in 1641, like the others we found near here." His eyes glistening, he unsuccessfully attempted to hide his smile. "This must be what you call a nest egg."

"Nest egg, huh?" Keya shook her head as she groaned.

Dropping the coins in her hand, he glanced at the churned-up sand. "Why don't you two keep watch, see if any more hatch, while I get the metal detector and a shovel." Woofing, Diesel followed him as he started back to his car.

After several minutes, another turtle emerged. Again, Keya stared as if mentally connecting with the turtle before it turned and rushed toward the sea.

"What did that hatchling have to say?" asked Ruth.

"Except for more 'shiny turtles that don't move,' she was the last one out. Looks like the nest's empty." With that, Keya knelt and gently sifted through the soft, damp sand with her hands.

With a smile and a parting wave, Maita disappeared.

Ruth joined Keya, and together they dug down over a foot, finding more coins the deeper they dug. By the time Auggie and Diesel got back, they had a small pile.

Handing Keya the metal detector and sifter, he picked up his shovel. "Here, let me dig while you two filter."

His first shovelful brought up a dozen or more coins. He continued finding more and more treasure to a depth of three feet, but the deeper he dug after that, the smaller the return. He tried widening the search, digging several feet down in each direction until he found more scattered coins.

"We need to put these in something. Their weight's pressing them back into the sand," said Keya. "I'll run back to the house for a box while you keep digging."

As she sifted, Ruth studied the layout. "Look at the pattern. I think the coins are leading us toward that sandbank."

Nodding, he continued to dig toward the hill, where they found larger caches of coins.

Then just as Keya returned with the box, Auggie's shovel hit something. He glanced at her without speaking and began shoveling away the sand, creating a broader cavity. Time and again, his shovel thumped against something solid, but as he shoveled, the sand kept reclaiming it, obscuring it.

Finally, a wooden platform appeared. Built at a sloping angle, it was part floor and part door.

After jumping into the shallow pit, Ruth brushed away the sand with her hands to reveal a boarded-up trapdoor in the side of the dune.

"The wood's rotting." Auggie pounded a decayed board with the shovel. Within minutes, he broke through, allowing him to grip the other boards and pry them away, one by one.

A musty stench escaped the crypt—the stale, fetid odor of decaying wood and four-hundred-year-old mold.

Then just as the sun's last rays shone into the grotto, its contents lit up like a golden sunset.

"I'll be darned." He dropped his shovel and squeezed into the space. "Doubloons."

"How many?" asked Keya. "A dozen?"

He snickered. "More like several dozen, thirty, forty scattered about…maybe more." His steps resounded as he moved around the space. "We'll need a flashlight, but I see what looks like a rotted wooden chest full of coins." Climbing out with a handful, he showed them. "Maybe the family stories were right. They always said Aunt Libby had a stash. Was this it?"

"What do you mean 'had a stash'?" Keya studied him.

"No hard evidence, but family gossip claimed Aunt Libby built the house with money from buried treasure. According to rumor, she paid for the labor and building materials with antique coins. Like I'd said, until the mid-eighties, she'd lived on a pension in a two-bedroom bungalow. Then with no apparent change of finances, she built the house you now own."

Lounging on a warm rock, Earnestine lifted her head and seemed to call—*meow*.

Keya perked her ears, concentrated, and then translated. "The images Earnestine's sending me show a vintage coin pressed into the house's foundation."

"Really?" Auggie's tone and raised brow were skeptical.

Again, the cat meowed and started back down the path.

"She wants us to follow," said Keya.

Auggie snickered good-naturedly. "It's getting dark, anyway. Why don't you two head back while it's still twilight? I'll join you after I take what I can carry and cover up the rest till morning. We don't want anyone 'happening' on the cache tonight."

Nodding, Keya and Ruth followed Earnestine to the house. She led them to the purple-flowered shrubbery that screened the house's foundation.

Keya looked at the bushes. "What were you doing behind the blue porterweed? Chasing mice?"

Meowing, Earnestine ducked beneath the leafy bushes.

The two got on their hands and knees and crawled behind the cat until Earnestine rubbed against something mortared into the foundation.

As Ruth brushed away the accumulated leaf litter, an embedded colonial-era copper coin gleamed faintly against the gray mortar. "This looks like the first coins we found." She laughed at the irony. "And it reminds me of Hemingway's last cent."

Keya turned toward her cat. "Why didn't you tell us about this sooner?"

Earnestine yawned and stretched nonchalantly.

"She obviously didn't think the find was important." Keya pursed her lips as she shook her head.

Ruth studied the coin. "Though it looks like the others, I can't be sure of the mint date without a flashlight. We should look again in the morning light."

After they had crawled out and brushed themselves off, Keya glanced at the house. "Do you think Auggie's aunt built this place with her 'stash'?"

Ruth shrugged. "If she'd led a modest lifestyle, then out of the blue built this place, a windfall could explain it."

"I've read stories about hermits in the Keys paying for their groceries with gold coins. Until now, that's all I'd thought they were." Keya shrugged. "Stories."

"Where there's smoke…" Ruth let her half smile finish the adage.

The box of coins in his hands, Auggie and Diesel met them at the patio door. "It's too dark to see these outside," he said. "Where's the brightest place to study them?"

"The kitchen island." Keya led them in, set the alarm, flipped another switch for the smart windows to darken, and then turned on the lights. "Can't be too careful." She gave them a cynical sneer.

Ruth grimaced. "I wonder how much Heath knew—"

"And Gerald," added Auggie.

Ruth nodded. "No matter what he told the police, it's still hazy who masterminded the Erskines' lawsuits against Keya and why they want this land."

"And how much they knew about the treasure," said Auggie.

"The cache we found didn't look as if anyone had discovered it," said Keya.

"No"—Auggie shook his head—"but it might have been one of several hideaways."

"That's true," said Ruth. "Heath confessed to

finding coins near shore."

"And the more I think about the family rumors of Aunt Libby finding buried treasure, the more I'm starting to believe them." Auggie's smile was twisted. "Was this treasure what split the family?"

"Who knows?" Ruth thought of similar family squabbles. "Lesser reasons drive people apart. Sometimes, all it takes is a small wedge."

Spreading out the coins on the kitchen's island, Auggie gave a low whistle. "These are in almost pristine condition."

"Do you think the wood chest protected them?" asked Ruth.

Auggie nodded. "It saved them from being worn down or scratched by sand, at least until the chest rotted, and this was *buried* treasure as opposed to deep-sea treasure."

Keya glanced at him. "Other than the obvious— found on land instead of underwater—what's the difference?"

"Water's corrosive. Besides the ebb and flow of the tides scouring the coins against the sand, the water's acidity damages them. Warm water speeds oxidation, and submerged coins are often covered with lime deposits, coral, or barnacles."

"What about buried treasure?" asked Keya.

"Coins hidden on land aren't subjected to that." Auggie's eyes glinted. "I'm no numismatist, but I'd bet these coins are worth a pretty penny on the market."

Keya's enthusiasm faded. "Are they legal?"

"Yup, since you dug on your land, it's all legit."

"Just don't forget to report the income on your taxes," Ruth wisecracked.

"Or the twenty percent the U.S. District Court in South Florida takes," added Auggie.

****

After Ruth retired to her room, she called Brett about the latest adventures. "Though Florida's proving quite an experience, *I miss you.*" She sighed, remembering the feel of his arms around her, and she regretted her decision to stay longer. "Other than brunch Sunday, I haven't seen you in over a week."

"I miss you, too." His smile came through his voice. "But it won't be long now—just three more days."

"The time can't go fast enough. Love you." Despite wanting the time to pass, she considered the downside. *I can't leave without finishing Bart's memoirs.* As she hung up, she touched her earrings.

Bart appeared—sort of.

"Bart?" She studied him, unsure. "Is that you?" She stared at his form, no longer solid, but semitransparent.

The feather of his translucent hat bobbing as he nodded, he spoke in a thin, reedy voice. "In a manner of speaking."

Thinking his sheerness might be an optical illusion or a play of light, she stood and walked around him, but he looked the same from all angles. Filmy. Hazy. "What's going on?"

"I'm not sure, my dear." He looked at his nearly transparent form. "This fading started soon after we finished our transcription. I seem to be…disappearing."

"Does it…?" She caught herself. *Of course, it doesn't hurt. He's dead.* Instead, she asked, "Do you have any feeling, any sensation?"

He shook his head. "No."

"Has this ever happened before?"

He shook his head.

"Why's it happening now?"

Shaking his head, he shrugged.

"What?" She smiled. "The cat's got your tongue?"

His voice hoarse, he shook his head. "It's difficult to 'speak.' "

"Bart, did you finish telling me your stories this afternoon?"

He half shrugged. "Not exactly," he whispered in a reedy voice.

Ruth frowned as she tried to interpret. She did not want to force his speech, but she needed more information. "Sorry, I'm not following."

"Review," he whispered. "I want to review."

"Oh." She brought out her laptop. "You want to go over your memoirs one more time to make sure you've left nothing out, is that it?"

Wearing a wan smile, he nodded. "Yes, m'dear." His voice sounded weak. His robust physique had shriveled into an old man's wizened body.

Bart's a frail shell of himself. Empathizing with him, she asked, "How 'bout I read your notes to you? If they're right, nod your head. If they're not, whisper your edits, okay?"

He gave a faint nod.

Starting from the beginning, she read aloud.

Every so often, Bart held up his finger, signaling her to reread a section. Then he either nodded or motioned her to bend her ear toward him, and he whispered his changes.

They worked until morning, editing and adding

anecdotes or details Bart had originally overlooked.

As Ruth read through his accounts, his memories more than came to life. They took on a life of their own, and she visualized a book.

The guide's words at Earnest Hemingway's house came to mind. "He reported...The only things he fictionalized were the names of actual people." And she recalled her response. *If I'd ever find a story—a true story—to write about...*

She gazed at the shrunken wisp before her. "Bart, I don't want to exploit our friendship. Are you sure you don't mind if I craft your memoirs into a novel?"

He motioned for her to bend her head closer. "As long as my daughter reads my words, exactly as I've told them"—he pointed at the laptop—"write what you will."

"Thank you." Grateful for his gift, she wanted to interact with him—shake his hand or hug him—but physical contact was impossible. Besides being bodiless, he had become so sheer, he was almost transparent, like breath on a chilly day. *No, more like smoke backlit by a sunbeam.* "Bart, I can barely see you."

Nodding, he whispered, "I'm beginning..."

"What?"

"My greatest adventure." As his face lit up in a smile, he dissolved like the mist at dawn. For an instant, his smile lingered, and then he vanished.

"I'll miss you," Ruth whispered to the empty air. Stunned by his abrupt departure, she sat reflecting. *Now that you've moved on, where have you gone?*

Chapter 12

Fictionalized Facts

The next morning, while Auggie inspected the treasure cache in the sunlight, Ruth broke the news to Keya.

"He's gone?" Blinking, she snapped her fingers. "Just like that?"

"It was time. He completed his mission, so he was free to leave." Ruth handed her a thumb drive. "But he wanted you to have this."

"What is it?" Her brow creasing, Keya stared at it.

"It's a word-for-word transcription of Bart's memories." Ruth sighed. "It's what held him here, bound him. He wanted his story told, *and* he wanted you to read it, exactly as he told it. *Verbatim.*"

Keya crooked her neck. "Why do you emphasize 'verbatim'?"

"Because," Ruth took a deep breath, "when I fictionalize Bart's tales, the story may stray from his memoirs."

Keya was silent a moment, seeming deep in thought. Then with a smile, she gave Ruth's shoulder a friendly shake. "Good for you! I'm glad you made the most of your time here." She winced. "I've felt guilty about keeping you here till Friday…"

"Don't." Ruth gave her a quick hug. "I'm just glad

to help my favorite cousin."

Wearing an amused smile, Keya studied her. "So you're going to write about my great-something grandpa, huh?"

Ruth nodded. "I got the idea at the Hemingway house. Remember how the guide said the only thing Hemingway fictionalized 'were the names of actual people'?"

"No." Keya shrugged. "Funny how we hear only what's important to *us*." She held up the thumb drive. "I'm looking forward to reading this, learning about my ancestor." Then she caught Ruth's gaze. "*And* I'm looking forward to reading how you wield his memories into a swashbuckling novel."

"Hey, if it's ever made into a movie," Ruth deadpanned, "you can play the romantic lead."

An ironic twist to her lips, Keya grabbed her car keys. "At least we'll start the day with a laugh." Then, her faint smile wilting, she sighed. "I'm not looking forward to this morning."

"Me, neither." Ruth shook her head. As her earrings swung against her neck, Maita appeared, wearing a radiant smile. "But we're doing this for Maita—"

"And Bart," added Keya.

"The funeral, yes," said Ruth, "but I mean, picking up Maita's cremains at the police station. This is for her…just for her."

"Actions make a family, not blood. T'ank you for treating me like family." Maita's smile faltered. "Better 'an family."

"Glad to help." Ruth would have hugged her if she could. Instead, she smiled her encouragement as she translated for Keya.

"I'm glad 'e turtles led you to 'e treasure," said Maita. "It's only right."

"What do you mean?" Ruth studied her.

"'at treasure will pay for any legal fees. If 'e court finds in Keya's favor and lets her keep her property, she'll bequeat' it to 'e turtles—tit for tat, one good turn for anot'er." Maita's smile dimmed. "I just wish I could help her somehow, repay her for her kindness."

After Ruth translated, Keya shook her head. "You don't owe us anything. I'm glad we were here for you, glad to do what little we did."

"It's more 'an a little." Maita's voice trembled. "You have no idea."

****

A half hour later, as Keya signed the paperwork at the police station, Detective Bell walked through the waiting room.

Ruth waved, and to her surprise, he joined them. "Good morning, Detective."

"Morning." His voice gruff, he turned toward Keya. "I see you're going through with it."

Keya turned toward him with a puzzled frown. "Going through with what?"

"Claiming Miss Rogers' body."

"It's only right to give her a proper funeral." Keya shrugged. Then her gaze hardened. "Why? Has anyone else has inquired about her?"

He shook his head. "No one's claimed them."

Ruth did a double take. "Them?" She caught her breath. "That's right. She was pregnant."

"So it'll be a Mass for *three* souls," Keya half whispered to herself.

"By the way," said the detective, "the fetus was a girl, and the autopsy's DNA test confirmed the paternity. Heath Hawkins was the father."

Maita's ears perked. "My baby was a girl?"

Ruth nodded as she asked the detective, "Does he know?"

"If the pregnancy didn't register while Miss Rogers was alive, Mr. Hawkins understood the consequences when he signed his formal confession. He admitted to the murders of both Miss Rogers and their unborn daughter. According to Florida's fetal homicide laws, he's guilty of—and is being prosecuted for—not one, but two counts of murder."

Arching her eyebrow as she inhaled, Keya glanced at Ruth. "I'm glad he recognizes the scope of his actions."

"God forgive him," whispered Maita.

The clerk placed another document in front of Keya. "I'll need your signature on this release, and that's the last of the paperwork." After Keya signed, he double-checked the stack of papers for signatures and initials. Then with a sad smile, he handed her a corrugated cardboard box about two-thirds the size of a shoebox. "My condolences, Mrs. Erskine."

Staring at her cremains, Maita wilted. Her smile sagged as her jaw trembled.

Ruth wanted to hug her or at least offer a few compassionate words, but human touch was out of the question, and with the detective standing beside her, conversation was inadvisable. Managing a sympathetic grimace, she mumbled, "Sorry," hoping the detective thought the condolence was meant for Keya.

They stopped by the house, transferring the ashes

to an urn Keya had bought, and picked up Auggie and the critters. No one spoke in the car, each apparently lost in their own thoughts.

Except for Diesel sniffing the urn and Earnestine rubbing back and forth against it, the mood was somber.

Then, as they drove north from Marathon toward the church, Ruth smothered a giggle.

"What?" Auggie leaned forward from the back seat.

"Duck Key." She pointed to the road sign at Mile Marker 61. Then, grateful for any comic relief, she deadpanned as she turned toward him. "Isn't that just *ducky*?"

They passed people fishing from bridge embankments and the parallel bridges alongside the highway at Tom's Harbor Cut, Long Key Bridge, and Channel Two Bridge.

"Have you ever fished from a bridge?" asked Ruth.

Eyes on the road, Keya shook her head.

"I have," said Auggie. "When the sun's high like this at noon, the fish like to hide in the bridges' shadows." He shrugged. "You know what they say. A *reel* expert can tackle anything."

She groaned. A few minutes later, they came to a raised drawbridge over Snake Creek. "Look at the line of cars."

"Traffic will move in a minute," said Auggie. "See? They're lowering the bridge now."

Ruth looked at the line, seeing not just cars, but the passengers, each on their separate journeys, waiting to move forward, *move on*. Glancing at the urn, she thought of Maita.

Along the highway bridge between Key Largo and the mainland, just before entering Dade County, they passed a man riding a unicycle. She exchanged an ironic smile with Keya. "Can't say I've ever seen that before."

"Many paths, one destination," said Keya, turning off the highway.

Ruth considered her words. *Many paths, one destination. Bridges.* She thought of Bart, needing to connect with his family one last time and share his story before he could move on. She glanced at the urn again. *What'll help Maita reach her destination? Bridge the gap?*

Within minutes, they arrived at the church, where a priest greeted them. "I'm Father Peter. We spoke earlier on the phone about having a funeral Mass said for two souls."

"Three." Keya explained the situation as she handed him the urn.

Nodding, he considered the vessel. Then as he led them to the cemetery chapel, he asked, "Did I understand correctly? All three souls perished at sea, including Maita's premature daughter?"

"I hadn't thought of their deaths that way," said Keya, "but you're right."

After entering the stone chapel, Father Peter said, "Please be seated. We'll start with a short funeral Mass and follow with the Rite of Committal."

As they sat, Ruth touched her earrings and Maita appeared, sitting on the pew beside her. Her hands folded and her eyes misty, she wore a faraway expression.

Father Peter opened with a prayer. "The people

we've gathered here to remember were all connected by the sea. Maita Rogers was an avid sailor. Her daughter was also a mariner as she floated in the saline amniotic fluid. Bartolomé García de Castillo began his career as a cabin boy, then rose through the ranks to become a ship's captain and explorer.

"Seafarers all, they were in good company. Even Jesus traveled by boat. He used one as a floating pulpit to speak to crowds on shore. He calmed a storm that threatened to capsize a boat carrying his disciples. He even walked on water.

"Christianity was born near the Sea of Galilee, so it's not surprising the ship appeared as an early Christian symbol. Sometimes the ship appeared in full sail, symbolizing safe passage through this world's troubled waters. Other times, it appeared with the sails furled, resting in port after this life's voyage.

"Maita, her child, and Bartolomé were seafarers twice over—mariners who plied the waters and Christians who traveled through life aboard God's vessel. Now they've launched on the greatest voyage of them all. These sailors have embarked on a tide that will take them beyond the boundaries of space and time to where, in their final, safe harbor, their Pilot will welcome them home. May they rest in peace."

After Communion and a closing prayer, they carried the urn to the cemetery, where the priest gave the final farewell before blessing and interring it.

Maita stood at Ruth's side, still silent, apparently deep in thought.

When the service ended, Father Peter escorted them back to the church, where Keya thanked him.

"Glad to help in their transition, but keep in mind:

From birth through death, from alpha to omega, the Captain of our souls is always steering us and piloting us"—Father Peter's gaze rested on her—"from creation to cremation to culmination."

While Keya and Auggie continued talking with him, Maita walked toward a sculpture of a ship's anchor that resembled a cross.

Following her, Ruth read the plaque beneath it. "Hope anchors our souls, Hebrews 6:19."

Maita continued to stare at it, mumbling, "'e Mariner's Cross."

"Why are you still here, Maita?"

She shrugged.

"I thought all you had to do was forgive Heath and let go your resentment," said Ruth. "I'd expected you to move on by now."

"I had, too, but…" Maita turned toward her. "I'd like to repay Keya for her kindness."

"She's already told you. You don't owe her anything. She just wants you to be at peace. We'd hoped this Mass and funeral would help." Ruth frowned.

"'e Mass, being buried in holy ground, and forgiving He' all helped, but…" Maita gave a frustrated sigh. "I don't know what's holding me here…except maybe helping Keya, making sure she keeps 'e land, so she can donate it to 'e Turtle Refuge."

Ruth studied her. "Why's that so important to you?"

"I want 'e turtles to have a safe place to nest."

"Why?" Ruth watched her body language.

"Maybe because *I didn't*." Closing her eyes, she sighed. "And maybe it's because I can relate to turtles—afraid to stick out my neck, afraid to come out of my shell." Maita fidgeted. "I respect Keya, admire her, wish I were"—shoulders slumping, she grimaced—"wish *I'd been* more like her."

"Why?"

"Lots of reasons." She shrugged. "'e way she dresses, 'e way she acts, 'e way she fights for 'e turtles, fights for her land. She's so self-confident, bold." She turned toward Ruth. "She reminds me of Bart, fearless—not like me."

"She reminds you of Bart?" Ruth did a double take. "Why do you say that?"

"She goes after what she wants. She's adventurous—like Bart."

"Keya takes after him for good reason." Ruth smiled. "They're related. Maybe she's inherited his sense of adventure."

Maita seemed to turn inward. "All my life, I've—" She made a face. "*While I lived*, I was too timid, too insecure to speak up for myself."

"What made you so self-conscious? Your speech impediment?"

"Partly, but I've always felt inadequate—incompetent." Then her spine straightening, Maita held her head high. "Except about one t'ing."

Ruth studied her. "What was that?"

"Bookkeeping. I could juggle two sets of books and still reconcile bot' accounts every mont'." Suddenly her face lit up as if getting an idea. "I know!"

Ruth asked the void, "Know *what?*"

****

The next morning, Ruth finalized the brochure while she babysat Earnestine and Diesel. After emailing the files to Keya and the Turtle Refuge, she took a deep breath and began her next project—revising Bart's notes into a novel. By the time Keya and Auggie returned from their errands at dinner, Ruth had finished the first chapter.

"How 'bout amberjack steaks for dinner?" asked Auggie, checking through the stash of frozen fish Brett had caught.

"I'm sure anything you grill will be delicious," said Ruth, "but I can't say I've tried amberjack before."

"Then you're in for a treat," said Auggie. "It tastes a lot like swordfish but juicier."

"Add to that some creamy cilantro lime slaw and a Mediterranean cucumber tomato salad," said Keya, "and voila! Dinner."

When they sat to eat, Keya opened a bottle of Gamay Noir.

Ruth did a double take. "Red wine with fish?"

"Wait till you taste how the amberjack's robust flavor pairs perfectly with the Gamay's earthy overtones." Keya handed her a glass. "Try it."

Ruth expected a tart clash of flavors but was surprised when they complemented each other. "You're right. They do pair perfectly." Gazing at her friends, she made the connection. "Just like you and Auggie—robust with earthy overtones."

"I'll drink to that." After toasting, Auggie raised his glass again. "May your anchor be tight, your cork be loose, your rum be spiced, and your compass be true."

Clinking glasses with Ruth, Keya said, "That reminds me. Have you seen Bart?"

Ruth's gaze homed in on her. "Bart's moved on—"

"You'd told me, but..." Keya's smile drooped.

"After reading his memoirs last night, I wanted to thank him."

"He'd have liked that. Your reading his chronicles meant a lot." Ruth gave her an encouraging smile. "It was his last request."

Keya's smile was shy, reflective.

Reminded of Maita, Ruth watched her face. "What are you thinking?"

"After reading about Bart's life, it's almost like I knew him." Keya's lips rose in a wistful half smile. "Wish I'd known him."

Ruth sat back in her chair, assessing her. "Don't tell me you finally believe he's your great-something grandpa?"

Nodding, Keya grimaced. "But now it's too late."

"At least you have his memoirs." Ruth smiled, trying to cheer her. "And I promise you'll get the first copy of the novel I've started about him," adding with a self-conscious cringe, "if it's published, that is."

The pupils of Keya's eyes dilated. "You've already begun the book?"

"I finished chapter one." Ruth sat a bit taller in her chair.

"That was fast," said Auggie.

Ruth nodded. "Thanks to Bart's swashbuckling life, the book almost writes itself. I just add context."

"Good for you!" Then, glancing at her fiancé, Keya added, "*And* Auggie's got some news of his own."

"What's that?" Ruth turned toward him.

"A coin dealer in Key West confirmed it." Auggie's eyes danced. "These coins are from the *Nuestra Señora del Rosario*, a galleon that left Havana in 1641 and went aground on the reefs."

"That's interesting…" Ruth crooked her head, sensing she was missing something. "But why are those details important?"

"Knowing the *provenance*, that is, the place of origin and the past ownership of these coins, increases their value." He gave a crisp nod. "With their history, these gold coins are worth a fortune."

"You mean, worth more than just their weight in gold?"

****

Thunder woke Ruth early Friday morning, and she peered out the window. A thick bank of clouds obscured the sun, casting an odd twilight color, more like dusk than dawn.

The earrings on the nightstand glimmered in the silvery-gray light, reminding her of Maita's baffling statement. She slipped them on, and the girl appeared. "Yesterday when you said, 'I know,' what did you mean?"

"You'll see." Maita gave her a mysterious smile.

"Maybe, maybe not," said Ruth. "I'm flying out tonight."

Maita's jaw fell open. "Already?" At Ruth's nod, she frowned. "I'd hoped you could stay here until I…"

"Move on?"

"Pass over, go into 'e light." Sighing, Maita briefly closed her eyes. "Whatever you call it, I'm still here. I'm still not…ready."

"You've forgiven Heath, let go your resentment, and been properly laid to rest." Ruth scratched her head. "I'm out of ideas. What's holding you back?"

"I don't know." Maita lifted her shoulder in a half shrug. "I'm worried Keya will lose in court, afraid 'e turtles will lose 'eir nesting beach." She gave a frustrated groan. "I'm so tired of 'is neit'er-nor limbo…yet I'm afraid to move on. I don't know what to do."

"Then pray." Ruth hoped her smile was reassuring. "Don't let fear control you."

"Fear's *always* controlled me. All my life, I've been"—Maita grimaced—"*had been* afraid."

"Of what?"

"Everyt'ing. Not fitting in, not being liked…not being loved." Maita's eyes and lips tipped down at the corners, giving her face a defeated look. "I've always been unwelcome, unwanted, excluded, not good enough—"

"So you stayed in your shell?"

Maita nodded.

"You've got to break free of that to move on."

"How?"

"Pray."

A wistful look came into Maita's eyes. "I used to pray. I felt God here"—she pressed her fingers into her breastbone—"right here in my solar plexus, my fort' chakra, *my heart*, I felt Him *right here*." Again she stabbed her fingers into her chest. "He was 'e one t'ing I could count on when people let me down. I always felt God was wit' me."

"You said 'felt,' past tense," said Ruth. "Don't you feel Him now?"

Maita shook her head.

"What happened?"

Gazing into the distance, her eyes seemed to focus inwardly. "I haven't sensed His presence since I started helping He'." Looking at Ruth, she grimaced. "Aiding and abetting him."

"Heath." Ruth stared at her, recalling how, at their first meetings, Maita had always been sobbing and crying. Then a few days before, she had seemed to glow. "You were so happy when you let go the hatred. You said, as you forgave Heath, your resentment faded." Ruth studied her hunched shoulders and drawn face. "What's changed?"

"Fear holds me back—prevents me from taking 'e next step."

Choosing her words carefully, Ruth said, "It stole your joy in life. Don't let fear destroy your hope now. We're all afraid at one time or another. Just trust that God has a plan for you."

"That's just it." Maita's voice faltered. "I'm afraid I'm not good enough for Him."

"You're just as good as anyone." Hearing herself, Ruth wanted to bite her tongue. *She doesn't need platitudes.* "Why wouldn't you be good enough?"

Maita hunched her shoulders, looking fragile. Brittle. "I don't deserve His love...His or anyone else's."

"Why do you say that?"

"Experience." Maita gave a dry laugh that verged on tears. "I've dealt wit' failure all my life. Everyt'ing I did was eit'er wrong or not good enough. My classmates made fun of me and 'e way I spoke. My family was ashamed of me. Even 'e man I loved just pretended to care for me. After he used me, he destroyed me."

"If your best wasn't enough," said Ruth, "maybe you wasted your time on the wrong people, the wrong person."

"I didn't blame He' for not loving me." Maita caught her breath. "I blamed myself for not being good enough." Her eyes misty, Maita lifted her trembling chin to meet Ruth's gaze. " 'ere's a reason no one's liked or loved me. I'm not good enough."

Not good enough. Her tone striking a chord, the words echoed in Ruth's mind.

All the pain came shooting back like an exposed nerve or a cracked tooth—like biting the inside of your cheek when it's already chewed raw. Reopening the wound hurt twice as much.

Ruth took a deep breath, grounding herself. *It's over. I've moved on.* But the wound burned like frozen fingers scraping a windshield in sub-zero weather—icy hot, burning cold. Only oxymorons could describe the intensity of the relationship that no longer was. *It's over.*

Still the memories of their time together came flooding back. Not just the cold, bittersweet loss of love, but the anger and humiliation—the heat of its conclusion without closure—the scorching freeze, the glacial blaze.

Yes, theirs had been a toxic relationship— poisonous, venomous. Though it had started off nurturing, gradually, like pernicious anemia, the connection had sucked her lifeblood dry—frigid warmth, icy heat.

Breaking up was like a cold burn, a controlled fire in winter. The prescribed burn should have burned away the noxious remains of their love-hate relationship, renewed the scorched earth of her soul and restored her, but instead, the blaze left her fallow and barren.

Thank God, Jack's out of my life.

Affectionate loathing, tender revulsion filled her. Though Ruth despised Jack—detested him—she reasoned, if love hadn't been involved, he wouldn't have left such deep scars. Despite his mental cruelty, somehow, she *had* loved him, and for that, she could not forgive herself.

After the breakup, the worst times had been late at night, when she was alone in bed and her thoughts wandered back to Jack. Reliving the past, she replayed her final conversations with him over and over. *If only I'd said or done* this *instead of that.*

"Learn from your mistakes," friends had told her, but during her self-examinations, she blamed herself. When she "lit a match" to view the past, she burned her fingers.

Phone calls to girlfriends had been lifelines, helping her through the initial breakup, but Brett enabled her to weather the post-breakup trauma.

Her friends told her a rebound relationship would backfire. They warned her not to jump from the frying pan into the fire. They said her new relationship wouldn't last, that she was still attracted to her old flame, but Brett eased the pain and filled the void in her life. He kept her from being alone, lonely, afraid. With Brett, her thoughts had returned to the future, but without him in it, her future loomed like a terrifying abyss, and she would seek refuge in the past, only to loathe herself more.

If Brett had been the answer to a prayer, writing was a godsend, the surest way to clarify her thoughts. After the breakup with Jack, she recorded her feelings in a journal, using the pus of her festering wounds as ink to scrawl her anger onto paper. Only then did she begin to heal.

She started a freelance-writing sideline to her teleworking job. She threw out or gave away everything that reminded her of Jack. Not stopping there, she reorganized her closet and cleaned out her junk drawers, celebrating the therapeutic catharsis of purging.

She lost five pounds, updated her wardrobe, got a new haircut, and started going out. She reconnected with her friends, something Jack had discouraged, and she began to enjoy life again.

Slowly, she had regained her self-esteem and, more importantly, her self-respect, but hearing Maita's words brought back her own painful memories—*not good enough.*

Ruth breathed deeply, grounding herself before answering Maita. "You're not the first person to feel this way. At one point in my life, I'd lost all my self-confidence and self-worth. It took months to undo the emotional damage."

"But you got back your self-respect...didn't you?" At Ruth's nod, she asked, "How?"

"I redefined how I envisioned myself." Ruth stopped looking inward and turned toward her. "Don't let others hijack your self-esteem. Don't internalize their lies. When your family or Heath said you weren't good enough, maybe the truth was, you were overqualified...too good for them. You deserve more, Maita. Much more."

****

Later that night while she lay in bed, Ruth mentally replayed Maita's question. "But you got back your self-respect…didn't you?"

As if caught in a flash flood, memories of Jack surged over her like a swollen river brimming its banks, the clear, spring-fed water mingling with the sewage and silt, the good jumbling with the bad. *Tender*, affectionate memories merging and conflicting with *tender,* inflamed memories that were still raw…

Ruth squirmed, embarrassed as she remembered how her emotions had betrayed her. Then she recalled Maita's words earlier that afternoon. "I didn't blame He' for not loving me. I blamed myself for not being good enough." She empathized with the girl, cringing at how her own feelings of inadequacy had governed her actions more than she cared to admit.

She turned on the bedside lamp and recorded her feelings in her journal, detailing how Maita's dilemma had dredged up memories of Jack. As her anger diffused, her soul moved a step closer to healing.

Maita's helped me move on. Can I repay the favor?

Chapter 13

Two Souls but a Single Thought

The next morning, just before they left for the hearing, Ruth called Brett. "Since the Monroe County courthouse is in Key West, I'll fly out from EYW instead of Miami and avoid the drive."

"Just hurry back." The smile came through his voice. "Can't wait to see you."

"Neither can I." Mentally picturing the welcoming glow in his eyes, she imagined Brett's arms around her. "Love you so much. See you in a couple hours."

****

Ruth, Auggie, and Keya met the attorney, Brian Baines, in the courthouse waiting room a half hour early.

After introductions, Keya asked, "How long do you think this hearing will take?"

"Plan on several hours." He shrugged. "Don't expect your case to be the first one called."

Keya caught Auggie's eye before asking Brian, "Do we need to wait here, or could we get a cup of coffee?"

"As long as you're within ten minutes of a phone call, you should be fine, but skim through this before the hearing." He handed her a copy of the paperwork. "Have the facts fresh in your mind and remember courtroom etiquette. Be sure to stand when the judge enters the courtroom and address him or her as 'Your Honor.' "

"Got it." Nodding, Keya glanced at their faces. "Anyone else want coffee besides me?"

Ruth shook her head. "I'm coffeed out."

"Thanks," said Brian, "but I need to be here when they call our case. I'll ping you the moment they announce it."

"I do…" Auggie gave her a broad smile as he reached for her hand.

Returning his smile, Keya called over her shoulder, "We should be back in ten minutes, sooner if you need us."

As Ruth and Brian found seats in the waiting room, she spotted Gerry at the far end, working on his laptop. "That's Gerald Granger," she whispered.

"And the man beside him is his attorney, Jason Roberts," said Brian. Then he paused, listening to the PA system announcement.

"The first case on the docket is CC M 18 9993284."

"Might as well relax," he said. "It'll be at least an hour before our docket number is called." With that, he texted Keya, took out his laptop, and read over his notes.

Taking her cue from him, Ruth pulled out her laptop. *Maybe I can start chapter two.*

She had no sooner booted up than a ping announced she had mail from Gerald Granger. Glancing at him across the large waiting room, deep in conversation with his attorney, she blinked. *Why's he emailing me? And how did he get my email address?*

Even stranger, the message had no subject line or text, just two attachments. Opening them, she found a contract and a spreadsheet, listing people, all with the surname Erskine, followed by columns marked Check Numbers, Dollar Amounts, and Dates.

Ruth squinted at the documents. *What are these, and why did Gerald send them to me?* Again, she peered at him, but he neither looked up, nor acknowledged her.

Then she remembered the earrings in her pocket, and she slipped them on, hoping Maita might shed light on the paperwork. When the girl appeared wearing a sly sneer, Ruth mouthed her words, so Brian would not hear. "Why would Gerald send me these?"

Maita snickered. "He wouldn't."

"Then who would?"

Standing at her full height, Maita beamed. "Me."

"How can you type?" She thought of the earrings. "You can't touch or grip anything."

"True, but *somehow*—the same way I can write on Heath's skin—I can press the keys on Gerry's laptop."

Blinking, Ruth stared at her, amazed.

"What?"

"It's gone."

"What's gone?"

"Your speech impediment," said Ruth. "You said *the* and *Heath*."

"I did?" Placing the tip of her tongue against the back of her upper teeth, Maita repeated, "The." As she pronounced it, her eyes bulged. "Heath." She gave a disbelieving snort. "Would you listen to that? I've had a speech impediment all my life. I never could pronounce dental fricatives like *this, with, other, Heath*." After perfectly enunciating the words, she shook her head. "What's going on?"

"You're changing," said Ruth. "I think you're beginning to transition."

Maita's brow wrinkled. "Why do you say that?"

"The same thing happened with Bart. His physical imperfections fell away." Ruth gave her an encouraging smile. "I think you're moving on."

Maita hesitated as if weighing the possibility. "Maybe you're right. For the first time, I'm speaking up for myself, speaking up for what's right—the turtles, Keya." Then glancing at the laptop, she became all business, pointing to the spreadsheet. "This is a list of signing bonuses Gerry paid to the Erskine family members. These columns contain the check numbers, the amounts of their bonuses, and the dates the checks were written."

"Bonuses for signing this contract?" At Maita's nod, Ruth scrolled through the second attachment—a long legal document. "What's the gist of it?"

"The Erskines agreed to an exclusivity clause, giving Gerry's company the right of first refusal."

"What's that?"

"Should the Erskine family win Keya's property, this contract gives Gerry the right to purchase it from them before they put it on the open market."

"Is that legal?" Ruth studied her.

"Yup, although the deal benefits Gerry." Maita nodded. "He can lowball the purchase price to below market value, and the Erskines would have to accept whatever he offers." She pointed to the spreadsheet's columns. "These signing bonuses were all 'under the table.' In fact, that's how I reconciled both sets of books—Gerry's manipulated figures countered Heath's skewed numbers. I hid both sets of irregularities because each offset the other."

Ruth squinted, trying to understand. "I'm not following."

"Gerry had me bury the bonuses under 'miscellaneous business expenses' in dozens of accounts. When I helped Heath cover his expenditures, he overcharged customers or substituted inferior products and then skimmed off the top. Both sets of books tallied because one set of misappropriations compensated for the other."

"Was that legal?"

Maita made a face. "With Gerry, let's say it's common business practice. It's fine until you're caught."

Ruth recalled Gerald's "surprise" the day he'd taken them to lunch, when he confided auditors had discovered that Maita had "cooked the books" and hadn't been "the loyal accountant" he'd believed. *What a double-dealing hypocrite.*

Maita's eyes took on a distant expression. "With Heath, I believed he'd repay the company. I trusted him, covering for him *temporarily*, until 'his ship came in,' as he put it, and he reimbursed the corporation."

Trying not to judge, Ruth bit her tongue.

"I know." Maita sighed. "I was naïve to believe Heath. Scratch that. I was so afraid of rocking the boat, so afraid of losing him that I couldn't speak up for myself. Instead, I just talked myself into trusting him."

"What about Gerald?"

"With him, I didn't speak my mind because I was too afraid to speak up for what's right." She cringed. "I was always afraid of losing my job. Since I've never felt good enough, I always overcompensated. Working twice as hard as anyone else, I tried to be the perfect employee. Afraid to make waves—terrified of being a whistleblower—I kept my mouth shut. It's the story of my life. I've *always* been too afraid to speak up for myself."

Glancing at Gerald, Maita jerked her chin defiantly. "Well, not anymore!" She turned back to Ruth. "Forward those documents I sent you to Keya's lawyer. That should put an end to any hostile takeover."

Nodding, Ruth leaned over and tapped Brian's shoulder. "What's your email address?"

"Why?" His eyes narrowed.

"Gerald Granger just sent two attachments you may find interesting."

After she forwarded the documents and explained their significance, he studied her. "Why would Granger send you something so incriminating?"

Ruth deadpanned. "A guilty conscience?" Then her eyes drilled into his. "The question is, at this late hour, will they be admissible in court?"

Rubbing his jaw, Brian seemed to consider the possibility. "Once I email a copy to the court clerk and Granger's counsel, the documents will be legal, *but* before I submit these as evidence, I need to establish the Erskines cashed their checks."

"How can you prove it?"

"By confirming the dates the checks cleared the bank." He took out his cell. "My legal assistant can verify them." After he made the call, he pulled up another document on his laptop. "Thinking positively, I'll add these to our list of exhibits. As soon as Linda gives me the all clear, I'll submit it."

She glanced at the clock. "Do we have enough time?"

****

When Keya and Auggie returned from coffee, Ruth updated them, while Brian spoke on the phone with his legal assistant.

Smiling, he hung up, hit *send*, and turned to them. "Linda confirmed the Erskines cashed their checks, and I just sent the documents to the court clerk and opposing counsel."

"Now what?" asked Keya.

He shrugged. "Wait till the clerk calls our case."

Across the waiting room, Gerald and his attorney began an animated discussion.

Ruth tugged at Keya's arm. "Looks like they've seen the updated list of exhibits."

As they turned toward him, Gerald glared, his gaze throwing daggers. Then abruptly looking away, he resumed his heated conversation.

Ruth caught Keya's knowing gaze.

She responded with a throaty chuckle.

An hour later, their case was called over the PA system, and they filed into the courtroom.

As the court came to order, the judge asked the two attorneys to approach the bench.

Keya sat alone at one counsel table while a man sat at the plaintiff table, looking uneasy, his eyes shifting left to right.

"Who's that man?" Watching from the gallery with Auggie, Ruth nodded toward the plaintiff.

"Granger's pawn." Auggie's lip curled in distaste. "Some second-cousin, shirttail Erskine I *vaguely* recognize."

Gerald sat at the other end of the gallery, sullen, his face as pinched as if he had sipped vinegar.

When the attorneys returned to their seats, the judge addressed the court. "Two pieces of evidence were submitted recently. While the right of first refusal is not illegal"—the judge stared at the plaintiffs—"the contract implies collusion, and the spreadsheet demonstrates prior knowledge and complicity in what has all the earmarks of an attempted hostile buyout."

He glanced at Keya and her attorney. "Character witnesses are unnecessary."

Ruth breathed a sigh of relief as she caught Vera's eye.

Sitting several seats away, the veterinarian gave her a thumb's-up.

"Regarding the allegations of Mrs. Erskine's mental incompetence to act as the estate's administrator..." The judge paused as he thumbed through the thick stack of documents and transcriptions. "The court finds the assertions *irrelevant*."

The gallery buzzed with hissed whispers.

"One more outburst, and I'll have this courtroom cleared." The judge paused until the murmurs subsided. Then he peered at the plaintiff over his bifocals. "The *issue* is the complaint itself. The lawsuit names the estate of Jules Erskine as the party being sued. In Florida, the complaint would not sue 'the estate of Jules Erskine.' Rather, the claimant would file a suit against 'Keya Erskine, personal representative of the estate of Jules Erskine.' " The judge glanced at Keya as he banged the gavel and motioned to the clerk. "Case dismissed."

"All rise," called the clerk.

Her eyes round with disbelief, Keya turned toward Auggie, Ruth, and Vera as she stood. Then, after the judge had vacated the courtroom, she and her attorney met them at the exit.

"I've got to get back to the clinic," said Vera, hugging her, "but I'm so glad for you. Congratulations!"

"Thank you for being here," Keya mumbled, her gaze vacant and unfocused.

With a wave, Vera smiled and left.

"I still can't believe it's over." As they walked outside into the sunshine, Keya shook her head as if dazed. "Just like that." She snapped her fingers.

"And on a technicality." Brian smirked.

"Why didn't you tell us?"

"Sometimes it's better to play the cards close to your chest." His lips lifted in a crooked smile. "My legal assistant will be in touch. Thank you, Mrs. Erskine." Shaking hands, he said his goodbyes.

"Mrs. Erskine." Auggie rolled the name off his tongue as if listening to the sound for the first time. "Has a nice ring to it, doesn't it?" He turned to Keya, his amber-brown eyes dancing and a smile playing at his lips.

Her lip curling, she watched him sideways. "What's going through your mind?"

"We're at the courthouse." Auggie's eyes blazed.

Keya regarded him. "So?"

"So…" He paused as a radiant smile lit his face. "We have our marriage license. What do you say we get married?"

"What?" Keya's face paled. "Now?" Cringing, she

glanced at the courthouse. "*Here?*"

"Yes." Playfully mocking her, Auggie parroted her words. "Now. Here."

"But…" Her eyes bunching, she glanced at Ruth as if looking for backup before turning toward Auggie. "We have to be married in church."

He nodded. "We will…next week, next month"—he shrugged—"as soon as we can, but what about spontaneity? Doesn't impulse count for something? Let's get married legally today—*now, here*—and then get married in church later?" His eyes sparkling, he took her hand in his as he dropped to one knee. "Mrs. Erskine, would you do me the honor of becoming Mrs. Erskine?"

Her other hand to her chest, her shoulders shaking, Keya threw back her head and laughed.

People passing through the courthouse doors smiled.

"Come on. Give a guy a break." His knee still bent, Auggie's smile stiffened. "I'm making a fool of myself down here."

Keya's laughter subsided, and a fond smile lifted the corners of her mouth. A glow lit her face as her eyes caressed him.

The look of love. Ruth stifled a sigh.

"Of course I'll marry you," breathed Keya. Then her face took on the no-nonsense expression she had worn in court. "But in church as we agreed."

"We will," Auggie said solemnly. Then his eyes glimmered. "*Again*, later."

Helping him to his feet, Keya whispered, "Marriage is more than just a certificate or a ceremony. Let's wait and do it right the first time."

Caught in each other's gaze, they hugged. Then applause from the spectators broke the spell.

"They think you said *yes*." He gave her a mischievous grin.

Amid the congratulatory smiles, Keya broke away from him. Then she looked at her ecru outfit—a fitted top over a flowing, ankle-length skirt. "Besides, I'm not dressed for a wedding."

"Other than your vivid parrot earrings, you *are* wearing white." Ruth shrugged. "Okay, pale beige, but close enough."

Auggie wore a lopsided smile as he took a small bundle from his pocket and handed it to Keya. "I was saving this till after the hearing, either as a consolation prize or a celebration gift, but it *is* white."

Her brow wrinkling, Keya unrolled the bundle to find a printed T-shirt—*Talk to animals? How else can I answer their questions?* Rolling her eyes, she shook her head. She pulled the shirt over her top, knotted it fashionably at one side, and kissed his cheek. Then hands spread wide at her sides as if presenting herself, she said tongue-in-cheek, "Ta-dah! The latest in haute couture bridal fashion."

"So what do you say to marrying me today?" Auggie gazed into her eyes. "Carp a D. M.?"

"I don't know..." Keya winced. "Things are moving so fast..."

"But they're all *good* things," said Auggie, "like today's hearing—a happy ending to what could've been bad."

"True..." Her tone rose, insinuating another thought.

"But...*what?*"

"A civil ceremony isn't a marriage." Keya shook her head. "I want to be married in the eyes of God, not just in the eyes of the law. I want a church wedding with flowers and music."

"You'll have all that," he said, "next week, next month, whenever you say, but let's be impulsive. Let's get 'legally' married now, and then really married in church as soon as we can."

Her forehead puckering as her face glowed, Keya seemed to wage an internal battle.

Ruth pulled out her phone and scrolled to a street map showing specialty shops. "While you two work this out, I've got to run an errand." With a parting wave, she glanced at her friends still deep in an animated discussion. "Be right back," she called over her shoulder.

Running three blocks, Ruth bounded into a florist shop, jangling the doorbell.

The startled shopkeeper whipped around to face her. "Can I help you?"

Gasping for air, Ruth nodded as she took a deep breath.

"What can I get you?"

"Something fast." Winded, Ruth gulped air. "My friends are getting married at the courthouse. *I think*." Crouching forward, hands on knees as she took deep breaths, Ruth held up her index finger. "One sec." She filled her lungs.

"So, a wedding bouquet?" The lady's half smile was amused.

Still out of breath, Ruth nodded.

The doorbell jangled, and a man walked in.

"Be with you in a minute," called the shopkeeper

before asking Ruth, "What color? White?"

"Anything but white." Ruth shook her head, recalling Keya's vibrant fashion sense. Then she smiled, remembering Keya's ecru outfit and white T-shirt.

Nodding, the lady peeked into the glassed floral coolers. "What about something orange?"

Still breathing deeply, Ruth nodded. "Yup."

The woman pulled out several stems of orange tiger lilies. After further searching, she asked, "Fuchsia?"

"That works."

When she had chosen several stems of hot-pink roses, she turned toward Ruth. "What about these purple carnations?"

"Perfect!" Starting to breath normally, Ruth added, "Sounds like you know her."

The saleslady acknowledged her with a quick lift of her head and a flash of a smile while she arranged the flowers. "Lilies symbolize honor; roses mean joy, and purple carnations signify deep love." She gave a modest shrug. "Even if they're not white, they're ideal for a wedding."

"She'll like the bright colors ever so much more," said Ruth.

"Is someone getting married?" The customer wore a Hawaiian floral-print shirt with a guitar strapped to his back.

"Yes." Ruth turned toward him. "At least, I think so. My impulsive friend just asked my cousin to marry him at the courthouse. Even if she doesn't 'walk down the aisle,' I want her to have a bouquet."

"What are they doing for music?" The man rubbed

his stubbled jaw.

"Nothing." Hunching her shoulders, Ruth held up her palms. "This was a spur-of-the moment, fly-by-the-seat-of-his-pants proposal." She chuckled to herself.

"At the courthouse, you say?"

Ruth nodded. "Why?"

The man swung his guitar around and smiled. "It's on my way to Duval. Maybe they'd like live music?"

"Would they ever!" Ruth's smile widened. "What's your name?"

****

Ten minutes later, Ruth found Keya and Auggie standing under a palm tree, still deep in discussion.

Keya glanced at her. "Where've you been?"

"Getting this." Ruth presented the multicolored bouquet. "I couldn't let you get married without flowers—"

"That's still up for grabs." Auggie winced.

"—or without music," finished Ruth. "This is Troy. Troy, this is *possibly* the bride-to-be, Keya, and Auggie, the impetuous, wannabe groom." As they shook hands, she added, "Troy's part of a Jimmy Buffett tribute trio, and he's offered to play for your wedding."

After shaking hands and thumping Troy on the back, Auggie turned to Keya, his eyes glinting and his expression hopeful. "Well…what do you say?"

"I don't know…" She made a dubious growling sound in the back of her throat.

Auggie took her hand in his, tugging at her fingers. "You've got your ring, and now you have your music and flowers."

A tentative smile flickered at Keya's lips as she inhaled the fragrance of her bouquet. Her parrot earrings reflected the flowers' vibrant colors, their hues enhancing the violet-blue of her panic-stricken eyes. Holding up her index finger, Keya seemed to weigh her options. "But—"

"We'll get married in church just as soon as we can. *I promise*." Auggie's eyes pleaded. "Come on…What else do you need?"

Her gaze connected with his. "Only you…"

"Is this gig on or not?" Troy pressed his lips together, swallowing a smile.

Auggie studied Keya, waiting for a sign. "Was that a *yes*?"

Her lips teetered between a grin and a wince. A dozen emotions swept across her face before she settled on a smile and gave him a curt nod.

"Heck, *yeah*, this gig's on." Hand in hand, Auggie walked Keya into the courthouse, their fingers intertwined.

Witnessing the brief ceremony, Ruth videoed it while Troy accompanied himself on the guitar, singing Jimmy Buffett's "Changes in Latitudes, Changes in Attitudes."

"By virtue of the authority vested in me under the laws of the State of Florida, I now pronounce you husband and wife." The deputy clerk turned to Auggie. "You may kiss the bride."

His eyes never leaving Keya's, Auggie clasped her waist and shoulders as he tipped her backward in a lingering kiss.

Ruth captured the moment on her phone with Maita looking on, smiling. Then she forwarded the video to Keya and Brett.

Though flushed from the amorous kiss, Keya

beamed ear to ear when she turned to Ruth. "How about being my maid of honor at our *real* wedding?"

"I'd be honored." While she hugged Keya, Ruth caught Auggie's eye. "Just let me know the date."

"Aye, aye." He gave her a mock salute, then tried to slip the musician a fifty.

Troy refused the money with a shake of his head. "Just glad I happened along when I did." Holding up an imaginary glass, he said, "As lovers of harmony, may you never be in want of a note, and may your enemies be hanged by a common 'chord.' " Smiling, he hugged Keya and shook Auggie's hand. "Hope this is the start of a happy life together."

Auggie stuffed the fifty in Troy's back pocket. "After that 'toast,' have a drink on us."

Ruth studied the bride. "Do you realize you're following tradition?"

"What do you mean?" Keya squinted.

"Like your grandmothers before you, you're wearing Bart's parrot earrings on your wedding day." Ruth smiled. "Incidentally, I sent you the video. Maybe you can have a portrait painted from one of the stills."

"Good idea." Wearing a wistful smile, Keya fingered her earrings. "I wore them today for luck, but now that you mention it, I *do* feel connected to my grandmothers…and Bart." She hugged Ruth. "Thank you for the video"—she held up the bouquet—"the flowers, and music, *for being here*, for introducing me to Auggie, *and* for giving me my heritage."

Before Ruth could answer, her cell rang, and she glanced at caller ID. "It's Brett."

Auggie held out his hand. "Can I answer it?"

"Why?" Ruth gave him a perplexed frown.

"You said to let you know the date." Auggie's face warmed in a smile. "I'll do better than that."

Shrugging, Ruth handed him her phone. "Here you go."

"Hey, Brett. Keya and I want you to be the best man at our wedding." Laughing to himself, he paused as he listened to the receiver. "Yes, we did just get married, but now we're planning our *real* wedding just as soon as we can. Ruth's already agreed to be maid of honor, so let's keep the wedding party in the family and make a foursome." Auggie smiled as he listened to Brett's answer. "Great, then we'll see you soon. I'll be in touch with the date and details. In the meantime, here's your fiancée."

As Auggie handed back the phone, Ruth said, "A *lot's* happened since we talked this morning, but here's the gist."

Auggie glanced at his watch as Ruth hung up. "Your flight doesn't leave for another four hours." He turned to his bride. "Why don't we celebrate our *first* wedding"—he hugged Keya's shoulders—"with a champagne supper on the houseboat?"

"Sure." Ruth and Keya caught each other's gaze and nodded.

"Besides, I want to show you Brett's suggestion." After giving Keya a mysterious smile, he turned toward Ruth.

Keya eyed him suspiciously. "Now what's up your sleeve?"

****

An hour later, Auggie's skiff was cutting through the sea toward his houseboat.

"Since you've won the lawsuit, and the property's

indisputably yours"—Ruth looked from Keya to Auggie—"where are you two going to live—the house or the houseboat?"

"We'll have to go back to Marathon for Earnestine and Diesel after your flight leaves tonight, but then..." Keya spread her hands wide as she exchanged a perplexed look with Auggie.

"I remember your words the day we met," said Auggie. "You like to flit about the world and then relax in your nest."

"Just not concurrently," said Keya.

"How 'bout sharing time between the house and the houseboat?" he asked. "What do you say to sailing off into the sunset tomorrow? Maybe moor near the Dry Tortugas and spend our honeymoon snorkeling in the reef—the most active turtle-nesting site in the Florida Keys?"

Keya's eyes lit up. "Sounds wonderful."

Then Auggie peered ahead into the blue. Slowing the boat's engines, he pulled out a pair of binoculars. "Would you look at that?"

"What?" Ruth turned in her seat to see as Keya reached for the binoculars.

"It's Sargassum weed." He steered them closer yet skirted the edges. "And look what's in it!"

"Baby loggerheads." Keya caught her breath as she handed Ruth the binoculars. "I've never seen them in the open water before."

"Me, neither." Auggie shook his head.

After Ruth adjusted the binoculars, dozens—hundreds—of baby sea turtles came into view, either swimming in or floating on the seaweed. "Wow!" She glanced at Keya and Auggie. "We witnessed a clutch of loggerheads hatch, and now we're seeing them on their journey."

"It must be nature's wedding gift to us." He smiled at Keya.

Returning his smile, she nodded. "Until recently, no one knew what happened to the baby turtles, but studies show they use these giant seaweed mats as drifting nurseries and ride the Gulf Stream toward the North Atlantic currents. Then like a huge lazy river, the currents carry them in a wide circle around the ocean."

"Must be like catching a *magic* carpet ride." Watching the sea turtles through the field glasses, Ruth breathed a contented sigh.

"Pretty much. It's a new beginning for them"— Keya turned to Auggie—"just like for us."

He met her gaze. "It is, isn't it?"

Five minutes later, the skiff approached the houseboat, and Ruth gave a low whistle. "Would you look at this!"

"Look at what?" Keya deadpanned, gazing at Auggie. "Today I have eyes only for my husband." Then pretending to tear her gaze from his, Keya turned to see.

Ruth pointed to the ship's new name freshly painted on its stern—*Our H2Ome*.

"Our *Water* Home," Auggie read. "Like I said, Brett came up with the idea."

Keya covered her face with her hands, peeking through her fingers to stare at the surprise. Then, her eyes dewy, she looked at Auggie. "How long have you planned this?"

"Brett suggested it Sunday." Auggie shrugged as he maneuvered the skiff alongside the houseboat. "I had it painted the day you two drove to Saint Augustine, but I never really planned it. Everything just fell into place."

"A coincidence," said Keya.

Ruth shook her head. "I don't believe in coincidences."

"I don't, either, but this is a"—Auggie seemed to pick his words—"*happy happenstance*. When something's meant to be, everything fits together as though planned."

"Divine alignments for divine assignments." Keya gave them a pixyish smile.

"As the fisherman said, good things come to those who...*bait*." He snickered as he cut the engines and gave them a hand boarding the houseboat. "Now on to the celebration. Who wants champagne?"

"I do! Let me help." Winking, Keya glanced at Ruth. "Back in five minutes."

Ruth swallowed a smile. "Take your time." Walking to the boat's bow, she gazed at the seascape, contrasting the sky's crystal blue against the water's shades of azure, aquamarine, and indigo. Feeling somewhat blue herself and missing Brett, she sighed. *Just a few more hours till I see him.*

Then the hairs rising on the back of her neck, she sensed she was being watched. She turned and caught her breath. Maita stood beside her, pale as ice, almost blending into the air. "I didn't see you," said Ruth. "Scratch that, barely see you."

Maita nodded with a feeble smile. "I feel like a favorite chambray shirt I've washed and worn so often I'm fading."

Ruth winced. "You make it sound like you're

becoming less than you'd been, diminishing."

Maita shook her head. "I meant, I needed washing—several 'rinses' to remove the stains and several 'stitches' to repair the rips and tears. Now I feel clean and mended…*good enough*…" Her words died off.

"To move on?"

Nodding, Maita gave a breathy sigh.

Ruth closed her eyes as a stiff sea breeze forced her back a step. "Maita," she called into the wind, but when she opened her eyes, she was alone on deck.

She said a silent prayer as she stared at the merging colors of water and sky, their blue palette peaceful now, serene. She missed Maita—*missed Brett*—but she was no longer isolated. Instead, she was at one with her surroundings.

"Goodbye," called a voice.

About facing, Ruth expected to see Maita one last time, but instead, a seagull cried into the wind.

A cloud emerged from what had been an unblemished sky.

Ruth stared, not believing her eyes.

The lustrous white puff grew gradually, taking the shape of an angel with wings outspread. With the sun behind it, backlighting and illuminating it, the cloud blazed with a golden brilliance.

Then bit by bit, the wind swept the "angel" into wispy cirrus clouds, drifting in the breeze. The shape became less and less distinct as it morphed into the sunset's copper and lemony crimson streaks, its kaleidoscopic panorama mesmerizing Ruth.

"The golden hour." Keya nodded toward the sky as she handed Ruth a champagne flute. "Now is the gilded moment before twilight when everything's glazed with a rich, fiery glow."

Ruth raised her glass to her favorite cousin. "May *all* your hours with Auggie be golden."

"I'll drink to that." After toasting, Keya hugged her. Then as the first star glimmered overhead, she caught her husband's eye. "To a stellar day—"

"And to the first of many star-spangled nights." He linked arms with hers as they clinked glasses.

Happy for their newfound love, Ruth thought of Brett, and her pulse quickened. *Just a few more hours…*

Unbidden, Maita tiptoed into her mind. Ruth recalled the sacrifices she had made—and the price she had paid—all in the name of love.

Then Bart strode through her thoughts, and she smiled. *That swashbuckling sentimentalist waited four centuries to see his wife again.*

She turned back to the newlyweds, their body language bristling with silent messages, the pheromones flying. Breathing in the heady atmosphere, Ruth lifted her glass. "To love, the only true adventure."

Keya's Conch Chowder Recipe

Ingredients:
    3 slices of bacon
    1 medium onion, diced
    2 stalks celery, diced
    2 large carrots, diced
    1 red bell pepper, diced
    3 cloves of fresh garlic, minced
    ¼ teaspoon cayenne pepper, optional
    4 large tomatoes, diced
    ½ teaspoon of ground allspice
    3 bay leaves
    4 sprigs thyme, minced
    1 (16-ounce) can clam juice
    2 tablespoons fresh lemon juice, or to taste
    1 quart vegetable broth or water
    1 medium potato, diced
    1 pound fresh conch meat, cleaned and chopped
    ½ cup white wine
    salt and pepper to taste
    Juice of 1 fresh lime
    6-8 sprigs of parsley, minced

Preparation:
    Using a large stock pot, fry the bacon over medium heat until browned, about five minutes. Remove the bacon, leaving the fat.

    Add the onions, celery, carrots, and bell peppers and stirring occasionally, sauté over medium-high heat until soft, about 4-5 minutes.

    Add the cayenne and garlic and sauté for about a minute.

Stir in the diced tomatoes and cook for 2 minutes.

Add the clam juice, lemon juice, water, and diced potatoes. Bring to a boil.

Place the allspice, bay leaves, and thyme in a piece of cheesecloth. Tie closed with string. Place in the spice packet in the soup, reduce the heat, and simmer, stirring occasionally for 30 minutes.

Sir in the conch and white wine and cook over medium heat until the meat is tender, about another 25 minutes.

Remove the pot from the heat and discard the spice packet.

Add the lime juice and parsley, stir to combine. Adjust the seasonings to taste and serve hot! Yields 6 to 8 servings.

Creamy Cilantro Lime Slaw

Ingredients:
    1/4 cup mayonnaise
    1/4 cup sour cream
    1 tablespoon fresh lime juice, or to taste
    1/2 teaspoon lime peel, finely grated
    1/2 serrano chili, seeded, minced
    2 garlic cloves, minced
    1/4 cup fresh cilantro, chopped
    4 cups cabbage, thinly sliced
    2 green onions, minced
    1/2 teaspoon salt, or to taste
    1/2 teaspoon pepper, or to taste

Preparation:

Whisk together mayonnaise, sour cream, lime juice, lime peel, chili, and garlic in a large bowl. Add cilantro, cabbage, and green onions. Toss to coat. Season with salt and pepper, cover, and chill before serving. Yields 3-4 servings.

Mediterranean Cucumber Tomato Salad

Ingredients:
- 3 cucumbers, diced, not peeled
- 3 plum tomatoes, seeded, diced
- 3 green onions, sliced
- 1/2 red bell pepper, seeded, diced
- 2 tablespoons garlic, minced
- 1/2 cup fresh parsley, finely chopped
- 1/4 cup fresh mint leaves, finely chopped
- 1/4 cup olive oil
- 1 tablespoon fresh lime juice, or to taste
- 1/2 teaspoon salt, or to taste
- 1/2 teaspoon pepper, or to taste

Preparation:

Lightly mix the cucumbers, tomatoes, onions, bell pepper, garlic, parsley, and mint in a large bowl. Drizzle with olive oil and lime juice and lightly toss to coat. Season and serve. Yields 3-4 servings.

A word about the author…

Dr. Karen Hulene Bartell, author of *Christmas in Cahokia: Song of the Owl*, *Holy Water: Rule of Capture*, *Sacred Heart: Valentine, Texas*, *Lone Star Christmas: Holy Night*, *Angels from Ashes*, *Christmas in Catalonia*, *Sacred Gift*, *Belize Navidad*, *Sacred Choices*, and others, is a best-selling author, motivational keynote speaker, wife, and all-around pilgrim of life. She writes multicultural, offbeat love stories and women's literature steeped in the supernatural that lift the spirit.

Dr. Bartell lives in the Texas Hill Country with her husband, Peter, and her "mews": four rescued cats and a rescued Catahoula leopard dog.

http://www.karenhulenebartell.com/